S0-ACV-474

Natalie could only stare into Shane's eyes. The room was so still, so suddenly intimate.

It amplified the stilted rhythm of her breaths. And his. He'd spoken about a person making an effort to understand someone else. Hadn't he done just that for her tonight? Strange how she'd never felt more understood.

It may have been surprise, or perhaps just want of a connection she hadn't even realized she craved, but something powerful held her in place.

Shane's gaze was unwavering, steady. A contradiction to the riotous feelings battling inside her, some calling for a poorly plotted charge and others, a hasty retreat.

She should listen to the one that told her to run for safety...

Dear Reader,

I am so excited to return with you to the True Blue series and to the world of the honorable men and women of the Michigan State Police Brighton Post. In the past few years, law enforcement has come under more scrutiny, and rightfully so for the bad behavior of more than a few officers. But I love writing about the much larger segment of the law-enforcement community, of brave men and women who wear the badge with pride and who make sacrifices and risk their lives daily for the safety and well-being of people they've never met. These are the officers I have met through the Lakes Area Citizens Police Academy and through interviews and ride-alongs with officers from several Michigan law-enforcement agencies. And these are the characters who populate the stories in True Blue.

In *Falling for the Cop*, I explored the impossible pairing of Shane Warner, an officer who is battling his way back from a possibly career-ending shooting injury, and Natalie Keaton, a physical therapist who blames all police officers for the high-speed police chase that left her mother a paraplegic. As with all of my characters, I loved challenging their wounds (both internal and external), their fears and their prejudices that keep them from having the lives of their dreams.

I love to hear from readers. Connect with me through my website, www.dananussio.com; through social-media channels Facebook, Twitter, Goodreads or Pinterest; or by regular mail at PO Box 5, Novi, MI 48376-0005.

Dana Nussio

DANA NUSSIO

—

Falling for the Cop

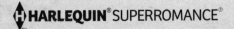

HARLEQUIN® SUPERROMANCE®

If you purchased this book without a cover you should be aware that this book is stolen property. It was reported as "unsold and destroyed" to the publisher, and neither the author nor the publisher has received any payment for this "stripped book."

Recycling programs
for this product may
not exist in your area.

ISBN-13: 978-0-373-64020-1

Falling for the Cop

Copyright © 2017 by Dana Corbit Nussio

All rights reserved. Except for use in any review, the reproduction or utilization of this work in whole or in part in any form by any electronic, mechanical or other means, now known or hereinafter invented, including xerography, photocopying and recording, or in any information storage or retrieval system, is forbidden without the written permission of the publisher, Harlequin Enterprises Limited, 225 Duncan Mill Road, Don Mills, Ontario M3B 3K9, Canada.

This is a work of fiction. Names, characters, places and incidents are either the product of the author's imagination or are used fictitiously, and any resemblance to actual persons, living or dead, business establishments, events or locales is entirely coincidental.

This edition published by arrangement with Harlequin Books S.A.

For questions and comments about the quality of this book, please contact us at CustomerService@Harlequin.com.

® and TM are trademarks of Harlequin Enterprises Limited or its corporate affiliates. Trademarks indicated with ® are registered in the United States Patent and Trademark Office, the Canadian Intellectual Property Office and in other countries.

Printed in U.S.A.

HARLEQUIN®
www.Harlequin.com

Dana Nussio began telling "people stories" around the same time she started talking. She has been doing both things, nonstop, ever since. The award-winning newspaper reporter and features editor left her career while raising three daughters, but the stories followed her home as she discovered the joy of writing fiction. Now an award-winning fiction author as well, she loves telling emotional stories filled with honorable but flawed characters. Empty nesters, Dana and her husband of more than twenty-five years live in Michigan with two overfed cats, Leo the Wondercat and Annabelle Lee the Neurotic.

Books by Dana Nussio

HARLEQUIN SUPERROMANCE

True Blue

Strength Under Fire

Visit the Author Profile page at Harlequin.com
for more titles.

To my father, James Corbit, who passed away in 2016. You were always my biggest fan, showing off my books and bragging about me to anyone who would listen. I hope when you look down on me now that I still make you proud.

A special thanks goes to Melissa Erickson, a compassionate physical therapist who works with special-needs students in the Novi Community School District. She not only gave up her evening hours to research medical issues and help ensure the believability of Shane Warner's injuries, but she also became invested in the story and rode the ride-along with me as I wrote. (I hope you enjoy the finished product.) And a continued thanks to the many law-enforcement professionals from the Lakes Area Citizens Police Academy who helped me build the fictional world for the True Blue series. I appreciate your dedication and daily sacrifices for the safety of Michigan residents.

PROLOGUE

"OFFICER DOWN."

The words came to Shane Warner in a dream. At least it felt like a dream, its edges blurred and spreading like spilled wine. Flashing lights penetrated the fog in angry bursts, so bright that they seemed to have a sound all their own. The piercing squeals came from somewhere inside his head. The sounds built to a deafening pitch.

And something was dripping on his face.

"Hold on, buddy. They just got here."

Shane blinked several times, trying to identify the vaguely familiar voice next to him. A voice that sounded too real to be a part of any dream. Hold on to what? Where was he, anyway? But the only words his mouth could form were "Who is—"

A rustle of cloth interrupted even that question as an umbrella unfurled over him. Of course. Rain. Not snow, though early December flurries had fluttered earlier in the day. His thoughts flicked to the windshield wipers that had been turned on in his patrol car. In a series of quick connections, he remembered. A domestic call.

The angry shouts. The screams. The female victim crumpled inside the backyard gate.

Then the earsplitting blast.

As the stray dots of his memory scrambled back into a straight line, Shane jerked to lift his head.

And something set his back on fire.

Lying on his side, Shane tried to reach behind him to examine the pain's source, but his hands refused to cooperate.

"Stay still, Trooper Warner," a woman called out from somewhere nearby.

"Listen to her, Shane," Sergeant Vincent Leonetti said, taking possession of that earlier voice.

He knelt in front of Shane, some towels in his hand. "You've been hit."

"Shot?" Shane managed, his words coming slowly as if spoken through sludge. "But…my vest?"

As Shane shook his head to deny what was becoming obvious—that the vest had failed—the pain struck again, branding him with an unrelenting iron. Bile rose to the back of his throat. The tree-nestled bungalow swam before him in the murky sky.

"Sorry." Vinnie pressed the towels to the back panels of Shane's vest. "But everything's going to be all right."

"Wait." He held back an overwhelming urge to retch. "The victim. She—"

"Not sure. They're checking her now."

He cleared his throat. "The suspect?"

"Dead."

Vinnie looked away, toward what had to be a body on the east side of the yard, and then turned back to him. "But you're going to be okay. *Have* to be okay."

That was the last thing Vinnie added under his breath as he tucked a blanket over Shane, but the words still echoed in Shane's ears. Just how bad was it? Wall-of-honor bad? Or just a forced retirement from a job that meant everything to him? He squeezed his eyes shut to block the misery of either option. Now the ground beneath him felt cold. So wet. Was it just the rain or was it…blood? A chill scrambled from the earth to his core, setting off a shiver he couldn't still.

In what could only have been seconds, a crowd surrounded him, his fellow officers mumbling something and EMTs asking impossible questions and then shoving an oxygen mask over his nose and mouth. Could he move his hands? Could he feel his feet? He wasn't sure. Yes, the pain had clutched him before, but now he felt eerily numb. Was it just swelling, or would he ever feel anything again?

"Now, Trooper, we're going to have to get you on this board so we can transport you," one of the EMTs told him.

But as they shifted his body, slipping the board beneath it, something shook him. Either pain or the anticipation of it. The lights around him crushed into some crazy kaleidoscope, and the voices splintered into hundreds of disjointed sounds. His world blinked in and out of focus until the darkness swallowed him completely.

CHAPTER ONE

DEAD WOMAN WALKING. Natalie Keaton cringed over the hyperbole of death-row-inmate proportions as she crossed through the activity room, but that didn't loosen the ankle weights slowing her steps or lift the dread bearing down on her shoulders.

Sure, she'd had frustrating days at work before. Like when clients expected range-of-motion improvements without doing their exercises, or when she had to come in on Saturdays for appointments. But never before had she wanted to walk away from her job at Brentwood Rehabilitation Services rather than meet with a new client.

Now she was dreading the whole day.

From the activity room, where two other physical therapists guided clients through exercises and stretches, to the shoes and the examination-bed wheels that peeked out from beneath the curtains of consultation areas, everything seemed wrong inside the clinic. The piped-in music was too loud, its notes jagged scratches over her eardrums. Even the usually comforting antiseptic scents from foaming hand cleaner and antibacterial cleansers only made her queasy.

The row of windows outside the activity room displayed an obstinately gray March afternoon, the stratus-striped sky belching and spitting without having the decency to really snow. That didn't keep Natalie from shivering until long after the windows were far behind her. As she passed her boss's closed office door, she gripped the file folder she held tightly. The file she'd just tried—and failed—to hand off to another therapist.

You're a professional. You can handle a challenge like this. Meg Story's words of support, sprinkled with censure, burned like a blister ripped wide. A challenge? How could Meg see it that way? Why had she matched Natalie with this client in the first place? Didn't her history matter? Natalie didn't doubt that this seriously injured client deserved compassionate care. They all did. She just wasn't the right PT to provide it for him.

She pulled at the sleeves of her sweater and brushed her free hand down her maroon scrub shirt as she neared the clinic side of the registration desk. If only she could swipe away her unease as easily. But she needed this job, so her only choice was to help this client get back on his feet as soon as possible. In and out faster than a playboy on a one-night stand, if she had her way.

Still, for a heartbeat too long, Natalie rested her hand on the door leading to the reception area instead of opening it.

Anne-Marie Long, the impossibly young receptionist with a perky ponytail to prove it, glanced over from her computer, a telephone handset tucked between her shoulder and ear.

"You okay?" Anne-Marie mouthed, her eyebrows escaping to behind her bangs.

Natalie nodded, wishing it were true. She pressed her lips together and pushed open the door.

The minimalist reception area through the doorway was always cramped, with barely enough seating for a family of five, but the man in the manual wheelchair at the room's center and his uniform-clad valet overwhelmed the tiny space. She had to force herself to close the door behind her when she longed to retreat behind that shield of hollow wood veneer.

The man in the chair was an exaggerated cartoon version of what she'd expected, his overdeveloped physique a contradiction to the benign nylon sweat suit and running shoes visible below his coat. And the state police uniform his friend wore might as well have been a billboard announcement for the both of them. Navy shirt with a knotted gray tie. Shiny silver shield. A telltale hat on his head, which he wore even indoors. Did they have to throw this awful assignment in her face by showing up at the clinic with everything but a squad car?

Oh, that was probably parked outside.

She swallowed as the image of another police

cruiser slipped from behind the veil of her memories with blurry lights and squealing tires. Her mother, once vibrant, now broken…inside and out. It was only a blip of a digression, like that pinpoint moment of impact from eight years before, but it left her raw and exposed.

Natalie blinked away the image and schooled her features as she returned her attention to the man in the chair. The one not wearing a uniform, though she could easily picture him in one. But she wasn't prepared for the fathomless blue-gray eyes that stared up at her from beneath a black stocking cap. Intelligent eyes that seemed to pick up on more than they should have in that moment. Things that weren't any of his business.

"I'm Natalie Keaton," she managed and then coughed into her sweater sleeve to clear her strangely clogged throat. "Sorry. Dry air. Anyway, I'm a physical therapist. You must be Mr. Warner."

"That would be *Trooper* Warner," the other man answered for him, gesturing toward her client as if they all weren't perfectly aware whom they were talking about. "Of the Michigan State Police."

Warner had been trying to pull off his gloves, something that required more effort than it should have, but at these words he stopped and frowned at the younger man. He then went back to work on the gloves and finally pulled them off before stretching his arm up to pluck off his hat. An awkward move, given his injuries. As light brown strands of an overgrown crew cut sprang to electrified life, he reached stiffly for his head a second time and gripped a disobedient fistful on top.

"I mean Troop—"

She was relieved when he dropped his arm and cut off her comment. It didn't feel right calling him by his title, anyway.

"Don't mind him." Warner gestured toward his friend. "He's all out of whack, having to start his shift here instead of stopping by the doughnut shop for a vanilla cream with frosting and sprinkles."

Then Warner flipped on a smile so dazzling that it hit Natalie like an elbow to the diaphragm and spread warmth over her skin faster than a steaming bath. She blinked. What was that all about? Maybe the rest of female society might have joined in a collective swoon at the sight of this guy's sculpted jaw, aristocratic nose and lips that were fuller and softer looking than any tough guy's should be, but she wasn't like other women. She could never be. They hadn't lived her life. Or experienced the guilt she carried.

Still, when the other officer chuckled, Natalie startled. Had she been caught staring at him? Ogling the last type of man she should have been seeing through anything other than the most remote, clinical lens. Her face warmed, and her pulse rushed to announce her humiliation.

The officer, who looked barely old enough to shave, kept laughing. "I'm a raspberry-filled man, and Trooper Warner knows it." He pointed at Natalie. "We miss his humor around the Brighton Post lately, but you'd better watch out. If he's already starting with the cop jokes, you're going to have some long sessions ahead of you."

He didn't know the half of it.

One side of Warner's mouth lifted as he allowed his friend to help him out of his coat. Even without the extra padding, Warner still looked like a football player, his broad shoulders and burly arms pulling at the sleeves of his warm-up suit. His lack of muscular atrophy suggested he'd been rolling that wheelchair around all by himself.

"Thanks, buddy." Warner glanced up at Natalie. "You see the quality of help you can find after you get your butt shot? Anyway, before the rookie's rude interruption, I was going to tell you to call me Shane." He gestured toward the other officer. "And this is Trooper Jamie Donovan. But he's just leaving."

The younger man gave a shy wave of hello, the introduction barely registering as Natalie glanced down at the information on the file folder.

Warner, Shane. Age twenty-eight.

It was all she could do not to roll her eyes. Of course, the officer recovering from a gunshot wound would have a name like *Shane.* He even looked like a Shane. Like he could have acted the part of the gunslinger in that old Western with the same title. Only this guy's version of the Wild West was a sanitized suburban wilderness some fifty miles from downtown Detroit.

Clearly, Trooper Shane Warner was just another cowboy in blue. Another risk-taking police officer who thought of no one but himself, just like—

Natalie cut off the thought with a firm clamp of her jaw. She couldn't let herself go there. Even if the cavalier way he'd referred to his injury basically proved her point. Even if every minute of working with him would force her to relive the worst day of her life. She still had a job to do.

"Well, let's move you to one of the exam rooms so we can do some range-of-motion and manual-muscle tests." She shifted so she was behind his chair. "Let me help—"

"No!"

At Shane's sharp tone, Natalie's hands stopped inches shy of the wheelchair's push handles.

He cleared his throat. "I mean, no, thank you. I can do it. Just tell me where you need me to go."

Natalie frowned. As if this assignment wasn't hard enough, now her client was going to be a difficult patient.

But Jamie only chuckled again. "It's not easy for this guy to accept help, so he's pretty grouchy."

She could figure that one out for herself. He probably also hated looking up to Trooper Donovan like hell, who was no more than average height, when Shane must have towered over him… before.

"Didn't I just say you were leaving?" Shane didn't even look at him as he said it.

"Guess those are my walking orders." Jamie snapped his heavy jacket over his uniform. "Oh. What time do you need me to be back?"

Shane turned to him this time. "Thanks, but you're off the clock. Kelly's picking me up."

Kelly? Natalie's gaze flicked to Shane, expecting him to answer the question she would never ask. The name shouldn't have surprised her. Of course, a guy with his looks and his mastery in the art of flirtation would have a Kelly. Or a Jenny. Or a Kelly, a Jenny *and* a Jill. But that made no difference to her. She didn't care if they all carpooled over in a minivan to pick him up as long as they showed up as soon as his appointment ended.

"Whew. That's a relief." Jamie brushed his hand back over his hat in an exaggerated gesture. "I don't know how much longer I could've put up with this guy."

But he paused to pat Shane's shoulder. "Text if you need anything. Seriously. Day or night. Just ask."

Shane couldn't have looked more uncomfortable, but he nodded. "Thanks, man." He waved and then watched as Jamie crossed to the door.

Natalie should have been going through a mental list of the exercises she might use to increase

Shane's flexibility. She should even have been checking her watch and counting down the minutes until this session would end. Instead, she found herself watching her client. Trooper Warner was exactly what she'd expected, right?

But the obvious friendship between these two officers didn't fit well with the mental image she'd painted earlier. Was that bond just some extension of the "blue code" that police officers used to cover for each other? Maybe, but she couldn't help wondering if it was more than that. The rookie appeared to have genuine respect for Shane, the type that self-centered jerks seldom earned. It didn't fit.

Shane glanced over at her, catching her watching him. Her cheeks burned so badly that she could only hope the waiting room's low lighting helped to hide it.

"Well, let's get to work then." She buried her nervous hands in the pockets of her cardigan.

"Good, because I thought we were going to spend the hour standing around in the waiting room."

He didn't crack a smile as he said it, though one of them was clearly *not* standing.

Instead of responding, she stepped over to the sliding window of the receptionist's desk. "Anne-Marie, could you—"

She stopped as the receptionist and the long-time office manager, Beverly Wilson, stared out from the suspiciously open desk window. At Beverly's wink, Natalie tightened her jaw and her hold on the medical file.

"The buzzer?" she prodded.

"Oh. Right," Anne-Marie said.

She reached below the counter, and a short buzz was followed by a click.

Natalie pulled the door wide. "After you, Mr. Warner."

He glanced up at her again, those unnerving eyes trapping her and searching for stories she wasn't prepared to tell. Her pulse dashed toward some unknown finish line, and her hands were so damp that she could barely grip the door handle.

"You mean…?" he prompted.

"Shane," she choked out.

He smiled as if he'd won a competition and then carefully rolled his chair past her and through the door. Annoyed, Natalie stepped in behind him. She shouldn't let this guy get under her skin any more than she should notice how his shoulders and arms flexed as he rotated the wheels. If only she could stop looking at those things.

"Which way?"

She didn't know why he bothered asking for directions when he didn't even pause as he rolled down the hall. He probably didn't look both ways before crossing the street, either. Or check the date on the milk before chugging it right from the carton.

At the intersection where the hall and the activity room connected, Shane stopped so suddenly that Natalie bumped into the back of his chair. A whoosh of air escaped her where the handle hit her at the top of her thigh, and his file fell from her hands, pages fluttering to the ground.

"Sorry," he said with a muffled chuckle. "You didn't say which way."

She crouched to pick up the papers. So much for the nice guy. And so much for streamlining his clinic visit. At the slow rate they were moving, they might as well forget ever getting a treatment plan set up today. In fact, they would probably spend the rest of their lives in this hall...

Natalie took a deep breath to keep from directing him through the nearest window. "Turn left. Then go to the open evaluation room on the right."

Shane wheeled to the part of the clinic with laminate floors and curtained cubicles.

"About time! All right, let's do this," he said with another of those grins.

She couldn't agree more. She might not have this police officer running marathons overnight, but she would work tirelessly to help the man to walk again. Then she could get the guy who reminded her of everything she'd lost out of the clinic and out of her thoughts for good.

SHANE FOLLOWED NATALIE'S movements as she closed the evaluation-area curtain, moved to the tiny desk to grab a clipboard and then crouched near the foot plate of his wheelchair. She moved one of the feet he should have been able to at least lift for himself, pushed the foot plate to the side and rested his shoe on the ground. Afterward, she repeated the whole process on his other foot.

It was bad enough having to accept help from people, but what bothered him most this afternoon was that the therapist he was counting on to help him get out of this damn chair seemed to want nothing to do with him. He'd picked up on it the moment they'd met. Sure, she was doing her job in a distant, clinical fashion, but he was trained to pick out liars.

He was looking at one of those right now.

Unfortunately for him, Natalie Keaton also happened to be an exotic beauty with the kind of willowy body that could tempt a guy to tell a few lies of his own. Her café au lait skin, with a dusting of freckles across her nose and cheeks, made him think of Spanish coffee with whipped cream and nutmeg sprinkles. And those eyes, wide-set and nearly black, challenged him to take a deeper look.

One look too many, he guessed, from her frown when she glanced up from the floor and caught him watching her. Her loose bun was doing its job of keeping her mass of black-brown hair out of the way, but she shoved a loose tress behind her ear, anyway, as if she needed something to do with her hands. Oh, he could think of a few things...

Clearly, they weren't on the same page, he decided, as she lowered her gaze again to his feet.

Shane closed his eyes and opened them again. Why was he looking at his physical therapist like some item on the menu? What did chasing after a beautiful woman have to do with him learning to walk again? No. *Run.* He needed to be able to sprint if he ever hoped to be approved for patrol. Besides, there wasn't a chance that a woman like Natalie Keaton would actually look back at him now. What did he plan to do, sweep her off her feet with his wheelchair?

"Today, in addition to looking at range of motion and doing a manual-muscle test, we're going to check sensation, coordination and balance," she said without looking up from the form on her clipboard. "Regarding balance, we'll look at seated and standing balance and static and dynamic."

"Thanks for not making me change into one of those cute little hospital gowns," he said instead of asking for more details. "Quick costume changes don't work well for me lately."

"Both for here and for the home exercise program I'll be giving you today, the sweat suit you're wearing is fine."

"And a whole lot less breezy."

He grinned, but she didn't look up to see it. Her jaw tightened, the same way it had when he and Jamie were joking in the waiting room. Those full, kissable lips curled in to form a grim line above her chin. She obviously didn't appreciate his brand of humor. Or much else about him.

Well, why the hell not? He'd never done anything to her. Was it because he was a police officer? He would never understand why some people hated the cops without any good reason. But then, not everybody owed as much to heroes in blue as he did. Not everyone knew without a doubt that the police—or one officer in particular—had saved his life. Even if Shane would never understand why the guy had gone to so much trouble.

Without responding to his joke that even he no longer found funny, Natalie lifted his right leg and extended it from the knee until it was nearly straight. He couldn't help but smile at the amount of effort it took for her to hold the weight of his leg. Maybe the muscle loss from inactivity wasn't as bad as he'd expected, but it would only be a matter of time until his leg was as skinny as one of her arms.

"That's pretty good, really," she said as she rested his foot back on the floor.

"Flexibility is not my problem. *Walking* is the problem."

"I know. But we have to start somewhere." She lifted the other leg, extended it and then set it down again.

But *did* she know? Did she understand that he probably needed a shrink now more than a PT, since his continued paralysis might be in his head?

Even his doctors had hinted at it. Did she have any idea how critical it was for him to get back on the job and at least work toward restitution over a debt he might never be able to fully repay?

Kent Sawyer's silly grin slipped into his thoughts then, as it often did when he was feeling sorry for himself. Kent had always been the first to tell him to buck up, but his argument was even stronger now that he gave it from his hospital bed, where Kent was giving cancer the battle of his life and losing a little more every day.

Where would he be now if the police officer hadn't stuck his neck out for him with the courts and refused to give up on a juvenile delinquent like everyone else had? He'd deserved to be forgotten after he'd been responsible for another kid's death, whether he could be held legally accountable or not.

Natalie cleared her throat, his silence clearly making her uncomfortable.

"Why don't we back up for a minute?" She did just that, backing away from him and then reaching for the rolling chair behind her. Once she was seated, she grabbed his file and flipped it open. "Let's talk a little about your injury."

"Okay."

"How long has it been since the accident?"

His gaze lowered to the file that probably contained all the information she could have asked for, but he decided to humor her...to a point. "It wasn't exactly an *accident*. That gun didn't go off by itself."

"Of course. I mean the incident. So how long?"

"Over three months." The longest thirteen weeks of his life.

"Three months," she repeated as she wrote something on the paper. "According to your file, you sustained an incomplete spinal cord injury between L5 and S1, and the surgeon was successful in removing the bullet." She looked up from the file. "You were lucky it was so low in your spinal cord."

"Yeah, the doctors also said if it had been a complete spinal cord injury, I would have permanently lost all movement and sensation beneath the point of injury." He used air quotes to indicate he was repeating the doctor's clinical explanation.

She nodded. "And were you wearing a Kevlar vest when it happened?"

Shane blinked, the off-topic question hitting him fast and low. He was the one gritting his teeth now, but she didn't notice. It wasn't the first time someone had asked that, but her question sounded more like an accusation. Was she suggesting that getting shot was somehow his fault?

"I don't see what that has to do with—"

She lifted her head and blinked several times. "Forget I asked that. I was just curious."

He studied her, noting again her light brown skin. Could she possibly be biracial? If so, she would have a better reason than most to resent those few bad apples in law enforcement who'd committed wrongs against the African-American community. But, again, that had nothing to do with him. The least she could do was get to know him before she hated his guts.

She fidgeted under his scrutiny. "I said forget I asked."

"Then to ease your *curiosity*, yes, I was wearing a vest. Funny thing about so-called bullet-proof vests. They're really only bullet *resistant*."

"Oh."

"That was my thought."

"Sorry...that it happened." Natalie glanced down, becoming engrossed with the file she held. She tapped the paper with her pen. "How long were you in inpatient rehab?"

"Eight weeks. And then four weeks of in-home PT after. Yet here I am." He gestured toward his chair. "I need to get back to the force *now*. No. Sooner than that."

"You have to be patient," she said. "Every recovery is different."

"Well, this one is taking forever. I mean, the doctors assured me I would walk again, but..." He shrugged.

"I'm sure you'll be back to playing cops and robbers in no time."

She chuckled when she said it, though her eyes darted to the right, as if she was suddenly uncomfortable. But he wouldn't let her get away with a comment like that again. Even if she had a good reason to dislike cops, she didn't get to take it out on him.

"I'm more concerned about getting back to work so I can help people."

Her gaze lifted to meet his. "Sorry. Long day."

"The day's only half over."

"I mean it." She paused, looking at the floor. "That was uncalled for. It won't happen again."

"That's good to hear."

He didn't doubt what she said was true. Natalie Keaton didn't appear to be the kind of woman who slipped up often, so part of him liked that he'd pushed her off her game. Was it because he unnerved her? Who was he kidding? He was the only one who'd been affected in any way by their meeting. And he'd better get over it in a hurry.

This wasn't about attraction, or lack thereof. It was about him learning to walk again. Soon. *Sooner* if he ever hoped to be out on patrol again instead of warehoused behind a desk or, worse, be thanked for his service and put out to law-enforcement pasture with the other officers who'd given *almost* all for public safety.

As his physical therapist, Natalie might be the one thing between him and that meaningless future. Well, she and whatever was messing with his head and keeping him from walking. But until he figured that out, she was all he had. So he didn't care what problems she had with him. He intended to win her over to his side. His future depended on it.

CHAPTER TWO

"It's about time."

Shane's words as they reached the reception area were the same ones he'd said before, and, again, Natalie couldn't have agreed more. The appointment had to have lasted longer than just an hour, at least if physical and mental exertion counted as minutes. For him and her. Even though Shane had worked harder than her last three clients combined, she still was relieved the appointment was over.

The woman seated in the chair across from them looked just the way Natalie would have predicted. Blonde. Flawless. A perfect match for someone who looked like Shane Warner. Now the police uniform the woman wore, Natalie hadn't expected that. Was this the Kelly he'd mentioned earlier?

The officer, who'd been engrossed in the screen of her smartphone, startled as if caught doing something she shouldn't have been and leaped to her feet. She frowned as her phone clattered to the floor.

"Now see what you made me do. If it's broken,

you're a dead man." She crouched and grabbed the phone from beneath the chair and examined it as she stood. Finally, she looked up at them. "Anyway, I'm here. Right on time."

"You're usually late, so thanks for the special effort."

"You're welcome." She grabbed her hat from the seat next to her and crossed to him, bending to give him a quick hug.

Natalie could only look back and forth between them. At first, their conversation had sounded like flirting, but it seemed no different from the way he'd spoken with the other trooper earlier. Minus the hug. Still, it sounded like workplace banter. Or a really dull relationship.

"Oh, Natalie Keaton." Shane gestured toward her then indicated the officer. "Meet Trooper Kelly Roberts, my second chauffeur of the day."

Chauffeur? No one could call someone he was involved with that…and live. But the question of the day was why Natalie cared who that woman was or what she meant to her client. She refused to call the feeling welling inside her *relief.* Whatever it was, there was no excuse for it. Hadn't her curiosity about Shane's injury already gotten her into enough trouble today without her heading in some other unacceptable direction?

Kelly smiled her way. "I drew the short straw today."

"Today?" She shouldn't have been asking. It was none of her business.

"He's fighting it every step of the way, but all of us at the Brighton Post have divided him up like a pizza," Kelly explained. "Everybody wants to help out. Since we have three shifts, our slices are pretty thin."

Wow, that many coworkers wanted to help Shane? Sure, Natalie and her mother had received some help following the accident, but no one had reached out to them like that. Of course, they hadn't required much assistance, since Natalie had taken on the whole job herself.

"They all just want to take turns bugging me," Shane said with a frown. "They barely leave anything for the visiting nurse or the aide to do."

"Except help with showers," Kelly said, grimacing. "Nobody volunteers for that."

A flash of steamy water pouring over that broad chest and those rounded biceps took Natalie by surprise. But the way Shane shifted in his chair, as if uncomfortable with anyone knowing he needed bathing assistance, threw ice on her off-limits reverie. Good thing Shane wasn't watching her now, since he would have read her as easily as he would a street sign.

Kelly continued, "Now let's get going before my lunchtime is up. I'm lucky Vinnie let me take a turn at all." She turned back to Natalie. "Sergeant Leonetti has got it in his head that he should do all the helping."

"Overachiever," Shane said in a tight voice.

There had to be a story behind that one. Again, Natalie was curious, but she wouldn't ask. She glanced at her watch instead.

"Well, I have another client in ten minutes, so I'd better get ready."

She met Shane's gaze as Kelly helped him put on his coat. "Remember what I told you. If you want to get stronger, you need to follow your home exercise program every day."

"I remember *everything* you said."

His steady gaze held her captive. Her pulse pounded, and her lips were suddenly dry. Good thing he looked away because she couldn't have done it. Oh, she'd bet he remembered what she'd said, even the parts of their conversation she wished he'd forgotten. How was she supposed to work with him three times a week now that she'd hinted about her personal bias toward police? She needed to show that she could do her job without letting her baggage—or her hormones—interfere.

She slanted a glance to the uniformed officer, who was handing Shane his hat. If Kelly had noticed anything unusual about Shane's comment, she wasn't giving anything away.

"See you Friday," she said.

"I'll be here," he promised.

Natalie signaled at the desk for the buzzer and pulled open the door. She glanced back one last time, only to catch sight of Kelly grabbing the push handles on Shane's chair. Something vaguely uncomfortable washed over her. Was she jealous that he'd allowed the officer to push his chair when he wouldn't let her do it? Or, worse yet, was she just jealous of the woman going with him through that door?

She turned away from the man and those thoughts and rushed into the shelter of the clinic. But her memories of Shane Warner refused to be dismissed without a fight, the colors still bright, that baritone voice too rich and appealing for anyone's good. Particularly hers.

What was she doing? First, she'd all but told a shooting victim that it was his fault for getting shot, and now she was daydreaming about him. Fantasizing over any client would be bad enough, but *a cop*? That was it. She had to get her head together. She had other clients to see and a boss who was probably watching her more closely today. Not to mention a couple of front-office workers with outlandishly good hearing.

At least she wouldn't have to go out of her way to find something that would straighten her out. Her big dose of reality, her reminder of how much could be lost through a combination of flashing lights and a sense of invincibility, would be waiting for her at home tonight.

HOME SWEET HOME. Shane's house blinked in and out of focus with each swipe of the patrol car's windshield wipers. Fat snowflakes peppered the glass with every pause. The three-bedroom ranch stood out in bleak inferiority to its neighboring colonials, but even with its drafty windows and a roof that was one good downpour away from its first leak, at least the place was his. Well, the bank's, but they let him live there as long as he kept the checks coming.

His house looked especially dreary today, snow-covered flower beds providing none of their usual pops of color against the ordinary white siding and charcoal-colored shutters. Would Natalie be surprised to know that he'd planted all of those perennials himself?

Shane blinked, the mechanical hum of the wipers suddenly too loud. Why was he thinking of *her* now? Were his hormones really so out of whack that he couldn't get *one* pretty woman off his mind when he used to juggle several with ease? No, that couldn't be it. Sure, he was still annoyed that she'd prejudged him for being a cop, but could it have been more than that? His thoughts shifted to that moment in the waiting room when he'd glimpsed something raw in her eyes. It was only an instant, like one of those silly snapshots that kids send to each other, and she'd shuttered it as quickly as it had appeared, but he'd sensed a connection. As if he wasn't the only one who carried at least some of his scars on the inside. And he couldn't help wondering if hers were as deep as his.

You'll be back to playing cops and robbers in no time.

Even now those words had him gripping his gloved hands in his lap. Whether she'd seemed vulnerable for a moment or not, nothing gave her the right to say something like that. He didn't care that she'd offered some lame apology. Who was she to presume to know anything about why he wore the uniform? She hadn't seen Kent's proud face at Shane's graduation from trooper recruit school. Or the pride in his parents' faces, for that matter—something he'd never expected to see again.

Just then the car door flew open, filling the interior with light and a handful of flurries. Shane jerked more obviously than a suspect hiding drug contraband.

What was wrong with him? He'd met many people who hated cops, but he wasn't sitting in a patrol car trying to give *them* excuses for the things they said. He'd probably invented his connection with Natalie, too, since it was easier than admitting that he couldn't stop thinking about her. Or forget those soft feminine curves that even her boxy scrubs couldn't hide.

"Jumpy, aren't we?" Kelly said, pushing his wheelchair into the space by the open door and locking its wheels. "I thought I was getting faster at this, but I guess I was wrong. You forgot I was even out here."

She couldn't know how close she'd come to the truth. He hadn't even noticed when she'd opened the trunk to pull out his chair.

"You *are* getting faster. Sorry you've had so much practice."

He hated that all of his coworkers had been forced to step up so that he could leave the hospital's rehab center sooner. Hated being in debt to his friends, but he guessed he should have been used to it by now. Even his Christmas lights would still be hanging as a sad reminder of a holiday he could barely recall if his pals hadn't boxed them up and put them in his attic.

"I really do appreciate everything you guys have done for me."

Kelly prattled on as if his gratitude made her uncomfortable. "The first time I tried, I couldn't even unfold the chair. Now it's no trouble at all."

If only he didn't still require her help. If only he could be back at the post, doing his job. But because the situation was what it was, he unbuckled his seat belt, accepted the transfer board she handed him and removed the chair's side panel to shift himself from the car to the chair.

"All set?" she asked after he slid the side panel back into place.

"Let's get inside before we freeze to death."

She pushed him over the gravel and then up the

wheelchair ramp that had magically appeared just as he was released from the hospital.

He turned the key in the lock, pushed open the front door and allowed Kelly to push him inside. She stepped past him into the dark family room, flipping on power switches and lamps as she went. Light, but never enough of it, flooded the dark-paneled room, with the overstuffed sofa and recliner he no longer sat on, the television that finally bored him now and the stacks of books that had saved his sanity over the past month.

With a glance toward the TV tray where Shane took most of his meals, Kelly turned back to him. "Want me to get you something to eat?"

"No. I'm good. I still have leftovers from last night." And from Saturday and two nights before that, but he didn't elaborate.

"Whose turn was it?"

"Ben and Delia."

"Then I bet it was something good." She took his hat and gloves and then helped him with his coat.

"If you guys keep feeding me like this, I'll have to diet for weeks before I can pass my physical."

Yet he was already salivating at the thought of the *mostaccioli* Lieutenant Ben Peterson and Trooper Delia Morgan Peterson had brought over. Judging by the dishes the newlyweds had delivered so far, he had to wonder if they'd spent their first year of marriage in cooking classes together.

"You have to keep up your strength until you get there."

Until. They all used that word, but how many of them still believed it? If one of his fellow officers had been shot instead of him, would he still believe after so many weeks?

Kelly helped him into the zippered sweatshirt he wore around the house and handed him a loose-knit throw for his lap.

"Is there anything else I can do for you before I go?"

"No. I'm fine."

"You're sure?"

He nodded, smiling. "Don't worry. Vinnie will be over in about an hour." And someone else a few hours after that. As much as he appreciated the help, he craved a few moments alone.

Because she probably would keep stalling, Shane rolled closer to the door. She took the hint and followed.

But just as her hand closed over the door handle, Kelly turned back to him. "Your new physical therapist seemed...nice."

"She's all right."

"Pretty, too."

"Didn't really notice." But dark, shiny hair and lips that just had to be pillow soft slipped into his thoughts before he could bar them. He cleared his throat. "Seems pretty good at her job. That's all that matters to me."

"Then why all the...tension in the waiting room?"

He was shaking his head before he met the other officer's gaze. "What do you mean, tension? I was just exhausted after that first session. Still am."

"Oh. That's good, then. Isn't your commendation ceremony coming up? Yours and Vinnie's?"

"About a month."

Twenty-eight days, but who was counting? Neither mentioned that the event had already been rescheduled once so he could be further along in his recovery.

With a wave, Kelly let herself out of the house. Visible through the sideline window, she tromped down the ramp to her car. And to think that Natalie had obviously assumed he was involved with Kelly. Him and Kelly? As if that ever would have happened, even if she'd been up for it. Even if it wasn't a complete pain—and a cause for a potential transfer—to become involved with a fellow officer.

So other than that obvious reason, why not someone like Kelly? He considered that as he backed away from the window and wheeled past his tiny living room toward the narrow kitchen. She was gorgeous. And built. Like so many of the women he'd dated...when it used to be easy. Too easy.

But nothing about Kelly piqued his interest the

way that Natalie Keaton did with her barely concealed disdain and exotic good looks. What did it say about him that he was only attracted to unattainable women? Like that waitress at Casey's Diner who never gave him the time of day. Was that what made Natalie so appealing? That she clearly didn't like cops and wanted nothing to do with him? Did he just love the chase, or was it something more troubling than that?

Stop. He rolled to the refrigerator when he would have preferred to stomp. The last thing he had time for right now was self-psychoanalysis over events that were best left in the past. He balanced a container of leftovers on his lap, somehow reaching the microwave without dumping the whole thing on the floor. Using his grabber tool, he moved the hot dish to the table and filled a plastic cup with water. He rolled his chair as far as he could beneath the table.

The moment the zesty pasta sauce hit his taste buds, his thoughts returned to the equally spicy brunette. Why couldn't he get her out of his head? If she appeared on his doorstep right now, wearing a trench coat and nothing else, he wasn't positive he would be able to accept her offer with more virility than a polite thank-you. Sure, the doctors had said that everything down there appeared to be in working order, but then, they'd also said Shane should be walking by now, and look how well that was working out.

He pushed his plate away without eating another bite. He couldn't worry about his other problems right now. His focus needed to be on walking again. That focus also depended upon him not wasting more energy on pointless fantasies about a member of his health care team.

In four weeks, he had to cross that stage to accept his commendation certificate. If he hoped to return to full-time patrol and not waste away behind a desk, he needed to accept that award under his own power. Which meant the next time he met with Natalie Keaton, he would pay attention only to her instructions. Not the curve of her collarbones as they peeked out from the neckline of her scrubs. Not that fine line in the center of her plump lower lip—the lip that just begged to be nipped and then traced with a line of kisses. None of those things.

He would focus only on the exercises and then the first step that absolutely needed to be followed by hundreds more if he planned to walk across that stage. And if he hoped to do it while Kent was still around to see it.

He had twenty-eight days. He was running out of time.

CHAPTER THREE

NATALIE SLID THE key into the lock and turned the knob in painstaking increments. Still, the click of it was as loud as a gunshot. Just a few more seconds. She just needed a minute to herself. Sometimes she felt like the oldest twenty-eight-year-old in the world.

"Is that you, Natalie?" her mother called out from the other room, asking the same question she asked every day.

Expecting anyone else? But, like always, Natalie didn't respond that way. They both knew the answer, anyway.

"Yes, Mom. I'll be right there." With her back to the door, she lifted one foot and pulled off her boot and then repeated the process on the other side. She carefully set both on the mat.

"Make sure your boots don't drip all over the floor," came the voice from the other room.

Natalie's jaw tightened. "I'll be careful." She would clean it up if she did make a mess, anyway.

She hung her coat in the closet, pausing to rub her fingertips over her temples and close her eyes.

But she couldn't stall any longer. Lifting her lids, she padded across the freezing tile in her socks.

"You're home late," Elaine Keaton said the moment her daughter came into view in the family room doorway.

"There was traffic."

And medical records to update. And one client in particular who had her feeling off-kilter.

Elaine nodded, accepting the excuse, and turned back to the television, where an '80s sitcom was streaming. She'd probably been watching for hours, unless her daytime caregiver had insisted that they play cards today or work on a crossword puzzle. Her electric wheelchair was parked in the middle of the room, and the lamps on the end tables that bookended the sofa provided little more than shadows on the wall.

"Hi, Mom."

Natalie crossed the room and dropped a kiss on her head and then adjusted the wedding-ring quilt Elaine had once hand stitched herself. *Before.* In what seemed like another lifetime. Because it was Wednesday, Elaine's hair looked clean from her shower day, but the straw-colored strands stood at odd angles. Natalie could only hope that the caregiver had been more insistent with Elaine's toothbrush than she'd been with the hairbrush.

"Laura left forty-five minutes ago."

Her mother didn't say it, but her message couldn't have been clearer: *You weren't here.*

"Sorry." Natalie busied herself by replacing the sweater that had fallen from her mother's shoulders. "I should have asked Laura to wait for me. Can I get you something? Are you warm enough? Do you need to go to the restroom?"

"No. Don't worry about me. I'm fine."

Of course she was. Her passive-aggressive antics just didn't work as well without an audience. Without a daughter to send on yet another guilt trip when she already had a passport filled with destination stamps.

Natalie swallowed. She really was a rotten daughter. Her mom might not be a grateful patient, but she deserved her daughter's respect and the best care she could give her. It was the least she could do.

"What have you been watching today?" Natalie indicated the TV with a wave of her hand.

Elaine barely looked back from it to answer. "Season three."

"How many seasons are there?"

"Ten."

"Then you'll be binge watching 24/7 through next Wednesday."

"It's not like I have anything better to do."

"Maybe you could cook dinner, then. Since you have so much free time and all." Natalie forced a smile.

"And maybe you could try it from a chair like mine."

Natalie swallowed. Was a flippant reaction better than none at all? She didn't know why she was so determined to spark her mother into action—any type of action—when Elaine appeared determined to set a record for how long someone could bask in self-pity.

Would it be easier if she finally gave up hope that Elaine would one day return to that funny, interesting mom she used to be instead of the shell that remained after the accident? It was as if her mother blamed the world for her unlucky lot in life. Or was it only Natalie she blamed?

"Bad day at work?"

Natalie startled as much from the odd question as from the surety that she'd been caught entertaining disloyal thoughts. She couldn't remember the last time her mother had asked her about her job. Or *her* life.

"Just a busy day, I guess."

"Your work is too stressful."

She studied her mother for several seconds. Did she care about what was going on in her daughter's life, after all? Was she just unable to show it?

"I have a challenging case," she said finally.

She didn't even know why she'd mentioned it. She never talked about work at home or about the clients.

"You just wish you'd finished music school so you could be living a stress-free *artist's* life now."

Natalie chuckled. This wasn't the first time her

mother had joked about her earlier career choice. "Stress-free? Except for wondering whether I'd be able to pay my bills."

"You're probably blaming me again for making you change your major. You probably hate me every day."

Natalie blinked as she realized she'd walked right into her mother's trap. Usually she was better at reading the signs and changing the subject, but now she could only backpedal.

"You never made me change anything, Mom. You know that. I just realized how much I enjoyed helping people." She massaged her mother's shoulders, hoping one day Elaine would buy her story. Hoping she would, as well.

I'm more concerned about getting back to work so I can help people.

Her breath caught as Shane's words slipped, uninvited, into her thoughts. She turned her head, hoping her mother hadn't noticed. Why couldn't she stop thinking about this guy? It couldn't matter that he was the first man who seemed to really *see* her when she'd felt invisible for so long, the first one to challenge her, even if only to call her on her bull.

He was a *cop*, after all.

How could she betray her mother by bringing thoughts of a police officer into their home? It didn't matter that this guy seemed different from those other officers. He wore a badge. They were all the same.

"So you'd better *help* put dinner on, or at least one of us is going to starve to death."

"Wonder which one." She smiled, but when Elaine didn't return it, she added, "Better get to it, then."

"What are you making? Hope it isn't chicken again."

Natalie's cheeks ached from the effort to keep smiling. "It's chicken, but I think you're going to like this new recipe."

"Probably not."

Natalie waited to shake her head until she'd rounded the corner into the kitchen. Since she'd stretched the truth about having a new recipe, she grabbed her phone and searched for chicken dishes. A series of colorful food photos covered the tiny screen. Orange chicken. Chicken à la king. Surely there was something her mother would eat. Now, to eat it without grumbling, that would be tougher.

If only she had the guts to call her mother on her childish behavior the way her client had blasted her on hers earlier. Shame washed over her again. How could she have acted so unprofessionally?

Sure, he didn't know what she dealt with outside the clinic, but she never shared that with any of her clients. She shouldn't have brought her personal baggage to work with her this time, either.

Even if it felt heavier than usual today. This was her life, the responsibility she had accepted almost from the moment the doctors had informed her that *she* would walk out of the hospital but that her mother would never walk anywhere again. At the time, she'd believed this was the worst news she could receive. No one had warned her then of the real tragedy: that Elaine Keaton would never really live again.

As she combined orange juice, lemon juice, rice vinegar and soy sauce for a makeshift orange chicken in a saucepan, she couldn't help wondering why her mother couldn't be more like Shane. In attitude only. Sure, his prognosis was more promising than her mother's had been, but why couldn't she have been as determined as he was to make the most of her situation?

She shouldn't have been comparing them at all. Their cases were too different. Anyway, Shane was a stranger, and her mother had been there for her all of her life—at least until the accident. Then it had been her turn.

"You owed her that much." Her words seemed to spill into the kitchen of their own accord, but she immediately recognized them as truth.

For the past eight years, she'd understood that her focus had to be on her mother's care. She couldn't allow one hour with a client—one she'd begged not to work with—make her question her mother's post-accident life. Or hers.

While she waited for the chicken to brown in the olive oil, she searched on her phone for scholarly articles on spinal cord injuries. The sooner she found out what was keeping Shane from walking, the sooner he would no longer need her help, and she could get back to her life.

SHANE MANEUVERED HIS wheelchair across the parking lot of the Brighton Post Building the next evening, stopping outside the rear entrance. If he hadn't already been convinced that it was a mistake to stop by the post after their visit with Kent at the hospital, the barrier beneath the steel door ahead of him would have changed his mind.

"Why aren't you going inside?" Vinnie asked from behind him. "You don't need an invitation."

"But I do need a little help." Shane waved with his gloved hand toward the step beneath the door.

Vinnie, whose brainchild this little detour had been, took in the situation with a frown. "Oh. I didn't think about that."

"*I* should have." Of course there would be no wheelchair ramp at the troopers' entrance. His gaze moved toward the front of the building, where there was surely an Americans with Disabilities Act–compliant entrance since citizens with disabilities filed police reports and applied for gun permits as often as anyone else.

"You want to go around?" Vinnie asked.

"Why don't we just forget it and go home?"

"Who's the prima donna now?" But Vinnie was looking back and forth between the door and Shane's chair as if weighing his options. "Have a problem with popping wheelies?"

"Why would I?" As a matter of fact, he did have a problem with that, but he refused to tell his friend that. He might have had to give up his dignity to accept help since the shooting, but there was no way he was surrendering his man card completely. "But it might not work—"

"Guess we'll see." Vinnie pushed the buzzer for entrance, pulled the door wide and popped up the chair onto two wheels, wedging it through the opening before the door could fall closed again. "You see? It wasn't that high."

"Guess not."

But Shane tightened his arms across his chest. With a few bumps and a loud scrape along the steel, they got his chair parked on the large textured mat inside the door.

"You see, the place hasn't changed much."

Shane bristled, not entirely because his friend was hovering the way he did too often these days. Vinnie was also dead wrong. Everything about this place felt different now. Foreign. As if someone else had changed into that uniform in the locker room just to his left. As if a stranger had joked with the others before daily announcements at the beginning of each shift, had called on them for backup and had met with them to decompress after work hours.

That man had been willing to give his life in place of any of his fellow officers. Nearly had.

"Smells the same," Shane said finally. "Like stale subs and gun oil."

"Our signature scent. We've been trying to bottle it for years, but so far distributors haven't bit."

"I wouldn't be waiting by the phone for that one."

Even the banter didn't feel right tonight. Shane rolled toward the open area at the squad room's center, a line of desks with desktop computers forming its perimeter. His chair bumped the first desk, the monitor rocking before settling back into place. Vinnie pretended not to notice.

Coming here today was a mistake, all right. It only emphasized the truth that he might never have any of this again, and just the possibility of it bore down on his shoulders so hard that he could barely sit straight in the chair. He shouldn't have let Vinnie talk him into coming. But Vinnie had been so desperate to do *something* that Shane had taken pity on him. Now he only had to endure a few more minutes until he could get out of there and return to his house—a sanctuary that most days felt like a prison.

At the sound of heavy footsteps, Shane turned toward the hall that led to the superior officers' offices. Trooper Nick Sanchez, a black-haired ladies' man who'd switched from the midnight shift just after Shane was shot, started toward them.

"Well, look who took time out from his vacation to pop in." He crossed to them and shook Shane's hand.

"Yeah, great vacation. I'd show you my tan, but I've been sunbathing nude, and it's pretty cold out today."

"Thanks for not sharing." Nick cleared his throat. "But seriously, man. How are—"

"He's great, Trooper," Vinnie answered for him.

Apparently, there would be no downer talk tonight.

"He nearly broke my arm, twisting it to make me bring him to Casey's tonight," Vinnie continued.

Shane shot him a glance, but Vinnie refused to look his way. They'd made no such plans. "Yeah, Vinnie's here to file assault charges. He brought me along to save time."

"You going?" Vinnie asked Nick.

"I'll be there if I get that report finished." Nick pointed to a desk with a travel coffee mug on top.

At the sound of voices behind him, Shane turned to find midnight-shift troopers Dion Carson and Clint McNally emerging from the locker room, one patting his duty belt and the other touching his breast pocket for his badge and nameplate. Both glanced over at the same time and crossed the room to them.

"Hey, look who's here," Clint said.

"Good to see you, man," Dion said as he took his turn patting Shane on the back.

Other officers trickled from the men's and women's locker rooms, each stopping to greet him, but Shane could feel their gazes on him after they stepped past, sensed their unspoken questions. Could he blame them? Wouldn't he have the same questions if one of them had still been in a chair like this one? Wouldn't he wonder if they would ever be back?

Lieutenant Scott Campbell emerged from his office as he was coming off his shift. "Didn't know there was a party going on back here. I would have brought balloons and root beer."

"You don't have anything stronger here?" Shane asked him.

"Nothing I'll admit to. What are you two doing here? Did Leonetti kidnap you?"

"Damn near."

Scott shrugged. "You have to forgive him. He needs work on his sweet-talking skills."

"I'm trying."

Shane exchanged a meaningful look with the lieutenant, one he hoped Vinnie would miss. They might joke about forgiving Vinnie, but the sergeant was nowhere near forgiving himself for not arriving at the scene quickly enough to prevent Shane from being shot. It wasn't anyone's fault, but nobody could convince Vinnie of that.

Vinnie had just been talking to Liz Gallagher, the midnight shift's only female trooper, about road conditions, but now he turned back to Shane.

"Ready to go?"

"Sure." He glanced to the door. The trip down the step would be jarring, though not as difficult as going up.

But before they reached the door, it flew open, with several troopers stepping inside and bringing the frigid air with them. They crowded around Shane, telling him how they couldn't wait for him to return to duty. Shane only wanted to get outside and away from all of them. He couldn't breathe.

As if Vinnie finally recognized his distress, he opened the door and moved in front of the chair to guide it over the step. Shane's back teeth crunched as the wheel bounced to the asphalt below.

"You okay?"

Shane nodded. Still, he paused for several long seconds, breathing in the chilly air until his lungs ached. He started toward Vinnie's SUV, but when he reached it, he couldn't help glancing back at the unimpressive, single-story brick building.

Why did it feel as if he was seeing the place for the last time? He pushed away the thought, but the sense of loss remained. It was like saying good-bye to a place that had felt more like home to him than anywhere he'd ever lived. The loss hurt more than any bullet wound ever could.

"You don't look okay," Vinnie continued.

Shane stared at him until it sank in that he hadn't answered Vinnie's earlier question.

"I'm fine." His laugh sounded strained. "Anyway, you've seen me far worse than this. Bleeding like a stuck—"

"Don't!"

"Not funny yet?"

"It never will be."

"Never's a long time."

"Yes, it is." Vinnie pushed the automatic button for the SUV's tailgate, opened it and pressed the transfer board into Shane's hands.

Apparently, the subject of the shooting was closed, at least for tonight. Shane wasn't the only one who carried scars from that night. His might be on the outside, but Vinnie's scars were every bit as real and, perhaps, even deeper.

"Any chance you'd consider just taking me home instead of going out tonight?" Shane asked as he shifted himself from the chair to the SUV's bucket seat.

"Is that what you want?"

"It's just that I'm pretty tired." Maybe his friend would let him off the hook after all.

Vinnie closed the door and, after loading the chair in the back, settled in the driver's seat. "The guys will sure be disappointed if you don't come."

"Is that right?" Shane grinned into the darkness. He'd spoken too soon.

"How about we just make an appearance?

Thirty minutes…tops," Vinnie said. "Just so they all won't think you're avoiding them."

"Okay. Fine," he said, although their visit tonight should have been enough proof that he wasn't dodging anyone.

"Great."

Shane gripped his hands in his lap. As great as it would be to spend time with the rest of the team, hearing the war stories and chuckling at Vinnie's classic jokes, going to Casey's would serve as a reminder of everything he'd lost when that bullet had penetrated his back. The laughter. The fellowship. The unique understanding of the risks they willingly faced every day, for each other and for people they'd never met.

All the things he might never have again.

APPLAUSE BROKE OUT the moment Vinnie pushed Shane's chair through the front door of Casey's Diner, the bells jingling like a charity bell ringer with an empty kettle.

"Thank you. Thank you." Vinnie took a bow. "I'll be signing autographs for those who would like to cover my dinner."

"Then put your signing pen away," Trooper Trevor Cole called from across the room.

Shane's coworkers usually sat at two booths across from each other, the separation wall between them lowered, but tonight they'd moved to a line of square tables. One of the chairs on one end had been removed, leaving an empty spot for Shane.

"Aren't you glad you came?" Vinnie said as he pushed Shane's chair into the spot.

"You knew I would be."

And he was. These were some of the best people he'd ever known. The most honorable. From the senior officers to the new arrivals. A dozen officers crowded around the table, more than would usually go out on any given Thursday. It couldn't have been more obvious that they'd come because they'd heard he would be there.

As Vinnie took a seat farther down the table, Ben Peterson leaned over and patted Shane's shoulder. "It's a little overwhelming, isn't it?"

"What do you mean?"

"Wondering how you'll live without all of these people if you can't come back."

Shane blinked at Ben's directness, but the lieutenant knew what he was talking about. Not so long ago, Ben's job and freedom had been in jeopardy when he'd been a suspect in an evidence-tampering investigation at the Brighton Post. The officer responsible was in a cell now, but Ben had faced his own long days of uncertainty.

"You've got that right," he answered finally.

"You'll have to forgive Vinnie for trying too hard. He's still beating himself up for not being there."

Shane shot a glance down the table, but Vinnie was deep in another conversation. "It wasn't his fault."

"Yeah, try telling him that."

"I have. Repeatedly."

"And yet here we all are."

Shane shifted in his seat, sweating but not ready to take off his coat. A waitress, a little older and harder on the eyes than their usual server, stepped up and started taking orders.

"Too bad Sarah isn't working tonight," Lieutenant Scott Campbell said. "She could pretend you're invisible, like always."

At the opposite end of the table, Kelly leaned forward.

"Hey, Shane, I was just telling Delia about your new physical therapist." She paused long enough to exchange a meaningful look with the other female trooper across the table. "That she seems to be keeping you on your toes."

As if all the officers took a collective breath and held it, the side conversations stopped. Only a clattering of pans could be heard coming from the kitchen.

Kelly cleared her throat. "Well…you know what I mean."

Shane did the only thing he could do—he started laughing. "She's right. The PT's not even bothering with regular steps. I'll be dancing *en pointe* in no time."

When a collective groan replaced the awkward

silence, he was relieved. The elephant in the room had at least garnered a mention.

A short while later the waitress delivered their orders, and they all got down to the business of consuming too many late-night calories. Shane couldn't help watching them as he ate. These unique individuals shared something larger than any one of them: the commitment to serve and protect.

With a gesture toward his phone, Shane signaled to Vinnie that his thirty minutes had run out. Instead of stalling, Vinnie stood up from his seat.

"I'm gonna call it a night. Days off are exhausting." He glanced Shane's way. "You ready to go?"

"I could go, I guess."

After zipping his coat, Shane backed away from the table, waved and started toward the door. He wouldn't think about not being able to work with these people again, of losing a family built on mutual respect and shared risk. He would have to find his way back to this work and these people, just like Ben had. And he would look at these past few months as more a temporary detour than a permanent road closure.

CHAPTER FOUR

"SO WE MEET AGAIN."

A startled sound escaped Natalie's throat as she froze in front of the closed curtain. She didn't need to see the spoked wheel and the running shoes beneath to identify the voice that filtered out like a sneaky caress from the base of her neck to her tailbone, but she peeked anyway.

Shane.

Her mouth was suddenly dry. Of course, his name was on the appointment schedule. She'd set those appointments herself. And two days had seemed like plenty of time to prepare herself to have to work with him again. Apparently it wasn't long enough.

How had he known she would be the one passing by his exam room right then, anyway, and not one of the other PTs or the office staff? In her navy scrubs and basic white tennis shoes, she could have been any one of them. Was there something unique about her shoes or the way she walked? And had he been watching her closely enough to notice? But then her gaze caught on the narrow opening where the two curtains met. He grinned out at her.

She schooled her surprise into a frown, but she couldn't stop the sudden rush of her pulse or the dampness on her palms. Proving what a coward she was, she opened the chart in her arms and studied it as if she hadn't just reviewed it with her last client. She hoped he wouldn't notice it wasn't his.

"What are you already doing in here?" She stepped to the counter outside his visual range and switched charts. Once she opened his, she pulled the curtain wide.

"That young receptionist helped me out since you were running late." He waved a hand in the general direction of the front desk. "She was very helpful."

"I bet," she said under her breath and then grimaced, hoping he hadn't heard. But he was reading an exercise chart on the wall, the one designed for clients with knee injuries. She would speak to Anne-Marie about her *helpfulness* later, though she wasn't sure what she would say beyond *hands off the clients*. She could have used that reminder herself the other day.

"My last appointment ran over. Sorry." She stepped to the sink and washed her hands, even though she'd just done so prior to switching clients. She spoke over her shoulder as she dried them. "Did one of your chauffeurs have to get back on patrol?"

"Four-car pileup on Interstate 96. Trooper Cole took the call. Priorities."

"Trooper Cole?" She pursed her lips, trying to recall the name of the attractive woman she'd met the other day. "So it wasn't…either of the officers from last time?"

His smile was slow, knowing and so sensual that it was all she could do not to fan her face with the chart. Heat rose up her chest and neck. If only she'd worn a turtleneck under her scrub top. She didn't even want to think about any of the other places she felt warm.

She wished he would look away, and at the same time, she dreaded the moment he would. What the hell was wrong with her? Why couldn't she stop asking dumb questions? She shouldn't even be *thinking* the things she had been. She was acting as if he was the first guy she'd ever met. Well, he wasn't, and she refused to get all flustered by this guy, who had probably turned that sexy smile on every woman in the office by now, including dowdy Beverly Wilson.

She cleared her throat, banishing thoughts that could only get her into trouble. "Have you been doing your exercises?"

"I was supposed to do them at *home*?"

"Are you—" But she stopped herself before adding "kidding" as Shane's grin spread wide.

"Gotcha."

Natalie rolled her eyes and looked at the chart. She couldn't just keep staring at him.

"You're not the first of my clients to say something like that on a return visit," she said without looking up.

"I'm not like your other clients."

He had that right in more ways than he could know. "How do you know you're different?"

"Because I did my homework. Five times a day."

She set his chart aside, stood and opened the curtain. "You put in the work. Probably more than you should have. Let's see how much improvement you've made."

Deftly maneuvering his chair out of the tight space, he followed her into the hall.

"You're about to be impressed. Which of the exercises do you want me to demonstrate first? I'm an expert at each."

"None of them."

When the grind of his rotating wheels stopped behind her, she turned to find him watching her.

"What do you mean?"

She started forward again, hoping he would follow. He did. Continuing into the activity room, she led him past some of the machines they'd used the first time to a low-tech area filled with gym mats. She stopped in front of a pair of parallel bars on a wooden platform.

"I thought we'd give these a try."

He just stared at the contraption. "Already?"

"Why not already?"

But he was still looking at those parallel bars the way some people gawked at a line of fire trucks and ambulances racing toward someone else's tragedy.

"I just thought we'd build up to that," he said finally. "You know…try some other things first."

He still wasn't looking at her when he said it, but she couldn't stop watching him. This didn't fit. For the first time since he'd appeared in the clinic, Shane exuded something less than unshakable confidence. His face looked downright ashen.

"You were already using the parallel bars at the intermediate treatment center, weren't you?"

"Just once." He paused and licked his lips. "It was too soon."

"But you're stronger now."

"Maybe."

He didn't sound convinced. Which didn't make sense. He'd been so determined to get back to work. And he'd worked so hard in the clinic and at home. So why was he reluctant to even try the most important step? Why was he stalling? Was he afraid of trying to walk again…or terrified he never would?

Natalie turned her head toward the wall of windows as if she could find answers in that angry sheet of gray. She shouldn't become personally involved. Her only job was to use her skills to help an injured client become stronger. If he chose not to—or was too scared to—improve the quality of his life, that was none of her business.

It couldn't matter that his reticence reminded her of her mother's choice not to reclaim her life. She couldn't go there. Shane and her mother might both be in wheelchairs, but they couldn't have been more different. One knew the risks when he'd put on that uniform. The other had just been living her life until she became collateral damage in a public-sanctioned joy ride.

She shouldn't allow herself to be drawn in by someone who represented all her family had lost. She shouldn't wonder if he was hurting in a way that had nothing to do with the bullet-size scar on his back. She shouldn't stick her nose into other people's problems when she had enough of her own. But something was keeping Shane from walking when he should have been, and now that something was keeping him from even taking the critical first steps. And, God help her, she had to find out what it was.

SHANE STARED UP at the pair of parallel bars and then lowered his gaze to his gripped hands, his nail beds turning white halfway down from his tight squeeze. He could feel the sweat building just under his hairline, but there was no way he would reach up to swipe his forehead. Not with Natalie already watching him closely enough that she had to know what he was feeling, and it wasn't confidence. Chicken, maybe? He hated like hell that he couldn't shake off all those feathers.

Of course his PT would expect him to stand up from that chair eventually. Had he expected to walk again from a seated position? Maybe he should have tried it while lying flat on his back.

No, he hadn't expected either of those things, but like he'd told her, maybe it still was too soon. It probably didn't say anywhere in his file that he'd had a bad fall the first time the hospital PT staff had used that sling thing to lift him out of his bed and that half of his sutures had to be sewn again. If he'd believed that just by changing his treatment location he could exorcise his fear of falling again, he was dead wrong.

Was this why his recovery had stalled?

He glanced at the bars again, and a seed of panic embedded itself in his gut.

"Okay. Have it your way. For today, anyway."

Natalie had closed the file now, her steady gaze seeming to judge him a coward.

"You know, the sooner we get you up on your feet—"

"I know. I know. It's just…" He shook his head, the truth too embarrassing to share. He was like a toddler who'd fallen once and decided to settle in as a permanent crawler.

"I guess we can continue a few more days with

your first group of home exercises. But by the end
of next week—"

"Yes. Next week," he said to cut her off. The
sooner they stopped talking about it, the sooner
he could stop sweating like a marathon runner
hitting a wall near the twenty-two-mile marker.

"Well, let's get started."

She flipped open his file again to the sheet of
exercise instructions she'd given him on Wednesday. He didn't need to see it to begin the stretches
he'd already memorized. Filling the role his coworkers had taken during his home sessions the
past few days, Natalie lifted his leg, straightening and bending it several times before lowering
it to the ground.

"I'm getting an idea why the muscles in your
upper body haven't atrophied as much as we
would have expected by now," she said as she
lifted the other leg. "You've only been working
out from the waist up."

He couldn't help grinning at that. "So you noticed my upper body?"

She frowned up at him, the color in her cheeks
deepening.

"It's my job to pay attention to such details
about my clients." Without looking at him again,
she repeated the stretch on his other leg. "Besides,
who could avoid noticing when someone looked
like a cartoon character?"

"I guess there are worse things to be compared

to than a cartoon hero." He'd take her words as a compliment, even if she hadn't intended them that way.

"Whoever said hero?"

"It was one of the few things I could still do in bed."

Her lids fluttered, her blush deepening over his comment about his activities in bed.

"What was?" she managed.

There were so many things he could say, but he gave her a break this time. "Low-weight strength training. Sometimes I couldn't watch another minute of TV, and my eyes were strained from reading. So I had a friend bring over her hand weights. I started with the five-pound ones."

"You should have been exercising under a medical professional's care. It might have caused more damage—"

"More damage than a bullet?"

She shrugged. "Well, not that much."

"Anyway, there was hardly any moment when at least one medical professional wasn't watching me or telling me what to do."

"We tend to do that."

Shane smiled at that. At least some of the tension between them had dissipated. He just hoped she didn't ask him now why he was putting up roadblocks in the path of his recovery—because that would only multiply the stress again.

If he knew the answer to that question, he

would be pushing the obstacles out of the way as fast as his arms could move them. It wasn't that he was afraid of walking again—he couldn't think of a single thing he wanted more.

But what if it just wasn't in the cards? What if he got up there on the parallel bars and nothing moved, ever, except his arms as they dragged his legs behind him? How could he repay his debt to society then? He had to make some progress, had to have some good news to share with Kent. Especially now, since his mentor's cancer had failed to respond to the most recent round of chemo.

But he couldn't tell Natalie that. It probably wouldn't come off as such a great story, since Natalie definitely had something against police officers. He'd been wondering what it could be for the past few days, but had told himself he would only be opening a can of worms if he asked. But suddenly he had an irrepressible urge to pop open that can's lid.

"So, what do you have against cops, anyway?"

She dropped the file and had to pick it up again before she could look at him. "I don't have anything against cops. Why would you ask something like that?"

"That's the story you're sticking to after the other day with the cops and robbers comment *and* the question about whether or not I bothered to wear a vest?"

"It was just a bad—"

"A bad day. So you've said. But most of us have our bad days without offending an entire profession."

Instead of answering, she shrugged.

"Is it about the problems law enforcement has had with the African-American community?"

Her eyes widened as she stared at him.

He cleared his throat, his face suddenly hot. "I mean…well… I thought that maybe you might be…"

"Biracial?"

"Sorry. I shouldn't have assumed. It's just—" He cut off his words, but he couldn't stop his gaze from gliding over the smooth-looking skin of her neck before returning to her gleaming eyes. "Again…sorry."

But the side of her mouth lifted. "Usually I pass."

"For white?" Immediately, he wanted to know why she would *want* to pass for anything other than the amazing beauty that she was.

Her chuckle surprised him.

"It's only fair since my main exposure to the African-American side of my heritage is the two boxes I check on applications." She glanced at the exercise list, not meeting his gaze. "But race issues aren't the only reason I'm not a fan of cops."

"Then why not?"

"People become police officers for the excitement of shooting suspects or driving fast cars to chase down criminals," she said and then pulled her sweater tighter over her shoulders.

He lifted a brow. "That's it. Really? Even after the number of high-profile police shootings involving unarmed young black men, *that's* your reason?"

"I said those weren't the *only* reasons."

"Did you know that the majority of police officers work a full career without ever having to discharge their weapons, except in training? And in some cities, they don't drive fast cars or motorcycles at all. Some are on horseback. Or even riding bicycles in crowded areas."

She sighed as if she realized he wouldn't give up the point—she was right about that.

"I just hate...hate when they act like cowboys, racing around like no one else matters."

For several seconds he could only watch her. What wasn't she telling him?

"Present company excluded, right?" he asked when she didn't say more. "Lately, I don't drive anything fast or get to race around anywhere."

She shrugged. "Forget it. Let's get back to work." She stared pointedly at him. "And you'd better keep up your upper-body regimen, because you'll need those arms to support you on the bars next week."

"Guess so."

He shifted again, as she'd probably guessed he would. She was deflecting, and that told him that she was hiding something. Had something happened between her and a police officer? Had she dated a cop who turned out to be a creep? Just the thought of that had him strangely unsettled. He knew plenty of guys who wore the uniform and were jerks in the dating department. Some women he'd flipped through in his continual rounds of speed dating might include him in that category. But what bothered him more? That some cop might have burned her or that another officer might have *dated* her?

Too many questions, and he shouldn't have been wondering about any of them, let alone asking them. He had enough of his own problems right now. Natalie didn't appear to be in the mood to answer his questions, anyway. She'd suddenly become engrossed in his file, though nothing inside it had changed in the two days since his last appointment.

As Shane waited for her to finally look his way again, his gaze shifted around the room. The same machines and mats and gadgets that had been there during his last appointment had been left idle, waiting for PTs to begin torturing their patients. An open doorway led to another activity room with a miniature set of mats and equipment for children. Shrill laughter filtered from the room as if to clarify the space's purpose. A couple of glass-walled offices lined the opposite side of the room, their blinds tightly closed, rendering the open layout moot.

Not far from the intimidating parallel bars, a collection of framed certificates and photographs lined one of the walls. He'd noticed it the first time, but he'd been too busy checking out his therapist to take a closer look. Now that he had some free time while she pretended to study his file, Shane rolled closer to the display.

The certification documents were what he'd expected—one for Natalie Ann Keaton and a few for some other physical therapists. The other documents were thank-you letters and such from pleased clients, but the photos were what interested him most. They were of youth sports teams.

He blinked as he paused on the three wheelchair basketball team photos. In all three photos was none other than Natalie Keaton, wearing a bigger smile than she'd ever given him. He suddenly wondered what it would feel like to have her smile at him that way, but he tucked away the thought where it belonged.

"You've found out all of my secrets."

He started at the sound of her voice, surprised that he hadn't heard her approach. He'd been off the job too long if his senses were that dull. If nothing else, he should have felt this particular woman's nearness from the electric jolt she usually gave him.

"You mean that you smile really big when

you're not on the job?" He immediately regretted his words. Now she knew that he'd only been looking at her when he should have at least feigned interest in the other subjects of the photo.

At her frown, he grinned. "Oh, you mean that you coach."

"Guess it shouldn't come as a surprise."

He narrowed his eyes, trying to decipher her comment. "Why shouldn't it surprise me that you coach wheelchair basketball?"

"Oh… I mean…you know…that I played."

"How would I know that you played?"

"Isn't it obvious?"

She shrugged, but he could have sworn that she scrunched her shoulders more than she had been already. She couldn't have looked more uncomfortable if she'd been standing there beautifully nude instead of wearing those curve-masking scrubs. Then *he* would have been the uncomfortable one. At least he hoped his body would respond that way to seeing a sexy woman in the altogether. But he couldn't worry about that now, not when her discomfort over their conversation was still so obvious.

Was this about her height? Sure, she was tall. Her willowy frame had been one of the first things he'd noticed about her. Well, not the first, but close to it. Would it surprise her that she wouldn't look so tall if he were standing next to her instead of sitting?

"What position did you play?" He didn't know why he asked. He might understand the intricacies of the two-point conversion or a hook-and-ladder play, but he had no clue what happened on a basketball court. Still, it was easier than asking why she wasn't comfortable in her own skin. How could she not know how beautiful she was?

Instead of relaxing over his inane question, she winced.

"Center."

She watched him as if that admission should mean something.

"Were you good at it?"

She squinted at him as though he'd missed something, but she answered anyway. "High-school good. No D-1 colleges were chasing me, if that's what you're asking. Especially when I spent all of my time at practice."

He lifted a brow. "Why do you say that? Most of my coaches were all about putting in the work."

"Not that kind of practice. Five hours a day of piano practice."

"Piano?" He watched her for several seconds, trying to picture her playing. Strange, though—he could just as easily imagine her long and elegant fingers skimming over his skin as floating over ebony and ivory keys.

"But that was a long time ago."

She turned to study another therapist and his patient as if to signal that the subject was closed.

"Anyway, the Livingston Community Center was trying to build a youth wheelchair basketball team to compete with teams from surrounding counties, and someone suggested that I should coach. Probably because of my game experience and my medical background." She shrugged. "Anyway, the kids are great, and they work so hard. We have a game tonight."

"I bet you're a really good coach."

He didn't know why he'd said it, and he had no proof to back up his belief, but the way she smiled at the young faces in those photos told him he was right.

"Well, I'm not being a good PT right now, standing around talking about myself." She returned to the file in her arms. "We have work to do, so stop wasting time by asking me questions. I'm on to your game."

He was stalling today for more than one reason, so he appreciated that she didn't mention the other. Though he allowed her to direct him through the series of exercises, his thoughts were far from the strengthening of weakened muscles. He had so many questions about the woman instructing him that he kept losing count of his repetitions.

He'd planned to keep his distance from Natalie, to see her as his physical therapist and nothing more. But each little thing he learned about her only made him more curious. An athlete who played piano off the court. A tall, beautiful woman who was uncomfortable with her amazing body. A biracial woman who knew precious little about the African-American experience. Her contradictions drew him in as effectively as her beauty had. Possibly more.

Though she'd joked that he'd discovered all of her secrets, he really knew only a few. And he couldn't help himself. He needed to know them all.

CHAPTER FIVE

LOCAL WOMAN CRITICALLY *injured in police chase*.

Shane returned to the top of the article on his laptop and read the whole thing a second time. It had been too easy to find in a simple search, yet so much harder to read. Just another high-speed chase with tragic, unintended consequences. Only this time, Natalie and her mother were the innocent bystanders whose lives were forever changed by it.

No wonder Natalie hated cops. She could blame a couple of them for her mother's injuries. If the woman was even still alive.

Chewing his lip, he returned to the search results and scanned the headlines for follow-up articles. Most were from the initial accident and the ethical questions about whether the officers should have called off the chase once inside city limits. But one article, dated several months later, described a lawsuit for the care of a paraplegic accident victim. *Long-term* care, meaning she'd still been around to need it. Still another article spoke of a settlement reached as officers involved were cleared of wrongdoing.

At the sound of approaching footsteps behind him, Shane startled, bumping the TV tray and nearly sending the whole electronic setup onto the floor.

Trevor Cole set the tray of food on an end table and hurried to help with the tray.

"Easy there. Did you find what you were looking for?"

"Yeah." But Shane closed the laptop instead of showing his frend the results.

Trevor raised an eyebrow but didn't comment as he moved the laptop to the other end table and replaced it with the food tray.

"I told you I could do that for myself." Shane frowned at the sandwich, glass of milk and chopped strawberries.

"I know you did, but I was already getting something for myself."

"Yeah. Yeah." Shane waved away the other officer's excuse and took a big bite of his ham sandwich, chewed and swallowed. "But thanks."

"No problem. Anyway, you were busy doing research for…whatever you were looking for."

"Just keeping up on the news." He took a few more bites of the sandwich.

Shane pretended not to notice Trevor's speculative glance before he returned to the kitchen. It wasn't anyone's business what he was looking for, even if he thought Shane was surfing porn. Whether that was better or worse than searching for details on his physical therapist, he couldn't decide.

His gaze landed on the laptop again, the last article replaying in his thoughts. Natalie had every reason to be angry at the world. He could even see why she might blame all police officers, since there had been no repercussions for the cops involved. But that didn't make him like it.

Shane shifted, pushing the plate away.

"Is there something wrong with the sandwich?" Trevor called from the doorway where he'd been standing for who knew how long.

"Just not hungry."

"You need to keep up your strength."

If he had a dollar for every time someone had said that these past three months, he could retire today. But he forced down a few more bites of the sandwich, shoved in the strawberries and gulped the milk, so his friend would take away the tray. As soon as Trevor left the room, Shane rolled his chair forward so he could grab the laptop again. This time with the computer balanced precariously on his lap, he glanced at the list of articles again, becoming more perturbed by the minute.

He was guilty of a lot of things, but he refused to take responsibility for someone else's mistake. It wasn't fair for Natalie to blame him for the chase. He planned to tell her so the next time he saw her.

"Come to think of it," he whispered to the computer screen.

He began another search. There were a few things he needed to say to Natalie Keaton, and whether she realized it or not, she'd given him an easy way to do it. Sure, it might fall into a gray area where stalkers were concerned, but she was the one who'd volunteered where she would be tonight. He was only looking up the specifics. Still, he glanced over his shoulder to make sure Trevor wasn't watching from the doorway.

Since there was only one youth wheelchair basketball league in the area, details weren't tough to find. With just six teams in the league, all games were played at the same gymnasium. This was almost too easy.

He was just writing down the address on a notepad he kept on the end table when Trevor returned, this time empty-handed. Again, Shane shut the laptop.

"You know," Trevor began, "we're trained to pick up on when someone is hiding something."

"It's no big deal."

"I'm sure, but just let me know if you're conspiring for world domination or something."

"Nothing like that."

Was he really hunting for Natalie to give her a piece of his mind, or was he just looking for a way to see her outside the clinic? He chose not to answer that question.

"Maybe you're searching for better home care," Trevor said. "Free help tends to be subpar."

"I couldn't get better help if I paid top dollar for it."

"Then what?"

The wheels in Shane's mind were turning. His jaw tightened, the reality of his physical limitations battling his need for independence. There was no way he would be able to pull this off without help.

When Shane glanced over again, Trevor was watching him too closely.

"Just let me know what I can do to help."

This time Shane grinned at him. "How do you feel about watching some basketball tonight?"

CHATTER AROUND NATALIE died down as she crouched in front of the excited group of boys and girls in Wakefield Elementary School's new gymnasium, where the Livingston Community center team played all of its games. The players' outlandishly expensive sports wheelchairs were pressed wheel to wheel for the team pep talk.

"Now, I don't want any of you to get discouraged. We've had a rough season so far, but you've played your best, and you're getting better all the time." She made eye contact with each of her ten players, giving them her most encouraging smile. "Just go out there and have fun. If we win, we win. And if we lose, we'll try again next week."

"But it's more fun to win," ten-year-old Lucas chimed.

"Now, Lucas, remember, it's more important that we learn to play as a team. The other part will come in time."

"But when?" he whined.

She was beginning to wonder the same thing herself. Most of her players were returning from last season, and the team had finished last year without a single win. Lucas was her best player and hardest worker, so Natalie already knew that if individual efforts could have made a difference, they already would have won.

She leaned down to muss the boy's mop of tawny hair. "We'll get there." She turned back to the whole team. "Now let's go get 'em."

"Go, Junior Cats!" they called out in unison.

She wasn't sure from where they mustered their enthusiasm. These kids faced so many disappointments in their daily lives, from art classrooms with work tables too low for their wheelchairs to fit, to bouncy-house birthday parties to which they weren't invited. The least she could do was give them a win *here*, where they were all on a level playing field.

"Yeah, go, Junior Cats! Hoot! Hoot!"

Natalie jerked, and not just because it was the loudest cheer she'd ever heard at a Cats game. A shiver of familiarity shimmied down her spine. But there was no reason for him to be there. She shook away the sensation as she started back to the coach's bench, but the sound came again, as loud as before.

"Go, Junior Cats! Go, Cats!"

Finally, unable to resist, she turned toward the far end of the bleachers. Parked right next to the rows of seats, Shane grinned and waved at her. Lucas moved to center court for the tip-off, the other starters took their positions and the subs lined their chairs up next to the bench, but Natalie couldn't move. What was Shane doing here in her life outside the clinic? He had to know that he'd just thrown her a boulder-size curveball as his smile widened. She didn't recognize the man next to Shane, but even out of uniform, the guy practically had *cop* stamped on his forehead.

Somehow she managed to give a tight wave before turning to sit on the bench, hiding the heat rushing to her face.

Of course, she'd mentioned the game earlier, but she hadn't given a time or location. Was she flattered that he'd tracked her down? If she had any instinct for self-preservation, his appearance should have given her the creeps. So why was her discomfort tinged with flutters of excitement?

"Go Coach Natalie!" he cheered this time.

If there was any question as to whether he'd come to see her, that last cheer removed all doubt. Her jaw tightened as resentments from what felt like another lifetime resurfaced as if uncovered by a careless backhoe. Why had Shane come here? He couldn't know that this was a sensitive subject for her. He had no idea that he was the first person *ever* to attend one of her games. This was different, of course. She wasn't even playing. Yet she was nervous and excited and oddly proud, just as she would have been had her mother shown up for even one of her games.

That he'd disturbed her private web of feelings, intricately tied with the fragile thread of buried hurts, only made her angrier. So mad that she missed the tip-off. Only the cheers of the children next to her brought her back.

"Let's go, Junior Cats!" she called out, relieved that she hadn't asked for more defense, particularly when one of her players was taking a shot. It bounced off the rim, closer than most of her team's shots. Even so, she needed to get her head back in the game.

But she couldn't resist one more look at her unexpected fan. Of course, Shane picked that same time to glance her way. Her face heated. Shane only lifted his arm in silent cheer.

Just for her.

Somehow she made it through to the end of the game, but only by forcing herself to ignore him through all four quarters and the halftime break. She ended the game the same way she'd started it, by encouraging her players.

"You guys played a great game." She gave

them two thumbs-up for emphasis. "You should be proud of yourselves."

"We still didn't win," Lucas groused, pointing to the scoreboard where the 32–17 final score still showed. "Somebody didn't make any baskets at all." He glanced over at Chase, who looked as if he wished his chair could swallow him.

Natalie frowned. "You know better than that, Lucas. We don't single out players. We all did our best. And win or lose, we play as a team. Now, I saw some really good stuff out there today. We'll build on that in practice, and we'll be even stronger for next week's game."

But the solemn looks on all the players' faces suggested she wasn't getting through.

"We'd better have *extra* practice because we really need it," Kendall, one of the two girls on the team, called from the Natalie's left side.

"Maybe all night," piped one of the boys.

The children all murmured their agreement. She was losing them. They were giving up, and she worried she wouldn't be able to stop it.

"Hey, what are all of those long faces about?"

Natalie turned in the direction of Shane's voice. She'd been so aware of him throughout the game that it didn't seem possible that he could have wheeled his chair to the back of her team huddle without her noticing. But there he was.

The children turned their heads first and then swiveled their chairs to face the visitor they'd probably noticed from the sidelines. He was hard to miss.

"Hi, I'm Shane."

"That's Mr. Shane," Natalie corrected.

Shane grinned. "I just wanted to know what all this sadness is about. I saw some good basketball out there. You guys really played your hearts out."

Had he been watching a different game? If he'd seen any good basketball, it had been from their opponents, but she was grateful for his encouraging words.

"Are you Coach Natalie's friend?" Lucas wanted to know.

"Do you play basketball, too?" Kendall asked.

Without even receiving answers to their questions, the players suddenly sat higher in their chairs. Even Chase. Their loss was all but forgotten as they watched, with open curiosity, the muscular man, who traveled by wheelchair like they did.

"Yes, I'm Coach Natalie's friend," he said, responding to the first question.

Natalie could have sworn that his warm gaze on her felt more than just friendly.

Kendall rolled to the outside of the huddle to get a closer look at Shane. "You have a wheelchair."

Shane nodded. "Yeah, something happened at work."

"An accident?" Lucas asked.

"Something like that."

"I was in a car accident," Lucas said.

"Sorry, man," Shane told him.

Natalie braced herself, waiting for Shane to reveal what she already knew, but he didn't volunteer any details.

"What kind of job do you have?" Kendall wanted to know.

"I'm a police officer."

Shane met Natalie's gaze as he said it, so she forced herself to look away, toward the basket on the south side of the court.

"Really?" one of the players chimed.

"That's cool," another called out.

"You aren't a cop anymore, are you?" Lucas, ever the realist, asked.

Shane smile tightened. "Sure I am. I'll go back to work when I get better."

He blinked as if recognizing that he'd said those words to the wrong audience. But the children only nodded. Some of them still believed they'd get better, too.

"But I need something to do while I'm waiting to go back to work, so maybe I could be your assistant coach," he blurted.

Natalie could only stare at Shane. His eyes widened. Had he even shocked himself with his knee-jerk offer? She shook her head, even as her pulse rushed.

"I don't think that's such a good idea." Why had he offered? Did he know anything about basketball? "The season is more than half over, and the kids would have to get comfortable with another coach…"

"You're probably right."

She'd expected him to argue, so her disappointment that he was giving up without a fight surprised her.

Chase, who seldom had an opinion about anything, suddenly rolled his chair closer to Shane. "Can Mr. Shane be our assistant coach, Coach Natalie?"

"Yeah, can he?" another chimed.

Natalie was caught—had been from the moment he'd arrived at the gym with an agenda that still wasn't obvious to her. But as much as she couldn't disappoint the children, who were excited to be near an adult facing challenges similar to theirs, she reasoned that it might be good for Shane, as well. Somehow she needed to help restore his confidence if she wanted him to move forward in his recovery.

"We'll need to check with the league. And your parents."

Who was she kidding? League officials would be thrilled to have a police officer among the coaching ranks. As for the parents, they were already crowding closer, excited about the prospect of having someone with a physical disability serving as a role model for their kids. She couldn't blame them.

"If it's okay with them, then it's fine with me," she said.

What followed were the loudest cheers her players had made all day.

The man who'd been with Shane earlier strode across the gym as the players waved and started off with their families. He raised an eyebrow when he reached them.

"What have you gotten into now?" He turned conspiratorially to Natalie, gesturing toward Shane. "This guy. You leave him alone for a minute and he causes all kinds of trouble."

"I'm starting to realize that," she said with a wry smile. "Hi. I'm Natalie."

"Trevor." He shook her hand.

"One of Shane's police officer friends?"

Trevor waggled an eyebrow. "Did he already tell you about me?"

"Just a guess."

"Good. He didn't tell me about you, either." He exchanged a look with Shane and then turned back to her.

"I'm Shane's physical therapist," she explained.

"Oh, I see." He gave Shane a thumbs-up and then turned back to her. "Count on Shane to have a therapist like you. He always finds the pretty ladies."

"Just his PT," she clarified. And what exactly did the guy see? "Well, apparently, we're going to do some coaching together."

"Him? Coach basketball?" Trevor stifled a laugh. "So that's why you wanted to come to a game. To coach?"

"I'll be the *assistant* coach," Shane clarified.

"If everything checks out," Natalie couldn't help adding.

"Oh, don't worry about that," Trevor said. "You've got one of the good ones. The kids will be lucky to have him."

"I keep hearing that. He must pay you guys for endorsements." But even as she said it, the officer's words replayed in her thoughts. *You've got one of the good ones.* She didn't *have* him at all, and didn't even want to…right?

"He pays every month, just like clockwork." Trevor turned back to Shane. "So, since you're assistant coaching and all, you'll be needing rides to the practices and games."

"I can pick him up," Natalie heard herself saying. "I mean, since transportation is always an issue."

Both men looked at her.

"I can't ask you to do that," Shane said.

"But you can ask *me*?" Trevor said.

Natalie shook her head to squash the argument. "I'm already going to the practices and the games, so it only makes sense for me to pick you up."

When Shane opened his mouth as if to argue again, she added, "It would give your coworkers a break."

She couldn't explain why she'd launched the low blow any more than she knew why she'd offered to drive him, but when he blinked, she knew she'd hit her target. What kind of person used a guy's guilt against him like that?

"Hey, Shane, you know it's no trouble," Trevor began.

"Thanks, man."

Natalie studied the dry-erase play chart in her hands instead of focusing on either of them. The last thing she needed was someone else questioning her motives. She was doing a good job of that herself.

"Well, if you're sure," Shane said finally.

She glanced up to find Shane watching her. A tremor fluttered through her so quickly that she had to grip the board to keep from dropping it. This whole plan was a bad idea. Coaching with Shane was already not in anyone's best interest, especially not hers, and now she'd volunteered to put extra minutes on the time clock.

"Of course I'm sure," she said anyway.

"Then that would be great. Thanks."

Great. That wasn't the way she would describe the prospect of spending so much time alone with Shane Warner when it had nothing to do with his recovery. *Dangerous. Unwise.* Now those words offered a more apt description. Like tightrope walking on a fraying cord. But she'd promised to do it, and she always kept her commitments. Even if the men in her life had never kept theirs.

Shane probably would change his mind about being an assistant coach, anyway. He'd already almost backed out the moment she questioned his offer. As much as she hated to see these children face another disappointment in their lives, it would be easier for the kids to handle if he didn't come at all rather than to attend several practices and then be a no-show for an important game.

No, it wouldn't surprise Natalie if Shane backed out before she could pick him up for the first practice. But she had a strange feeling that she would be as disappointed as the kids if he did.

CHAPTER SIX

SHANE PEEKED OUT from behind the curtain Tuesday night as the van pulled to a stop in his driveway, its headlights aiming cone-shaped beams on his garage door. He dropped the cloth back into place, hoping she hadn't noticed. Natalie wouldn't appreciate it if he looked too excited about going tonight. She certainly hadn't seemed too happy about working with him when she'd let him know during his PT appointment the day before that his coaching application had been approved.

Maybe she preferred to work alone, but her reticence had felt much more personal than just that.

Now her offer of transportation afterward, he couldn't explain that one at all. He was tempted to think of it as some grand gesture, and she probably just felt sorry for him. Worse yet, she probably pitied the other officers who'd been carting him to his appointments.

By the time the bell rang, he'd almost decided to keep quiet and let her believe he wasn't home. But since he was the one who'd strong-armed *her* into accepting his help, he moved to the door and opened it.

"Right on time." He pushed the storm door open until she caught hold of it.

"We need to be at the gym before the kids start showing up." She stepped inside and glanced around stiffly before turning back to him. "You ready?"

"As ready as I'll ever be."

Maybe he wasn't the only nervous one. He was already sweating under his coat that Kelly had assisted him with before she'd left a half hour ago, but that was better than having to ask Natalie for *more* help.

When he started to put on his hat, she took a step forward but stopped herself.

"That's a really nice ramp out there," she said instead.

"It works so much better than that long drop off the porch." He grinned, but when she frowned back at him, he explained, "My friends built it for me."

"You have some really good friends."

"I do," he said as he locked the door.

At the top of the snow-covered ramp, she glanced from him to the wood structure as if asking for permission to assist him. He nodded. He couldn't fight help all the time.

She rolled him down the ramp at a tortoise's pace. "I bet this thing gets slick."

"It's not too bad. We keep it salted."

As they reached the wheelchair-accessible van,

Shane turned back to her, waiting for an explanation, although he already knew the answer. "Nice wheels."

"In my field, I have some connections."

She had more in her own family, but he didn't mention it. She must have had her reasons why she didn't want him to know about her mother.

"Guess I'm not the only one with good friends."

Natalie only smiled as she clicked the button for the side slider door and the lift. More practiced than his friends and with better equipment, she had him in the van in only a few minutes.

"Well, that was relatively painless," she said as she started the engine.

"Speak for yourself." But after her side glance, he added, "Okay, you did a good job."

"That's better."

"Wow, some people really need the affirmations."

"Some of us are starved for positive feedback."

She'd said it as a joke, but that only made him wonder how much truth there was in it.

"The kids are going to be so glad to see you tonight," she said in an obvious segue.

"I'm surprised the county people approved me so fast."

Her chuckle was low and unintentionally sexy.

"You must not realize how hard it is to get volunteers. Especially men. And especially those who've already passed a police background check. You were, in basketball lingo, a slam dunk."

"I guess you're right."

An awkward silence filled the van after that, making the hum of the engine and the muted tones of surprising retro-grunge music from the radio seem louder.

But as they pulled into a parking spot at the elementary school, she spoke up again. "We'll start with our regular drills tonight. Chest passes, bounce passes, layups. Do you have any drills you like to do?"

"First, you'll have to tell me what a layup is."

The van lurched as Natalie hit the brake too hard, a yellow haze from the parking lot light creeping inside. "I knew it! You don't know anything about basketball."

He had to grin at her frown. "That would be true. But I do, actually, know what a layup is, as long as I don't have to demonstrate."

"I should have known better than to agree to your becoming my assistant after you said you saw good basketball the other night."

"Yeah, that was probably too much."

She only shook her head and then turned to study him. "If you don't know anything about basketball, then why did you offer? Wait. Not just that. What were you doing at the game in the first place?"

He chose to answer the second question first.

"I was curious after you talked about coaching during my appointment."

"You were *that* curious?"

"A little creepy, I guess."

"Ya think?"

He shrugged. "I have a laptop at home and too much time on my hands lately." Not that it offered much of an explanation. He straightened and waited for more questions. The ones he would have asked if she'd shown up at *his* game instead of the other way around. Like just how curious a person had to be to track someone down at a kids' basketball game.

"What about the coaching thing?" she prompted.

"It looked like you could use the help."

At that she chuckled. "It must have been *really* bad for someone with no basketball experience to step up to help coach."

"You mean it won't help if I teach them about first downs or extra points?"

"Probably not."

"Punts and yellow flags?"

"You're about to be fired before your first practice."

"Okay. Okay." He raised his hands in surrender. "I'll keep my expertise to myself."

Was that a smile playing on her lips? Suddenly, he wanted to think up a dozen more clever things to say so he could make her smile like that again.

"Unless you tell the kids you know less about basketball than they do, they won't know." She tilted her head from side to side as if working out details. "Just follow my lead. I can also teach you a little about basketball during the drive to practices and games."

His gaze slipped from her to the van's interior. He could think of a lot of things she could teach him in that van.

"A few rules are unique to wheelchair basketball, like the classification system for determining the functional abilities of each player, but I can teach you those, too," she continued.

Shane chewed the inside of his cheek, trying not to grin. If only she knew about the type of lessons he would have preferred. "You're being so helpful, especially when you weren't thrilled to have me coach with you."

"I didn't mind," she began and then shrugged. "Well, not much. Anyway, the kids were so excited. You have something more important than basketball experience."

"You mean the chair?"

She nodded. "Whether you're just using the wheelchair temporarily or not, and we both know it *is* temporary, you share something in common with them."

He swallowed. This had been easier before she'd laid it out plainly. They did share something in common, but was he the kind of role model they needed? Would she see him as a good example for her players if she knew more about his history?

Instead of waiting for him to answer, she climbed out and hit the switch that moved his chair back and then down the ramp. As the lift retracted, she opened the hatch and pulled out a bag of basketballs.

"The kids are lucky to have you," she said as they started up the walk. "They need to see that they are not limited by their physical challenges, and it's generous of you to offer your time to help them see that."

Shane was glad it was already getting dark, so she couldn't see him wince. She might think he'd made this big sacrifice only for the sake of the children, but he knew better. He wondered just how much of his decision had been about the children and how much was all about proving himself to their coach.

"SHOOT AGAIN, BUDDY," Shane called out and then rolled closer to Chase. "You almost had that last one."

Natalie had to smile over Shane's exaggeration. Chase hadn't made a shot all night. Or once this season at practice, or in a game. As her own group of players continued to practice free throws, Natalie couldn't help but peek over as Shane demonstrated flawlessly for Chase the form she'd taught Shane only an hour before.

Who was she kidding? She'd been watching every move Shane had made all night, paying so little attention to her own group that she was lucky she hadn't tripped over one of their chairs. She'd observed while Shane demonstrated dribbling skills—surprisingly advanced for a wheelchair basketball novice, especially one in a regular wheelchair instead of a sports chair. She'd marveled at how quickly the children had accepted tips from him. And, despite her reservations, she'd been impressed by his determination and relentless positivity.

"Now remember, you need to team your shooting hand with your balancing hand to get ready for your shot," Shane told the boy, using the terms Natalie had taught him, as well.

This time Shane put the ball up in the air with a skill that suggested he should have been the head coach instead of her.

"Swoosh," Kendall called out.

"That's how it's done," someone else said.

When Shane glanced back and caught Natalie staring, he winked. Though her cheeks burned, she didn't bother looking away. She could justify watching her assistant coach do his job, couldn't she?

But as the ball he was attempting to scoop up slipped from his fingers and rolled across the floor, she had the reminder she needed that Shane was more than a fellow coach to her. He was her client. The next time he glanced over at her, she looked away.

Natalie turned to her small group of players. "Hey, let's join the others. We could all use some shot practice."

When she jogged over to them, Natalie found Shane offering Chase some tips, pointing a few times to the ball in the boy's hands and then to the basket.

She swallowed the knot forming in her throat. Shane just kept proving that he was a decent guy, no matter what preconceptions she had of him. But as Shane leaned closer and offered one last bit of inspiration for Chase's ears alone, and a new look of determination formed on the boy's sweet face, a disconcerting tingle began deep inside Natalie. She couldn't help but picture herself listening to whisperered words Shane intended just for *her*. Words that had nothing to do with basketball.

She'd successfully expelled those thoughts, like a player with five fouls in a game, when Chase lifted his arms and prepared to take another shot.

"You've got this, buddy," Shane told him. "Just point and shoot."

And he did.

Natalie held her breath as the ball went up, up, up and then skimmed the backboard, which was already a huge accomplishment for Chase. But then the ball seemed to move in slow motion as it hit the rim and spun around it. She braced herself for the echo when the ball hit the floor, and the sound came as expected.

After the ball dropped through the hoop.

For a few seconds, all sounds in the gym stilled. Chase stared, as if he couldn't believe what had just happened.

Kendall broke the silence with a squeal. "You did it, Chase!"

"Hoot! Hoot!" Lucas called out.

Soon all of the players were scooting closer to the boy for high fives. Natalie rushed forward, her arms outstretched, but even on wheels, Shane reached him first. Forgetting the high fives, he leaned forward and gathered the boy's tiny body in his arms, not seeming to care that he risked his own stability in the chair.

Jubilant, Natalie moved from chair to chair, hugging each player. By the time she reached Chase, Shane had moved on and was hugging them all as if they'd been playing together forever. She gave Chase's frail shoulders a gentle squeeze and then moved on to hug the occupant of the next chair.

Only this one's arms squeezed back with a man-size strength. Natalie's eyes popped open. She lifted up and away so quickly that she had to sidestep to keep her balance, but it still wasn't fast enough to stop the heat rushing to her face and other awkward places, given this was a children's sports practice. And nothing could prevent the tingles that began where his fingers had brushed and stretched like a grassfire across her shoulders and down her arms.

She licked her lips that had become desperately dry.

"You okay, Coach Natalie?" Chase looked over at her with concern on his face.

"Of course." She forced a smile. "I was just a little off balance."

Off balance didn't begin to describe this journey from her equilibrium without any sure direction home. She sneaked a glance at Shane. He looked as shell-shocked as she felt. Instead of watching her, he stared blankly at the far net where one basket had triggered this whole awkward moment.

He caught her watching, but instead of that cocky grin she'd come to expect, his smile appeared almost shy. Maybe she wasn't the only one who realized that they'd better roll, walk or run away from each other. And quickly.

Shane cleared his throat. "You see, guys, I won't say that practice makes perfect. But practice sure creates possibilities, doesn't it, Chase?"

He ruffled Chase's hair, and a grin split the boy's cherublike face. When Shane glanced back at Natalie again, his own smile was warm and direct.

Did she really want to get away from Shane Warner? The question returned, but this time, as she pushed the thought away, it clung with winding tendrils. Needing something to do with her hands, she moved about the gym, collecting the extra balls. The team members followed her example, helping out but finishing the task too quickly.

Parents who'd stayed for the whole practice, either watching the drills or paying attention only to their smartphones, gathered at the far end of the gym, coats piled over their arms. Had any of them witnessed the exchange she'd had with Shane? Would they wonder if there was more to their relationship than just basketball? *Was* there?

Shane didn't seem worried about anything the parents might have observed. He crossed the gym floor and greeted several of them, even speaking with Chase's mom, pointing to her beaming son. Natalie joined them all for small talk but was relieved when the children were bundled and out the door.

Natalie returned to the bench and collected her clipboard, dry-erase play board and the bag of balls. Sensing Shane's presence behind her, she turned to find him putting on his coat with no small amount of effort. She knew better than to offer help.

"You'd best be getting me home," he said as he pulled up the zipper. "I turn into a pumpkin pretty quickly these days."

As soon as he'd said it, Natalie had an answer to her question about whether or not she wanted space between them. It would be the wise thing to do, for her and the trooper to move quickly in opposite directions. But the truth remained that at least one of them might want the other to stay.

CHAPTER SEVEN

NATALIE HELD THE storm door open and pushed Shane's chair through the opening, waiting as he reached for a light switch.

The single light only threw shadows into the empty house. She stepped out of her boots in the entry and tiptoed into the dark family room. Once she located the table lamp, she traced her fingers down the shade to the base and flicked on the switch. The room was no longer dark, but it did nothing to relieve her discomfort.

They were alone in his house.

"I thought you said you always have someone staying with you?" She took in the tidy room with its simple decor.

"I never said that. You just assumed it."

"That's not safe."

"Now don't you be worrying about me."

She could hear the smile in his voice before she took a peek to confirm it. Her face felt hot though she'd barely warmed up after coming inside.

"I'm fine. Really. Someone is here every few hours, and someone bunks in the guest room every night." He shrugged. "I have almost too much help. I don't want to seem ungrateful, but I still appreciate the little breaks."

"But what if you fall or if you need to use the… er…facilities?"

She didn't sound like a medical professional right now, but she couldn't imagine if she left her mother home alone for more than a short while. Of course, her mother let her know it every time she did.

Without taking off his coat, he followed her into the family room. "If I fell, I would use my cell phone that I religiously have on me. And about the other—" he paused, glancing over at her "—I make do. My arms are still pretty strong."

Of course, he was more determined to be self-sufficient than her mother was.

"But if you'd like to check around the house for the boogeyman before you go home, help your-self."

He was really grinning now, and she could only frown. She doubted that any boogeyman would stand a chance against Shane Warner, chair or no chair.

"You could also stick around to protect me until reinforcements arrive," he continued. "I probably have a few beers in the fridge if the others haven't sucked them down."

Natalie's mouth went dry. Spending time alone with him in that house sounded like the kind of bad idea that made other bad ideas look like good ones with rough edges.

But as she shook her head, everything inside her nodded, as if unaware of the perils. "I really should get home."

"And leave me here to my own defenses? Won't you feel terrible if I break my neck trying to turn on the garbage disposal or fall off the shower chair?"

"You don't take risks like that when you're in the house alone, do you?" she asked sharply. She blinked as the image of him sitting in one of those functional shower chairs, wet and gloriously naked, stole into her thoughts. His only fall would be along with her as they tumbled to the bathroom floor.

He shook his head, not privy to her slippery and sudsy fantasy.

"Believe me, I've been read the riot act about the shower thing. I…uh…get help with that from the visiting nurse aide."

"Oh." Her daydream morphed then, but only to her back in scrubs, serving as his assistant and then slipping out of all that constraining cotton. She blinked away the image. She needed to get a handle on this unacceptable slide show.

"You could still stay a while to protect me. And have a beer."

"You're a cop," she said to remind both herself

and him. "Are you suggesting that I drink and then get behind the wheel of a car?"

He frowned. "I don't recommend that you guzzle a six-pack. One beer won't get you close to the legal limit. But if you're worried, I have juice. The faucet works, too."

She looked back and forth between him and the door. "How long did you say it would be before someone gets here?"

"I didn't say." He smiled like someone with the upper hand in an argument. "Maybe an hour or so."

She gave one last, flimsy try. "But you said you appreciate having time alone."

"But what if I do something dangerous like brush my teeth or use the can opener?"

"Fine." It had been a losing battle from the start, but she'd been complicit in her defeat.

"So beer?" he asked.

"Juice. In plastic, I hope. Wouldn't want you breaking any glass bottles."

Or her getting tipsy. She had to keep her senses sharp around him. She couldn't risk allowing alcohol to soften her rigid boundaries and make him seem too nice, too perfect. He was already a little too sexy for her to risk spending time alone with.

"Okay, law-abiding citizen. Follow me."

He led her into the long, narrow kitchen that never had been intended for anyone traveling by wheelchair.

He pointed to the wooden dinette with two chairs on the far end of the room. "Have a seat."

"I can—"

"I can handle it."

So she sat and watched his careful, practiced moves. She had to give him credit. He could easily have asked his friends to do everything for him, but it was clear that he'd found ways to do many things himself.

He opened a lower cabinet and placed a clear tumbler and two salad plates on his lap before closing the door. Then he reached in the drawer above it for two forks. He transported all the items to the table and then moved to the refrigerator.

"I thought this was just juice."

"Oh, no. With all of the food people keep bringing, you're not getting out of here without eating *something.*"

She shrugged. She was a little hungry.

"What do you have?"

"Everything, but right now we're having cake."

"Somebody brought you some cake?"

"A *whole* cake." He disappeared behind the refrigerator door, but when he closed it again, a two-layer chocolate cake rested on a plastic wrap–covered plate in his lap. A sizable chunk had been cut out of one side, but there was still plenty left. "People bring food when they don't know what else to say. Just like at funerals."

Because she understood that notion more than

she was willing to admit, she focused on the chocolate confection in his lap. She fully expected him to drop it, but he slid it on the table with the plastic intact.

"I'm getting a lot better at this. Lots of practice." Moving back to the cabinet, he pulled out a bread knife.

"I can imagine."

Her mother had never made that kind of progress in remastering simple tasks, but then Elaine had never even tried to do most of the things she'd taken for granted before the accident.

"These have helped." Shane tapped the edge of one of the plates with the knife, producing several dull thuds.

"Plastic?"

"This, too." He tapped the knife on the side of the glass.

"That looks real."

"It is real. It just isn't breakable." He pointed to the dishes on the table. "They were gifts. Everyone got sick of sweeping up broken things."

"Speaking of glass, you only brought one."

He waved his index finger at her. He opened the refrigerator door, blocking her view, and then he shut it. When he approached her again, he had a half-gallon jug of orange juice in his lap along with one can—not a bottle—of beer.

"Another thing that's a little easier." He pointed to the can.

"Beer with cake?"

"Any worse than *juice* with cake?"

"Probably not." She poured the juice, surprised when Shane didn't insist on doing it. "Anyway, you haven't explained yet why you have a whole cake."

"Not sure myself. Usually they just bring meals, but Delia was trying out a new recipe, I guess."

Rather than open his beer, he set it aside and uncovered the cake. He cut two large slices and handed her one.

"Do your friends bring a lot of food?"

He nodded. "I haven't had the heart to tell them I can't eat all of it. I have to sneak some into the garbage."

"Are you sure you can trust me with your secret?"

"Is there a reason why I shouldn't?" He eyed her for several seconds.

Natalie swallowed, her mouth dry. They'd been alone in his house for about twenty minutes, but the room suddenly seemed more intimate, the air too thin to draw a decent breath. He'd only said he could trust her with a tiny secret, but his steady gaze made it seem as if he was saying more. And she found she wanted to know more about him, details that had more to do with her curiosity and less with his recovery.

"You haven't told me about the…shooting." The

last word caught in her throat, but at least she hadn't referred to it as an *accident* this time.

His gaze fixed on hers, and then he lifted a brow. "You really want to know?"

"I wouldn't have asked if I didn't."

At first he said nothing, as if considering whether or not to share his story, but then he took a deep breath, exhaled slowly and started talking. "It was a domestic incident involving a woman and her live-in boyfriend. Domestics are our most dangerous calls because tensions are so high. Anything can happen.

"Anyway, I got the call from dispatch and was first on the scene. I was waiting for backup—my friend Vinnie was on his way—but I heard the screams. I couldn't wait."

A knot formed at the base of her throat, and her pulse thudded as she waited for him to tell the rest. She knew the end result, and yet she was no longer hearing his account as some distant listener. She had this strange urge to call out for him not to go, as a viewer might shout at a movie screen when the murderer waited behind the door.

"I know. I should have waited."

"You believed someone was in danger."

"She was." He paused before going on. "It was pouring, so I couldn't see that far ahead of me. I slipped in the backyard gate and found the victim crumpled just inside it. She wasn't moving. I checked the scene, and it appeared as if the suspect might have fled, so I called for an ambulance and tried to get to the victim."

He studied his gripped hands for several seconds before looking up again. "I needed to check if she was still alive, but I never reached her."

"The guy came back?"

"I never saw him, and because of the storm, I couldn't hear him." He shook his head. "They told me later that he'd been waiting on the other side of the house."

"Waiting for someone to try to help her?" Fury at a man she'd never met welled inside her, icy fingers creeping up her back. "Did he still want to get back to kill her?"

"We assume that was his plan, but we'll never know."

"Why not?"

He held up an index finger, asking her to wait. "I was about ten yards from her when the shot went off behind me."

"He shot you in the *back* without ever saying a word?"

"At least I don't remember anything. But then I don't remember much after that."

"Did they ever catch the guy?" The injustice of it burned inside her. He hadn't even had the chance to defend himself.

"Dead on the scene."

"Suicide?"

He shook his head. "Sergeant Leonetti... Vinnie. He apparently arrived just as I went down. He and the suspect exchanged fire."

"What about the victim?"

"He beat her nearly to death. But she survived and eventually was able to go home to her kids."

Because of you. She swallowed. At first she wasn't sure whether she'd spoken those words aloud or only in the privacy of her thoughts. But as Shane took a single bite of his cake and then pushed it away, Natalie surmised that she'd held her words inside. There was nothing she could do about the lump that formed in her throat, though. She took a swallow of her juice, trying to blink back the building emotion.

She'd imagined Shane as a cowboy, galloping in on his white horse to play the hero, and he'd really *been* a hero, possibly shielding that woman with his own body. If the man shot a police officer from behind, would he also have fired on an unconscious woman? They would never know, but Shane had nearly given his life trying to protect her.

At the pop of Shane opening his beer, Natalie jerked, drawn from a chasm of thoughts she'd never expected.

"That was a great practice tonight, wasn't it?" he said.

Natalie released a breath she hadn't realized she was holding. He might just have been uncomfortable with his memories, but the topic change felt like a gift to her, as well. Why did it matter so much that her preconception of Shane bore no resemblance to the man sitting next to her?

"Yeah. I was so proud of Chase."

He nodded. "He was proud of himself, too."

"You were so good with him. Do you work with kids a lot?"

"When I get the chance."

"Is it a calling?"

"More like atonement."

She drew her eyebrows together. "Now you have me curious."

"Chase is the little guy on the team, right?" He waited for her nod before he continued. "Even without his additional physical challenges, he would have been smaller than the boys his age."

"Maybe," she said, still not getting the connection.

"I can relate to Chase because I used to be that little guy," he explained. "The runt. The kid in the front row of the school photo."

"You? No way."

"I didn't start growing until a lot later. So I always had something to prove. I was this little thug, always shaking my fist at kids twice my size."

"I can't remember ever looking up to anyone." She smiled over the memory of her gangly self in the mirror. It was even worse before she'd finally started filling in. "Or ever being called the runt. Or even petite."

"Why do you do that?"

She blinked, startled by his question. "What do you mean?"

"Why do you always make comments about your height? So you're tall. Big deal."

Natalie crossed her arms, but Shane only grinned at her.

"I mean, you're tall, but not an Amazon or anything." He took a swig of his beer and set it aside. "You just worry too much about it. You're pretty perfect—I mean you're *proportionate*, and all of that."

At his surprising words, her heart raced. She couldn't look at him. *Pretty perfect?* Either he'd misspoken or she'd misheard.

"You encourage your players to be comfortable with who they are. Maybe you should take your own advice."

She rubbed her finger along the condensation on her glass instead of looking at him. "I'm just sensitive about it. Like you were about being small." She shrugged then finally met his gaze. "But you grew."

"Apparently, so did you." One side of his mouth lifted.

"That's what happens when your father was a pro basketball player who measured closer to seven feet than six."

"So you took after your dad. Did you start playing because you wanted to be just like him?"

Just like him. Now there was a laugh. She didn't want to be anything like him. "I might have wanted to if I'd known more than the basics about him."

"You didn't know your dad?"

"My mom didn't have much to say whenever I asked about *my father*," she clarified. "Oh, I knew the obvious things like that he was African-American. My mom could get sunburned under a beach umbrella with SPF 100 on, and I could stay in the sun all day and never turn pink. But that was all I knew.

"Mom always said it was just the two of us." She shrugged. "Same old story. Young woman gets pregnant, and the guy bails."

Shane's jaw tightened. "Except this guy played pro basketball and could easily have paid child support."

"Mom always said she never told the guy about the baby. That she *chose* to raise me alone. She's an accountant, so we got along fine."

"I take it there's more to the story."

"Let's just say that I found out a few years ago that Mom stretched the truth. A lot. I didn't even know until then that he *played* basketball, let alone that he was some big college star."

"I thought you said he turned pro?"

She nodded. "Apparently, just after he learned about me—just one of the lies—he took off across the globe to play in a European league. I guess he got traded a few times, spent a lot of time on the bench and then hung up his basketball shoes."

"Basketball. Great reason for a parent to desert his kid."

Natalie had to look at him twice to convince herself that the anger in his voice was real. His jaw was tight, and his hands gripped the edge of the table. On her behalf. She couldn't believe it. No one had ever been that mad at her father for her sake. Certainly not her mother. Elaine hadn't even bothered to tell her the truth about him. And not Natalie's college boyfriend, Paul, either. After the accident, and after she'd discovered the truth about her father, Paul had run away as fast as his skinny legs could carry him. Just like her father. Make that *birth father*. Genetic-material donor. He didn't deserve a term of endearment like *dad*.

"How'd you find out the truth?"

Natalie blinked as his question drew her back to the conversation. Did Shane realize just how far she'd traveled in her thoughts? "The truth?"

He lifted an eyebrow over her stalling as the wheels in her thoughts spun fast enough to make her dizzy. How much should she tell him? Strange how part of her was tempted to share the whole story. She couldn't do that. She couldn't put that much trust in another human being. Trust was dangerous. It gave people the chance to hurt her. She'd been hurt enough.

"Mom's journal," she managed finally, still

wondering whether she should have answered at all. "In it, she shared all of the pain she'd shielded me from knowing about."

From knowing her, she'd almost added.

"Did he claim the child wasn't his?" he grumbled.

She nodded because it was easier than saying that part of the story aloud. The truth that she wasn't wanted. "At first, Mom wasn't all that upset when she found out she was pregnant. They were an established couple. She was more excited as she wrote about the life she assumed they would have together. But then she told him. I've never read such gut-wrenching pain."

She had to pause as recalling it reminded her of how those words had sliced through her the first time she'd read them.

"He said he refused to give up on his dream just because she couldn't take her pills correctly. Or, worse, that she'd tricked him."

"Your dad is a real ass." He paused before asking, "Do you think that was possible? That she planned it?"

She shook her head. "That doesn't sound like her."

"So, his *dream* was a lackluster pro career?"

"Maybe not the dream, but it turned out that way." She had to smile at his hard tone. It was nice having someone in her corner. No one had been there in a long time.

"What did your mom do after he left?"

"Well, from her journal, I would say she pulled herself together. And fast. She was suddenly determined. Driven."

In fact, her mother's writing had changed so dramatically that Natalie had wondered if someone else had authored the entries. The romantic girl had been replaced by an unflappable woman who hadn't seemed to feel anything at all, even before the accident.

"She was responsible for two people instead of just herself," he said. "She couldn't afford to have any romantic notions."

She nodded. "But I became her whole life. Do you know how hard it is to be *anyone's* whole life?"

"I can imagine."

Could he? She'd been staring at her hands, but she looked up at him now, searching his eyes for... what? A connection?

"Were you ever curious about...him?"

"Not really," she said automatically. *Not anymore* would have been a more appropriate answer, but she wasn't ready to go there yet. Maybe never. She didn't want to hurt like that ever again.

"You didn't want to know anything?"

"There were a few things, I guess," she said, deciding to share at least part of the truth. "I was curious about my African-American heritage. There's this whole side of me I knew nothing about. It would have been nice to know my paternal grandparents, since Mom's parents are both gone. Did I have brothers and sisters? Did I have a big family with aunts, uncles and cousins who had potlucks every Sunday afternoon? Did they always live near Lansing, or was my father recruited away from somewhere else to play at Michigan State?"

"So you weren't curious at all then."

He grinned at her when she looked at him.

"It's more than not knowing about one parent," she said with a shrug. "I'm black and I'm white, but I was raised one hundred percent white. My poor mom didn't even know how to take care of my hair, so she just combed it until it was a mass of frizz and pulled it back in a ponytail."

She'd expected him to at least chuckle over the picture she'd painted, but his expression was serious.

"Did you face any racial prejudice growing up?"

"That's the ironic thing. I experienced it a few times from my white classmates though I had no idea how to even *be* black. Then the black students weren't exactly laying out the welcome mat for me, either."

"So you have spent your life wondering where to fit in."

"Well, I don't know if it was as bleak as all

that," she managed, but her chuckle sounded forced.

She couldn't believe it. This man who barely knew her, one she had no business getting to know, had just spoken her truth more succinctly than she ever could have. She gripped her hands around her juice glass. When she'd tried to talk to Paul about her questions regarding her heritage, he'd told her she should just leave it alone. As if that part of her didn't exist. Tonight she'd shared a little with Shane, and he only wanted to know more.

"I bet you're a good interrogator," she said, stalling. "You probably get criminals to confess to crimes they didn't commit."

He simply tilted his head.

Natalie shifted under his even stare. Why did he always seem to see too much? Wasn't all that she'd told him tonight enough? Did he really expect her to confess pieces she wasn't ready to admit to herself?

Shane drained his beer and spun the can between his hands.

Natalie found herself trying to fill the silence. "You probably think I'm a cliché. Raised by a single mother. Absentee father. Inferiority complex." She cleared her throat. "In short, a mess."

And she hadn't told him the half of it. That she was tempted to tell him the whole truth, to fillet

herself and let the whole thing spill out, scared
her to death.

"You're not a mess."

She fumbled with her glass. "I wasn't fishing
for compliments."

"If you were, you didn't catch a very good one."

"You know what I mean." Was it humiliation
that made her face burn or her pitiful need to believe his words?

"It's also the truth. You're doing well…consid-
ering." He cleared his throat. "I mean with all…
you…uh…found out."

She quirked an eyebrow. His words were odd.
She'd probably made him uncomfortable.

"But in the end, I don't think it matters what
kind of family you come from. Even a so-called
perfect one like mine."

"What do you mean?"

"I had a picture-perfect family with parents
who were involved in every committee possible to
make the community a better place for my brother
and me. Dad even coached my Little League team.
And yet I got into all kinds of trouble."

"What kind of trouble?"

"Long story."

"But wait—"

She would have argued more, but he raised his
hand and gave her a pleading look.

"Another time, okay?"

She considered and then nodded. Sharing about

the shooting had probably been enough for him for one day.

"Anyway, what I'm trying to say is that we're all just people. We're all capable of good choices and terrible ones. We can be kind or hateful. We can make decisions that can destroy our own lives and take others down with us. We can't figure out our own problems, much less make another person understand us."

He stopped as if deciding whether to say more, and then he did. "Sometimes we're just grateful that someone is willing to try."

CHAPTER EIGHT

NATALIE COULD ONLY stare into Shane's soulful eyes, the room around them so still that it amplified the uneven rhythm of her breaths. And his. He'd spoken about a person making an effort to understand someone else. Hadn't he done just that for her tonight? He'd done his best to figure her out when no one had bothered to even try in such a long time. Strange how she'd never felt more understood.

It could have been surprise, or maybe just the want of a connection she hadn't realized she craved, but something powerful held her in place as the seconds ticked on.

Shane's gaze was unwavering. Steady. A contradiction to the riotous feelings battling inside her, some calling for a poorly plotted charge and others a hasty retreat. She should listen to the one telling her to run for safety. That would be the reasonable decision, and if anything in these past eight years, she'd learned to be rational.

But then, as Shane stared at her lips, heat built somewhere deep in her chest, sliding up her neck. Her gaze moved in the opposite direction, follow-

ing from his eyes along the straight line of his
nose to that softly curved mouth she'd noticed the
first time she'd met him. But instead of smiling
in that sexy way that liquefied her bones, Shane
appeared serious now. Those amazing lips were
slightly parted, as if he was either asking or answering a question.

She had time for neither.

When exactly she'd leaned closer to him, she
wasn't sure. One moment she was tracing with her
gaze the fine line that separated the pale skin of
his face from the salmon color of his mouth, and
the next she was brushing hers over his. He stilled,
his lips feeling like those of a marble statue, perfectly formed yet icily impenetrable.

She froze right along with him as her swell of
courage collapsed upon itself. What had she done?
Had she misread his signals? Had there *been* any
signals, or had she only wished for them? But just
as she started to pull away, a hand came to rest
lightly on her shoulder. Seconds ticked by in an
interminable pause as their lips lingered only a
breath apart.

Shane bridged the distance between them with
a shift of his head. Far from her timid advance, he
swooped in with an urgency that made her gasp.
She might have even swooned if she wasn't almost
certain that they were already seated.

She could have predicted that Shane Warner
would know his way around a kiss. He'd proba-

bly been writing manuals about making the right moves since he was in his early twenties. But nothing could have prepared her for the strength, the finesse, the pure sensuality of his simple touch. Two days' worth of stubble blazed a trail of its own, abrading her sensitive skin as his lips moved from her mouth and over her jawline to her neck, but she didn't care if it left a mark.

Was he that amazing with everyone, or was it just with her? *Everyone.* She knew she should cling to the notion that there were probably others, but it rolled away on a wave of sensation.

With lips alone, he'd managed to touch every inch of her as effectively as any skilled lover's hands ever could. Her skin came alive, tingling with the need for touch. But then he pressed his tongue to the seam of her lips, and she opened for him, sighing as a curl of pleasure unfurled within her.

She knew she should think, should take a breath and bat away the fog that draped over her clarity. Only she didn't want to see clearly. She didn't want to breathe. Or think.

Or wait.

As his hand slipped from her shoulder to tangle in her hair, Natalie scooched to the edge of her chair to move deeper into his kiss. But that only made her more restless. It just wasn't close enough. She needed to touch him, to feel that amazing chest pressed against hers and allow him to enfold her in the cocoon of his arms.

So when his other hand curved over her rib cage, his fingertips accidentally skimming the lower curve of her breast and then tugging her forward, Natalie didn't even pretend to resist. She carefully shifted around the table leg and slipped over the arm of his chair. She was kissing him again before she'd even settled with her legs draped across his lap. His tongue was in her mouth again, and she welcomed it with a hunger she'd never experienced before.

She didn't care that they were cramped in that chair. All she could think about was this man and this moment. She wanted—no, needed—more. From the heavy pressure of him, obvious and enticing beneath her bottom, she was thrilled to realize that she wasn't the only one who wanted.

Was that her voice, moaning in protest when he slid his mouth away from hers? Where would he kiss her next? Her neck? Ear? Breasts? Oh, let it be there. She strained against the flimsy material of her bra at the possibility.

Only he didn't kiss her again. Anywhere.

Her mind still swirling with delicious thoughts, Natalie slowly opened her eyes. Shane had leaned back as far as his chair would allow and stared at her with wide eyes. Her face flooded with heat as quickly as it fled from her nether regions. What had she done? How had she ended up here, and how was she supposed to politely withdraw with a shred of her dignity intact?

She looked away from him and shifted back carefully. The last thing she needed to do now was land on the floor. The moves that had placed her on his lap might have lacked finesse, but they were downright smooth when compared to her jerky motions now.

He cleared his throat. "Sorry about that."

Sorry? Was he kidding? He'd said it like he'd hadn't just kissed the breath out of her and given her the ideal to which she would compare any make-out session from this point on. He'd said it like he'd just bumped into her boobs in the hallway instead of setting them on fire.

"I mean...oh, man...that was a mistake."

"What—" Somehow she managed to stop before saying more. Yeah, that was a mistake, all right. Only she was the one who'd made it.

Once back to her seat, she shoved back so quickly that the chair tipped and whacked against the cabinet. "I've got to go."

"Natalie, wait—"

But she was already too angry, too humiliated, too—what? She didn't want to answer that, though, because she was too freaking turned on by a guy who didn't want her back. Okay, he couldn't deny his physical reaction that he was still trying to hide. But that was just biology. His rejection was more personal than that. He might want her on some primal level, but not enough to risk the headache of acting on it.

The worst part was that she shouldn't want *him*. Had she forgotten that he was a cop? That he represented all her family had lost? And worse than even that, she'd been ready to climb into bed with a *client*.

She grabbed her purse from the floor and scooted past the table without bothering to right the toppled chair. Anyone who could embarrass her that way could pick up the chair for himself.

But at the sound of the garage door opening, Natalie froze.

"Are you…uh…expecting someone?"

"I told you—"

"Oh. Right."

The interior door squeaked open before either could say more. Would it be that Kelly or another female trooper arriving to take a turn helping him? It shouldn't have made a difference who was there, but a woman might be more perceptive about recent events.

"Hey, Warner. You here?"

At the sound of the masculine voice, she let herself breathe. She hadn't noticed that Shane had left the table when she had, but when she turned back now, he was awkwardly setting the fallen chair back in place.

Shane shrugged and then called out, "Well, I

was out partying, but I hurried home, knowing you would be here."

"Good. I'd hate to have to scour the bars looking for your sorry butt."

The officer must have followed the voice because he appeared in the kitchen doorway, still wearing a heavy coat. She didn't recognize this one. He was slightly older than the others, though still handsome in a rugged, broken-nose way.

"Right. I saw the van outside." The man glanced over at her speculatively. "And you are…?"

"Uh…Natalie Keaton."

He lifted a brow. "Are you sure?"

Smooth. So much for her acting like nothing had been happening before the guy showed up. The skin on her chin was so sensitive, and her lips felt swollen. Was it obvious to the guy just what she and Shane had been doing?

"Stop interrogating my guests, will you?" Shane said. "She's my physical therapist."

"You make house calls?" The guy waggled an eyebrow and turned to Shane. "Leave it to you to find a therapist like her. And one who makes *house calls.*"

"Make that one who gives me taxi service to practice so we can coach together," Shane added in a flat voice.

The introduction felt like a slug to the gut. Of course, those things were all she was to him. That she'd also been ready to play show-me-yours-I'll-show-you-mine with him mere minutes before hadn't fazed him at all. If only she could say the same.

The other officer turned back to Shane. "I still can't believe you're coaching basketball. Who made the mistake of letting *you* coach?"

"That would be me," she answered simply.

Allowing him to join her coaching staff was the least of her mistakes lately. The one she'd made tonight topped them all. How could she have given yet another man the chance to reject her? Weren't her father and Paul enough? Shouldn't she have learned by now that all men were the same?

"My friend here has forgotten his manners. This is Vinnie Leonetti."

"I was born in a cave," Vinnie said.

As he gripped her hand with his freezing one, Natalie swallowed. Of course, she recognized the name. He was the guy from Shane's story. The one who'd arrived on the scene just after Shane was shot. She'd just been worrying about what the guy might pick up on tonight, and he was probably thinking only about his own problems.

"Well, I was on my way out, so…"

She grabbed her coat off the side counter and forced herself to put it on right there rather than running from the house.

"Good to meet you," Vinnie said. "Maybe I'll see you at one of the games."

With a nod and a quick goodbye, she somehow

made it out of the house. Games. Practices. The clinic. Her head felt heavy with just the thought of those things. She wished she never had to see Shane Warner again, but she couldn't escape him. He was everywhere. She couldn't disappoint the kids by *firing* him as assistant coach. She couldn't stop driving him to practices and games because she'd made a commitment to do it. She couldn't avoid seeing him three times a week at the clinic, either.

But there was one thing she could do. It wouldn't be good for her reputation at work, but she hadn't exactly volunteered for this assignment. If her boss didn't understand, she would simply have to make her. She couldn't be Shane's PT anymore.

She'd crossed the line with a client, but it was more than that, and she knew it. At least if she didn't have to work with him so closely at the clinic, she wouldn't have to try to make light conversation with him. She wouldn't have to watch his discomfort as he had to be near her after pushing her away. And she wouldn't have to continually touch him and hate herself for wanting more.

"WHAT WAS THAT all about?"

Shane blinked at Vinnie's words, only now realizing he'd been staring at the empty space where Natalie had so recently stood. Instead of answering the question, he took a bite of the cake that tasted like sawdust now. He doubted anything would have any flavor for him, not after he'd experienced Natalie's sweet taste.

"What do you mean?" He was careful not to meet his friend's gaze as he said it.

"That's how you want to play it? As if I didn't just walk in here and practically catch you two in the act?"

Shane frowned at him. "If that's what you *think* you saw, then you'd better get some glasses and fast."

"And you need to remember to hang a towel outside the door next time. And forget glasses— you could have scarred my eyes." Vinnie splayed his hands over his eyes, peeking between his fingertips.

"You don't know what you're talking about."

"Maybe not, but there was enough electricity in that room to light up a Christmas tree. And I showed up right in the middle of it."

Vinnie might have been right about the rest, but he had that part wrong. Whatever had happened between Shane and Natalie was already over before he came through the door.

"Do you have anything good in your leftover collection?" Vinnie asked. "I'm starving."

Shane clamped his teeth shut to keep his mouth from falling open. If this were six months ago, Vinnie would never have given him a break and dropped the subject like that, especially when they both knew he was right and there might be details to share. But this wasn't six months ago, and Shane was no longer the lady-killer he used to be. Now Vinnie was treating him like he was encased in blown glass.

He didn't deserve a break, either, after the way he'd humiliated Natalie, but he took Vinnie's gesture for the gift it was. He pointed to the refrigerator. "Have at it. There's plenty."

Vinnie's head disappeared behind the door. When he emerged again, his arms were laden with containers of leftovers. "There's a gold mine in there."

"Which will turn into a *mold* mine if you don't eat some of it." He yawned and then lifted his arms halfway to stretch. "But, hey, I'm tired, so I'm going to bed."

"You need me to come…?"

Shane shook his head. He needed time alone to process all that had happened tonight. "Just heat up your plate. I'll call if I need anything."

His gaze wary, Vinnie went to work, opening and sniffing the contents of the containers. Shane headed into the bathroom. Vinnie hadn't missed that Shane was behaving out of character. Even with his injury, Shane never went to bed early when he had the chance to decompress with one of his teammates. Right now, though, he had some unwinding of his own to do, since he was wound so tightly that a spring inside him might pop.

What was that all about? He considered Vinnie's question as he brushed his teeth. He'd made so many mistakes tonight, starting from the moment he'd invited Natalie into his house. No, before today. From that first internet search. Why hadn't he just steered clear of her after he'd learned the story about her mother? It would have been the sensible thing. But no. Instead, he'd bulldozed his way onto her team and into her life. Was wanting to change her opinions about cops enough of an excuse? Had it ever been anything *but* an excuse to get closer to her?

Oh, he'd gotten closer tonight, all right. Deliciously close. And he had let her leave thinking he didn't want her.

She had no idea how wrong she was. Well, he hoped she had at least some idea. She'd been sitting right there in his lap, where the action down there had surprised him as much as anybody. Maybe he no longer had to worry that his favorite parts might sit on the bench when up to bat, but he still had no proof that he had any control or the staying power to make it around the bases. That he wouldn't end up humiliating himself. Or disappointing her. Or earning her pity.

So he'd humiliated her instead.

What was wrong with him? One minute he'd been touching the skin he'd dreamed about and kissing lips that were even softer than he'd imagined, and the next he was pushing her away as if she scared him to death. Because she did. He couldn't remember ever wanting a woman the way he wanted her. Could never remember craving a touch that went beyond erogenous zones. Or tiptoed dangerously close to emotions he would rather deny existed. Until tonight.

That was the part that had done him in.

It was also a flashing neon sign announcing that he needed to take a big step back from Natalie, at least as much as possible, given how inextricably he'd tied their schedules together. But before he could unweave that web, he owed her an apology for letting things get out of hand tonight, even if he couldn't explain to her why he'd put on the brakes.

Shane shook his head as he stared at his reflection in the mirror that his friends had lowered for his convenience. He barely recognized the guy looking back at him. The Shane Warner of six months ago would have accepted Natalie's timid offer with a *hell yes* and had her painted toenails peeking out from beneath his sheets without giving the act—*or her*—a second thought. But he wasn't that guy anymore.

Had the bullet changed him by penetrating his protective vest and naive belief that his walls would make him untouchable as well? Or was Natalie his catalyst for change, her boundaries and secrets pushing him to look at his own?

At the knock on the bathroom door, he jerked,

caught thinking of her as he had been so often lately.

"You okay in there?" Vinnie asked from outside.

"I'm fine. Coming out now."

Before he did, he took one last look at the guy in the mirror. It was more than just that his hair had grown out from the super-short cut he wore on the job or that his chin was often scruffy these days instead of clean shaven. Whether it was the shooting, his too-long recovery, meeting Natalie or some combination of all those things, he wasn't sure. But the one thing he knew for certain was the Shane Warner of six months ago no longer existed.

CHAPTER NINE

SHANE LACED HIS fingers together and stared at his hands the next afternoon as he waited for Natalie to take him in for his appointment. Kelly had balked when he'd asked her to drop him off at the front door of the medical services building, but at least she'd agreed to leave him as soon as they reached the clinic.

He didn't need another one of his coworkers observing when he faced Natalie today. The kind of awkwardness that this meeting promised would be hard to hide, and he wasn't ready to answer questions about it.

He braced himself when the door from the clinic side swung open, but Natalie wasn't the one standing there. Instead, a stocky woman whom he recognized from some of his other appointments smiled over at him. She wore scrubs like the other men and women in the office, but she was a little older, with a narrow strip of gray roots showing at her scalp next to her crop of short-trimmed blond hair.

"Mr. Warner, I'm Deborah Lang. I'm a PT, and I'll be working with you from now on."

His gaze shot to the open doorway, and then he looked back at her again. "But, uh, Miss Keaton…?"

The formality of her name sounded strange coming from his mouth. The same mouth that had been so familiar with hers last night.

The woman shook her head, but her smile remained in place as she started toward him. "There was a scheduling issue, but I'm sure the two of us will work great together. Your file is all up-to-date, so we won't even miss a beat during the transition."

When she gestured toward the handles of his chair, Shane shook his head, the reality that Natalie had requested the reassignment settling over him in a hard thump. He moved his hands to his wheels but had to loosen his grip before the chair would roll forward. Great. Now he wouldn't even have the chance to apologize to her today.

Once they reached the activity room, Deborah directed him to a set of weight machines closer to the wall of windows. "Okay, let's warm up with some gentle stretches."

Shane barely heard her as his gaze traced the length of the room to where Natalie stood on the opposite side, working with a teenage boy. The way the kid was eyeballing her—like she played a lead role in a porno film—had Shane shifting higher in his seat, something primitive and possessive flooding his veins. But Natalie didn't seem to notice. She jotted something on the file and then smiled up at Mr. Perv, as if he didn't deserve a long visit with the principal. Shane waited, unable to take his eyes off her and the boy. She had to notice him eventually, right? But when she did glance away from the boy, it was only toward the offices and then the wall of photos. Anywhere but at him.

She was still furious with him about last night. He could hardly blame her. He really was a jerk, wasn't he? What kind of guy turned down a woman like Natalie Keaton? Who had skin as soft as—

"Mr. Warner, I'm going to need you to focus."

He blinked and licked his suddenly dry lips as he turned back to his new PT. "Oh. Sorry."

Clearly, the little hormone across the room wasn't the only one having fantasies about the exotic brunette in scrubs.

"No problem," Deborah said. "Now let's get to work."

If she noticed just whom he'd been watching instead of her, she didn't mention it. But she started with exercises he'd been repeating for days instead of teaching him something new when his attention was, at best, divided. How could he focus, anyway, with Natalie so close that he could sense her presence, even when he wasn't looking at her?

Could she feel him, too, even as she refused to look at him? He sneaked another glance at her, but this time he caught her peeking. Then she pointedly looked away. She was still pissed, all right.

Convinced that he really was a jerk, he began his first set using the pull-down bar. But his frustration only built with each rep. She should at least give him a chance to apologize. And were his actions really so awful that she had to transfer him? Maybe she shouldn't have been letting a patient kiss her in the first place, but—

He pushed away the thought as he let the weights fall with a clank. Wait a minute. She'd kissed *him* first. He smiled as he recalled that initial, timid touch of lips, the one that had surprised and excited him as much as any striptease ever could. She might act all indignant now, but he wasn't the only one responsible for last night. He planned to tell her so.

He would also apologize for his part in it. For kissing her *back*. And for not stopping. If she thought she could keep avoiding him, she hadn't taken a good look at their schedule this week. She might have been able to dodge him at work, but she would have a tougher time Thursday when they stood side by side, coaching their team to another loss.

He would apologize to her when he saw her again. And she would listen, whether she liked it or not. Somehow, though, he had to find a way to tell her he was sorry for kissing her last night without taking her into his arms and kissing her again. And again. And again.

NATALIE HELD HER breath as the clock ticked down during the game Thursday night, not only because the score was actually close, but also because this had been the tensest game of her life. And she wasn't even playing.

The man who'd caused the butterflies to perform aerial dives in her gut wasn't even watching her now, but she'd felt his gaze on her all night. Her senses hummed, anticipating the chance to absorb his attention again. He had effortlessly collected hers, his polo shirt doing an even better job than usual at hugging firm muscle and masculine planes, the gray color only making Shane's eyes even bluer.

This wasn't fair. How was she supposed to pretend she was totally unaffected by their kiss the other night when everything about him shouted at her like a text in all caps? This was even worse than the day before, when Deborah had been working with him at the clinic. Why had she thought that removing him from her client list would solve all of her problems? That plan had only put her in a position to gawk at him from across the room when she should have been doing her job. And it had done nothing to help her avoid him at tonight's game *or* the games and practices for the rest of the season.

He'd rejected her. Whether she should have wanted him or not, the truth remained that he'd pushed *her* away. She should have been grateful. At least one of them had come to his senses before it was too late. She could have been angry at him, as well, for being first to put on the brakes when she would have gotten around to it…eventually. But that tight squeeze inside her chest and the sense that tears were building just beneath the surface suggested that she was far more hurt than angry.

Men rejected her. They'd been doing it all of her life. Her father. Paul. Guys didn't stick around when life became complicated. Shane had just been reminding her, even when she'd been too preoccupied to notice, that he was just like the others. That it would be a mistake to put her trust in him.

"There it is," Shane said, drawing her back to the game, where the laughter, cheers and thudding echoes of the bouncing ball should have held her attention in the first place. At least one of the coaches had been paying attention.

Her parent section was applauding, so it didn't surprise her that Lucas was doing a victory spin before rolling back down the court as his team switched to defense. Her other four players on the court were focusing on their games while those on the bench shouted their heads off. She was the only one not doing her job tonight.

As her gaze flicked to the scoreboard, she blinked. The board read 29–27.

"We're ahead!"

Her hand went to her mouth, but the words had already escaped. When Shane glanced her way and lifted a brow, she shrugged. The team had only been ahead a few times all season, and never during the fourth quarter. Still, with a razor-thin lead like that one, made closer by the other team's one successful foul shot, this game was going to be a nail-biter.

"Let's go, Junior Cats!" Shane had turned his attention back to the court, but he was still grinning.

It was the most significant exchange they'd had all night besides the awkward small talk in the van earlier. Maybe one day they would be able to work together without her constantly recalling what it was like to nestle in his arms. But that day wouldn't be for a while.

Natalie forced herself to focus on the game now as the other team's players passed the ball around in front of the basket, trying to set up a shot.

"Shoot, Titans! Shoot!" a parent called out.

Again, she and Shane exchanged a look. At each parent meeting, she reminded Junior Cat parents not to call out for players to shoot because it broke their concentration, but the other team's parents apparently hadn't received that memo. On the other hand, according to the Titans' record, that hadn't stopped them from winning. With less than a minute on the clock, one of the Titans drove up the right side of the basket and executed a modified layup.

The air rushed from Natalie's lungs, and all five of the players in red Cats jerseys sank into their chairs. They now trailed by that same precious one point, which might as well have been a double-digit deficit as likely as they were to recapture the lead.

"Work together, Junior Cats! Don't give up," she called out, though she was having a hard time not doing the same thing.

Just once she wanted to give these boys and girls a taste of victory. They'd worked so hard, and it just wasn't fair that they still wouldn't see any positive results from their effort. But then every player and parent in this gym understood as well as she did that life wasn't fair.

"Come on, guys, we've got this," Kendall said in a louder voice than she'd ever used at practice or in a game.

"Yeah, we can do this," Lucas chimed as he dribbled down the court and passed to Kendall.

Natalie could only grip her hands together and watch as the seconds ticked away. At least her players weren't giving up on themselves. She hadn't expected Lucas to pass at all if he could help it, but it didn't surprise her that Kendall passed back to him. They all knew which player was their best hope for a basket.

Lucas moved up to the key and stopped, looking for a shot near the heavily guarded basket. When he didn't find one, he made the predictable move of dribbling a second time since there was no double-dribble rule in wheelchair basketball. Of course, he would want to keep the ball.

Natalie held her breath, hoping one of the parents wouldn't lose patience and beg for him to shoot. Even if he was a selfish player sometimes, he didn't deserve to have his confidence blown when he threw an air ball at the buzzer.

"Come on, Lucas. You can do it," she said under her breath.

Then he did something she didn't expect. Chase was off, forgotten, on the far left side of the basket, where he'd spent much of the game. He'd probably only taken two shots all night, and both had bounced off the rim, so the other team probably didn't see him as much of a threat. But he suddenly awakened, like a wallflower finally asked to dance, as Lucas whipped the ball into his hands.

Natalie's hand lifted to her mouth of its own accord. Why had Lucas passed to him? He wasn't ready for that kind of pressure. He wasn't ready for the whole game to come down to his split-second decisions and the accuracy of his shot.

Chase didn't even hesitate as he lined up the shot and took it. The ball arched over players who appeared surprised that he'd taken a shot at all, and then it swished through the hoop. The buzzer blared just after the ball dropped with a hollow sound to the gym floor.

Applause erupted on their end of the bleachers, and the line of wheelchairs that had been serving as the bench broke up as the players rushed out on the floor to celebrate. Although most of the attention was going to Chase for his game-winning shot, Natalie couldn't get to Lucas fast enough.

"Such a smart play, Lucas," she said as she bent to hug him. "Such a sign of teamwork."

Shane had approached Chase and gave him a much deserved high five. She couldn't blame him. The two of them had worked together on that exact shot during the last two practices. She looked away quickly, before he could catch her watching him.

"But Chase's shot won the game," Lucas said in a small voice.

Natalie only shook her head. "You lost as a team, and now you've won as a team. You were being an unselfish player tonight, and I couldn't be prouder of you."

He glanced over at all of the attention the other boy was receiving as if trying to decide if the unselfish play was worth it. But then some of the wheels started rolling his way, and he grinned.

"Okay, everyone line up for handshakes," Natalie called out.

All of the players rolled into a row at the sideline, with Shane and Natalie taking their positions at the back. Since this was her team's first victory, she could only hope that the players would be gracious winners.

As the players moved forward and shook hands with the opposing players and then their coaches, Shane glanced back at her over his shoulder. His grin was wider than she'd ever seen it before.

"This feels better than scoring the game-winning touchdown," he said.

"I'll have to take your word for it."

Though she'd been determined to stay mad at him, or at least avoid him because of her humiliation from last night, she couldn't help smiling back at him.

He probably knew exactly what it felt like to be carried around on the shoulders of a bunch of burly football players, but now he'd experienced a coach's unbelievable high when players used the skills and plays they'd been taught and worked together to earn a victory. There was nothing like it.

"Learning to lose is important, too," he added.

She nodded, though he'd turned back around as he reached the first opposing player.

"Probably more important," she said to his back.

They both moved through the line, patting hands and saying "good game" to each player and coach. This was the first time all day that

Natalie hadn't felt on edge around Shane. Maybe now they could just pretend that the other night hadn't happened.

As they reached the end of the line, Shane turned his chair to face her and continued as if they hadn't taken a two-minute breath in the middle of their conversation.

"I know that learning to win *and* to lose is important," he said, "but these kids deserve to have some wins in their lives."

She nodded again, a knot forming in her throat. These children definitely deserved some small victories, and so did their assistant coach, who should get the chance to return to his life, to use the legs that had failed him. Even to return to the career he loved, whether it made sense to her or not.

Natalie's eyes filled, and Shane's eyes looked damp as well, but he turned away as if he didn't want her to notice.

She blinked away the moisture and turned back to her players. "Okay, everyone. Let's gather for a quick team meeting so everyone can get home."

"Go home? No way," Shane called out. "After a game like that, we need to celebrate."

"What do you have in mind?" She lowered her voice. "It's a school night, you know."

"We won't be long," he assured her before turning back to the players and their parents, who'd gathered behind them.

"Ice cream for everyone! On me!"

THE KIDS' ICE-CREAM cones had long since been gobbled away. The last of the milk shakes had been slurped. And a jingle marked the exit of the last player's family taking off from Brighton's only indoor ice-cream joint with enough seating for ten players and their families, plus a pair of coaches. Still, Natalie couldn't bring herself to suggest that she and Shane go home, as well. Tonight had been such a great night for all of them, and she hated to see it end. It didn't hurt that she and Shane had finally stopped acting so awkward around each other.

"You going to keep playing with that, or are you going to eat it?" Shane asked from across the long table.

The long, *empty* table, except for the two of them sitting in the center, preventing workers from cleaning it, refilling the saltshakers and prepping it for tomorrow's lunch crowd. Had it been an accident that he was seated directly across from her at the table where several chairs had been removed to accommodate wheelchairs?

He must have thought she hadn't heard him because he pointed to the paper bowl that contained her strawberry sundae. It looked more like strawberry soup now with lumps of berries. She wasn't sure why she hadn't eaten it, other than that she'd been having such a nice time with him—and the players and their families, of course—that she'd forgotten about it.

"I like my ice cream soupy." She stirred the liquid, making a whirlpool of the berry bits. "Why? Do you want some?"

He shook his head. "I like it best frozen. Or at least not warm."

"It's fine." To prove it, she carefully guided a spoonful to her mouth. Syrupy-sweet, *warm* strawberry soup. Somehow she managed not to gag and licked her lips for effect.

"Good, huh?" He grinned.

But instead of taking another bite, she glanced down the table where one leftover paper bowl and several sticky smears remained. "Today was great, wasn't it?"

"You mean the game?"

He watched her for so long that she couldn't help shifting. Her face was hot, and she didn't even want to think about the other places that felt strangely warm. She didn't bother taking another bite of her ice cream. She would be wearing it down the front of her coach's shirt if she tried.

"Of course. What else would it mean?"

But he grinned as he said it, a man who was well aware that he unnerved her.

"Maybe that thing at the clinic?" He folded his hands. "What was that about, anyway?"

"You mean the…switch?" She waited for him to answer, but when he didn't, she rushed on. "I just thought it was best. You know, after…"

"The other night?"

Her cheeks burned, but her jaw tightened. He was purposely making this hard on her. Did he have no shame? Wasn't it enough that he'd rejected her when she would have— She stopped herself right there because she wasn't sure *what* she would have done if he hadn't stopped them.

"I still can't believe you had my case transferred. Does that happen often?"

"Rarely." Or in her experience so far, never, but he didn't need to know that.

"But you know how important it is for me to get out of this chair? How could you trust someone else—"

She brushed her hand back and forth in the air to interrupt him. "You don't need to worry about that. Deborah is amazing. The best. I wouldn't have had your case reassigned if I'd had any doubt that you would be getting the best possible care."

"If she's so great, why wasn't I assigned to her in the first place?"

Natalie lifted a shoulder and lowered it. She'd asked herself that question several times before.

"So she's a better PT than you are?"

"She has much more experience than I do, so, yes, probably."

Again, he grinned. "Then I should take it as a sign of your generosity that you dumped me?"

Dumped? She swallowed. His smile was beginning to annoy her. "I know you think all of this is funny, but—"

"I'm sorry," he said before she could finish. "You were just doing what you thought was best after…everything."

Natalie nodded. She had to deal with this embarrassment if they were ever going to be comfortable coaching together.

"Anyway," he started again, "about the…other, I wanted to apologize for that, too."

Natalie couldn't even look at him. Instead, she stared at her gripped hands. Why was he apologizing for kissing her? Technically she'd kissed him first. And the fact that he was sorry for what had been the most explosive kiss of her lifetime frustrated her even more.

"Let's just forget about it, okay?" she said without looking up.

"I just wanted to explain why I…"

The truth struck her like a bowling ball to the gut, and her gaze shot up to meet his guarded one. He was apologizing, not for the kiss, but for not wanting her.

"Can we just not go there?"

"But I want to go there. I want to explain why—"

Whatever excuse he'd been about to give was cut off when Natalie's phone rang and her mother's photo appeared on the screen. Immediately, she grabbed it off the table and slid her thumb across the glass to answer the call.

"Hey," she said in a low voice. "Sorry I'm running late, but—"

"Where are you? Why aren't you home?"

Her mother's voice was so loud that Shane had to hear it.

"I'll be home soon," she said in the most soothing voice she could muster. "Just give me a few minutes to—"

"I don't have a have few minutes."

Natalie gasped. "What's wrong? Have you fallen?"

Already, she was out of her seat and slipping on her coat. Her gaze flitted to Shane, who was watching her closely. He gestured toward the exit with his index finger, asking if she needed to leave. She nodded.

"Don't worry about me. It's not like you care that Laura has been gone for over an hour."

She almost relaxed. "I know. It'll just be a few more minutes."

"Then I'll call the ambulance myself."

"Ambulance?"

"I'm sure the EMTs will be able to stop the bleeding."

"Stay put. I'll be right there."

Shane was already working his arms back into his coat sleeves, but she rounded the table and helped him.

"You don't have to drop me off," he said as she started wheeling his chair toward the door without asking permission. "I can get someone to come—"

"No time," she clipped and pushed him out the door and through some of the dirty slush.

"I just don't want you to waste time dropping me off when you clearly need to…" He let his words trail away as if hoping she would fill in the blanks.

"No time for that, either."

She hit the button for the wheelchair lift and had to force herself not to tap her foot while Shane was placed in the van. Hurrying around and hopping in the driver's seat, she turned the ignition and threw the vehicle into Reverse.

"Is there anything I can do? I think Vinnie is on duty tonight, so I can call—"

She shook her head as she pulled from the parking lot. "I don't know—won't know—until I get there."

"Are you going to tell me what's going on, or are you going to make me guess?"

She glanced at him once and then looked forward again as she pulled from the parking lot into the street.

"It's time for you to meet my mom."

CHAPTER TEN

SHANE GRIPPED HIS armrests tighter than he ever had before as Natalie hurried behind him up the wheelchair ramp outside her home. A ramp far more permanent looking than the one at his house. When they reached her front door, she unlocked it and then held it wide for him to enter first.

"Sorry about this," she said to his back as she closed the door behind them.

"No big deal." He quickly scanned the entry that led into a darkened formal living room where he was pretty sure no one had ever *lived*. "So where is your mom?"

A voice coming from the back of the house answered his question.

"Is that you, Natalie?"

"Yeah, it's me, Mom." She toed off her boots and set them on the mat.

"Then hurry, will you?"

"Coming." Natalie gave Shane an apologetic look and then in a lower voice told him, "Wait here." She jogged down the hall, leaving him by the front door.

But since he wasn't willing to remain in the

background, he started in the direction she'd just gone. He rounded the corner and stopped in the doorway of a family room that looked like a family actually spent time there. Natalie was crouched next to the wheelchair of woman who looked as much like Natalie as a blonde with almost translucent skin could. On a TV tray next to them, the bottom half of a broken glass had been placed next to a pile of blood-speckled tissues.

"Oh, Mom." She reached out to touch her mother's short hair. "What did you do to yourself?"

But her mother only shifted her head until Natalie's hand fell away. She gripped her hands together, another bloody tissue covering part of her fingers.

"Just a glass. I knocked it over. You weren't here."

Natalie didn't even pause over the accusation as she reached for her mother's hand. "Here. Let me see it."

"It's not like you cared enough to come home on time."

"Just show me."

Why didn't Natalie defend herself? Why didn't she at least explain that the team had finally won and they'd all gone out to celebrate?

With a petulant look, her mother extended her hand, and Natalie carefully unwrapped the tissue covering it until she came to the bloody smear on the woman's index finger.

"It's probably going to need stitches," her mother said.

Stitches? Hadn't she said something on the phone to Natalie about an ambulance?

Natalie shifted the hand a few times to get a better look and then glanced at the family room doorway where he waited.

"Hey, Shane, could you flip on that switch behind you? It's too dark in here."

Shane blinked. She'd known all along that he'd followed her. On the other hand, if she'd noticed his lack of surprise over her mother being in a wheelchair, she didn't show it. She had more important things on her mind.

He moved through the doorway and located the switch plate on the wall, flipping both switches and flooding the room with too much light from several rows of recessed fixtures.

Natalie returned to studying the cut that either hadn't stopped bleeding or had started again when the tissue had been pulled away, but her mother was looking straight at him.

"Who's that?"

"My assistant coach, Shane," she said simply. "Shane, I'd like you to meet my mother, Elaine Keaton."

Immediately, the woman sat up straighter, her uninjured hand lifting to pat her hair. Her demeanor shifted just as quickly. "Sweetheart, you didn't mention that we had a guest."

"I didn't get a chance."

Shane painted on his best smile. "I'm happy to meet you, Mrs. Keaton."

"It's Miss, but you can all me Elaine."

He ignored her coquettish tone, but he also didn't look at Natalie. She would probably get a kick out of the awkward moment.

"I would shake your hand, but you seem to be a little busy with it," he said instead.

"Just a silly accident."

And not an international incident? This time he and Natalie exchanged a look, and he had to bite the inside of his cheek to keep from laughing.

"We'd better get it cleaned up," Natalie supplied. "I know it's bled some, but I don't think it will need a stitch. Why don't we just keep pressure on it for a few minutes and see if we can get it to stop?"

"How do you know it doesn't need a stitch?" Elaine frowned at her and then stared down at her hand again, moving her fingers as if to determine if they still worked. "You're just a physical therapist."

Again, Natalie's jaw tightened, but she looked away instead of responding.

"You know, ladies, I had some first-aid training as part of my job. Would you mind if I looked at it?"

"That would be a good idea," Elaine said.

She hadn't even bothered to ask what job he'd

done that would require first-aid training. She just seemed to need a second opinion when the first was her daughter's.

Natalie's gaze narrowed, but he gave her a small nod. He could help her out if she let him.

"We have some gloves over here," she said, although she hadn't bothered to wear them herself.

Resting Elaine's hand on the tray, Natalie crossed to a section of built-in bookshelves with a row of cabinets stretching across the bottom. Inside, there wasn't just one box of sterile vinyl gloves, but a whole stack of them, plus all kinds of other medical supplies. She pulled two gloves from the box and carried them back to him.

"You'll have to be patient with me," he said as rolled closer to Natalie's mother and pulled on the gloves. "It's been a while since I've done this."

But Elaine only extended her hand. Taking it in both of his, Shane carefully pulled the tissue away, and, again, a line of tiny blood droplets appeared along the cut. He examined the injury for several seconds before turning back to Natalie.

"You don't happen to have any gauze in there, do you?"

"I think I do." She dug around inside the cabinet and pulled out a box of sterile gauze pads, returning to offer him one.

"Maybe this will keep it from opening up each time," he told Elaine. "It has to hurt, but, fortunately, I don't think it's deep. Natalie's right. You probably won't need stitches. We'll just keep pressure on it until it stops bleeding and then clean it up and bandage it. You'll be as good as new, but you might have a scar."

"You mean to go with all of my other scars?"

Shane grinned as he lined up the gauze pad and applied direct pressure to the cut. "Now I can't relate to that at all."

Because it was obvious that they both had their share of scars, they laughed, and after a few beats, Natalie joined in.

"Now how exactly did this happen?" he asked, rephrasing Natalie's question from earlier. Maybe she would answer this time.

"It started to fall. I tried to catch it." She shrugged as if to say that the rest was obvious.

"The glass? I can see how that would happen."

"So the two of you were at a game?" Elaine asked, looking at Shane instead of her daughter. "Was it a good one?"

Natalie's jaw tightened ever so slightly. As responsible as Natalie seemed to be, she'd probably told her mother where she would be and that she would be coaching a game, not watching one. He waited for Natalie to remind her, but she only dragged her front teeth across her bottom lip.

"Yes, the game was great," Shane answered to fill the awkward pause. "The kids won for the first time all season, so I treated everyone to ice cream."

"That was awfully nice of you. I bet the kids loved it."

Again, Shane and Natalie exchanged a look. If Natalie had said the same thing, her mother probably would have said something about how irresponsible it had been for her to go for ice cream instead of making it home on time.

"It wasn't so altruistic of me," he told her. "I just really like ice cream and didn't want to eat it alone."

"Still, I bet the kids love having someone like you—someone who understands what they're going through—teaching them about basketball."

He shook his head. "I don't do much teaching, since I know almost nothing about the sport."

At Elaine's confused expression, he explained, "Your daughter's the expert. I'm just backup since I have an obvious connection with the kids." He patted the arms of his chair for emphasis. "We make a good team, though."

Elaine rolled her eyes. "I doubt you're 'just backup.'"

Why had Elaine said that when she could have responded to his comment about their being a good team? Or even that he'd called her daughter an expert at something? But then, who was he to comment on awkward family relationships when he and his brother barely spoke?

"You're right about that, Mom," Natalie answered for him. "Shane has made such a difference on the team. The players love him."

"I can imagine," Elaine interjected.

Shane shifted in his chair, but Natalie only continued as though she'd missed her mother's gushing.

"The kids were excited when they found out that a celebrity would be helping to coach them."

For the second time, Elaine looked to Shane when the answer could have as easily come from her daughter. "Celebrity?"

He immediately shook his head. Unless they were talking about the infamy from his past, then there was no truth to that claim.

But Natalie nodded. "To them you are." Then she turned back to her mother. "Did I mention that Shane's a police officer?"

Elaine blinked several times and then looked from Shane to her daughter.

Natalie continued as if she didn't notice her mother's surprise. "You know how kids *love* cops."

Shane could only look back and forth between them. After everything that had happened to her, Elaine surely hated the police as much as Natalie did—maybe more—and yet Natalie had lobbed his profession in her mother's face. He could have sworn he'd just been at the center of a polite boxing match, dodging passive-aggressive punches by both sides but not quite escaping without bruises.

Turning his attention back to accidental injuries rather than intentional shots, he lifted the gauze square on her mother's cut and then stretched a bandage over it. "Now let's wait a few minutes and make sure it doesn't start bleeding again."

He laced his fingers together and focused on his hands, finding it safer than looking at either one of them.

"Was that from a car accident, as well?"

It took him a few seconds to realize Elaine was speaking to him, but when he looked up, she indicated his chair with a tilt of her head.

He shook his head. "Shooting."

"And I used to think I had bad days at work," she said with a chuckle. "I'm sorry that happened to you."

"Shane's hoping to get back to work real soon," Natalie supplied.

Her brows were drawn together as if Elaine's compassionate comment surprised her.

"So this isn't permanent?" Elaine asked.

Natalie left that question to Shane. Of course, she wouldn't be allowed to violate privacy laws by discussing his case, even if she was no longer his therapist.

"Hopefully not," he said with shrug.

"I hope not, too."

The woman's simple words brought his gaze back to her. She was wishing for a positive outcome with his condition when her own prognosis was far less promising.

"Thanks."

Elaine waved her injured hand as if to mark that the conversation had ended. "Look. Good as new."

"So we don't need to have 911 on speed dial?" Natalie asked her, this time grinning.

Her mother's frown had a touch of a smile in it. "I don't know about you guys, but I could use a cup of tea before bed."

Natalie glanced at her cautiously. "Sure it won't keep you up?"

"I'll drink herbal."

"Okay then." She turned back to Shane. "Just give me a minute. I'll make some tea for Mom and then take you home."

"I was talking about drinking tea *with* you two. I need to get to know your friend here." Elaine paused, looking from one to the other. "Are you going to make me drink alone? You don't know how much damage I might inflict on myself with a teacup."

As Natalie's gaze flicked back to Shane, he shook his head.

"We wouldn't want that," he said.

But Natalie didn't appear convinced. "Will it be a problem for you, getting back so late?"

He shook his head. "I'm a big boy. I don't have a curfew." He paused, glancing at her mother. "Besides, I want the chance to get to know this young lady, as well."

That it gave him the chance to spend more time with Natalie was just an added benefit. He shouldn't want it, knew it was a bad idea to allow himself to become more attached to her, but he couldn't resist. Her troubled relationship with her mother only drew him in more.

She still had a mother. Didn't she realize how lucky she was? Maybe Elaine had been selfish and angry since the accident, and she'd probably taken it out on her daughter sometimes, but there was good in Elaine Keaton. Good that Natalie couldn't see. Maybe he was just the guy to show her.

SHANE STILL SAT at her kitchen table an hour later, his hands wrapped around an empty coffee mug, when Natalie returned from helping her mother to bed. She tried to ignore the jolt inside her when he grinned up at her. Would she ever get past that?

"I think I'm a hit with your mom."

"Ya think?" But she couldn't help grinning as she said it. No one had inspired that kind of spark in her mother since the accident. Maybe even before that. It had been like watching a sunflower turning to blossom under the sunlight. Part of her resented Shane for causing that spark when she hadn't been able to do it, but the other part of her was grateful that someone had.

"Did you see how hard she was trying to stay

awake, just to keep talking to you?" she said as she returned to the table.

Natalie sat across from him this time, even though her seat had been next to him when the three of them had been at the table. No sense in aiding her temptation to climb into his chair again.

Although he watched, he didn't comment on the change. "She just relates to me the same way the kids on the team do. We all need someone who makes us feel understood."

"She was giggling like a schoolgirl."

"Maybe it didn't hurt that she was getting attention from a guy, too, but I stand by what I said."

"Okay, you stick to your story. I do have one question, though."

He tilted his head. "What's that?"

"Why weren't you surprised that my mom is in a wheelchair?"

"Why do *you* think—" But he stopped when she frowned at him. "Okay, I knew."

"How?"

"The accessible van for starters. Sure, a 'connection' might have let you borrow a van once in a while, but two or three times a week?"

She nodded. "That's fair. But was that it?"

"Not exactly."

"And…come on. You're a cop. What would it tell you if someone answered like that?"

"That there was more he wasn't saying."

She held her hands wide and waited.

"I was curious about why you hated cops. And because I was—am—one, I did some research." He shrugged. "The answers weren't so hard to find."

"I guess not." Her gaze narrowed. "Just how long have you known about our accident?"

"Awhile. Since last week after I asked you about why you didn't like cops."

"And you didn't say something before?"

He shrugged. "I figured you would tell me when you were ready."

"How did you know I ever would be?"

"I hoped."

He'd *hoped*? Why had it mattered to him that she would share her story? Why had he been so curious in the first place? She couldn't be the only person he'd met who wasn't a fan of police officers. She wasn't sure what to do with this feeling of vulnerability. Like Hans Christian Andersen's story about the emperor and his invisible clothes, she was the only who hadn't known she was walking around with her secrets exposed.

"But you knew when I…when we—" She had to stop herself now before she said something she would regret even more.

A smile pulled at his lips.

She swallowed but didn't say more. He should have told her what he knew before they'd shared such an intimate moment, but would she have preferred it if he'd pushed her away before that amazing kiss? Her obvious answer to that revealed how vulnerable she was to him. Even now, he seemed to draw her to him, making her long for sensations and emotions she had no business craving.

"So, how much did you find out?" she couldn't help asking.

"Details about the accident. The lawsuit. The two officers ultimately being cleared."

"Then I guess you know all of it." She played with her empty mug, turning it back and forth in her hands.

"Not all."

"What more could you possibly want to know?"

"What happened *after* the accident?"

"Besides Mom's long recovery and the lawsuit to cover her care for, hopefully, the rest of her life?"

"Yeah, besides that."

Natalie thought for a second. Should she answer that? Would she be able to stop if she started? But finally the words came, despite her reluctance.

"Everything changed. Mom began her long recovery, and after my bruises healed, I just went on with my life."

"Was it really as simple as that?"

She tilted her head side to side. "I guess not. I was still in college when it happened. A music major in piano performance, if you can believe that. I had my music and my boyfriend, Paul. And then the accident happened."

"I take it the boyfriend bailed?"

"He just hadn't signed on for all of that," she said with a sigh. "The accident, my decision to take a break from school to care for Mom and then my discovery about my birth father. It was too much for him."

"Did he have anything to do with your decision to go back and study physical therapy?"

She shook her head. "No. I'd just discovered while caring for Mom that I liked helping people. So I decided on a career in the medical field."

"That's a big change from music."

She nodded. "I also needed to make a better living so I could provide for Mom's needs. The settlement only covers so much. Since I wasn't the next Beethoven, music wouldn't have cut it."

"You've had all of this to deal with before you've even reached your thirtieth birthday?"

SHE WAITED. PEOPLE praised her for her sacrifices to deal with her mother's needs so often that she'd come to expect it. Instead, Shane studied her for so long that she could barely sit still.

"Do you feel guilty that your mom was injured in the accident instead of you?"

The empty mug she'd been tilting on its side toppled on the table. No one had ever asked her that before. A counselor that her mother's doctor had suggested Natalie contact might have, but she'd always been too busy taking care of her mom to make an appointment.

"I don't know. Maybe."

"Was that why you gave up your dream?"

She shook her head, the need to deny as strong as if he'd asked if she'd committed a crime. "No. It wasn't like that. I guess by the time I went back to school, my priorities had changed. How could they not have? I'd seen too much. Life wasn't as simple as I'd pictured it. Understand?"

"Yeah, I get it."

His sad expression made her wonder if he understood too well. Was he remembering his own injury and recovery, or was there something more putting that raw look in his eyes?

"But your mother resents you sometimes, doesn't she? And you're angry at her for that."

Natalie blinked and started shaking her head as his incisive gaze bored right through her. How had he cut so close to a topic she'd never been able to broach with her mother all of these years?

"It's not like that."

"It's not? It was hard to miss that game you two were playing, with her trying to make you feel guilty for not being at home when she cut herself." He pointed to her. "And you weren't so innocent, either, telling her that I was a cop to get a rise out of her."

It hadn't worked, either, something she couldn't figure out. She looked up to Shane again and shrugged. "I was just annoyed with her tonight. She nearly called an ambulance over a tiny cut, and, well, you know the rest."

He nodded, digesting her answer. "Have you ever thought about pursuing your dream now that everything's more settled?"

"What?" She shook her head, trying to catch up with him. "You change subjects so fast. Is that how you keep suspects off balance during questioning?"

"Sorry. Career hazard."

But he only waited, watching her, until she squirmed, trying to recall his last question.

"Oh, you mean that dream to play the Isaac Stern Auditorium at Carnegie Hall, the pinnacle of a musician's career, in front of two thousand, eight hundred and four of my biggest fans?" She grinned. "Yes, I memorized the capacity. But I don't really think about it anymore."

"Really?"

His tone said he didn't believe her, but she tried anyway. "It was a long time ago. A pipe dream even then. I have different dreams now."

"Like what?"

This time she met his gaze steadily. "That one day Mom will really live again instead of just existing."

"Tonight was a start, wasn't it?"

She shrugged. "Maybe. There was definitely a

spark, but she's so comfortable in her misery now that I don't know if she even wants anything else."

"Is it okay with you if she doesn't?"

At that question, she stared at her hands. Could she handle it if her mother lived like this another ten years? Twenty? Could she bear to continue this daily game they played for the rest of her mother's life? Of course she could. She had to. Like always, they only had each other.

"Do you still have any dreams for yourself, Natalie?"

Her gaze flitted to his, but she looked away quickly. She hadn't allowed herself to have dreams for a long time, and then Shane had come along, awakening her from what felt like a long, dark sleep. Did he realize the disruption he'd caused?

"You ask a lot of questions, you know that?"

"Did I mention that I'm a cop?"

"Yes. I think we've covered that material."

He grinned. "You keep answering, so I keep asking."

"Any chance I could get you to stop?"

"Okay. But may I ask just one more question first?"

She nodded, wondering what he could possibly still want to know.

"Will you play for me?"

CHAPTER ELEVEN

SHANE COULDN'T HELP but stare as Natalie's fingers danced across the ebony and ivory keys of the upright piano tucked in the back of her home's formal living room. A piano that for several years had served only as a shelf for a half-dozen photographs from Natalie's childhood. Though his definition of music included drum solos and guitar riffs, he'd asked her to play, curious how this musical side of her fit into the puzzle of Natalie Keaton that he'd been putting together with excruciating detail.

And from the first moment she'd lined up her fingers—drawing them up and down along the narrow keys in a caress before causing the instrument to emit a single note—Shane realized he'd missed a puzzle piece right in the center. The one closest to her heart. She'd been reluctant to play at first, a bashful genius, but he could see now that it was more than that. Maybe she'd worried if she started playing again she wouldn't be able to stop.

A musician. He couldn't put that thought together in his mind along with the competent therapist, the encouraging basketball coach, the talented basketball player. Yet the amazing sounds spilling from the piano told a different story. Of a private passion. Of dreams that had been lost the day of the accident.

He'd never known that a piano could make sounds like that, never realized its music could stand alone, rather than serve as accompaniment to a great vocal track or bass line. And Natalie was the one massaging those sweet sounds from it, her fingers whipping up and down the scales like a bicyclist who'd been injured and away from his machine for so long but whose body had never forgotten how to ride.

How could he have believed he knew her at all and not known *this* about her? She didn't really know him, either, though she probably thought she did. It felt as if, through her music, she was inviting him to see her soul, and he wanted to do just that. More than that, for the first time ever, he was tempted to let another person really know him, too.

Why would he risk it? That was dangerous. The truth about him wasn't pretty. It was easier to keep his distance, to invite her only to the fringes of familiarity. It was safer, too, since he was a coward, after all.

But the thought continued turning inside his mind as she played on, so lost in the joy of her music that she appeared to forget he was even there. She'd made herself vulnerable, so maybe he could allow himself to be that exposed with her, as well. He gripped the armrests of his chair, uncertainty battling with the desire for connection. Maybe, just maybe it was time to finally introduce a woman to the real Shane Warner.

THE MELODY CONTINUED to play in Natalie's head as she drove Shane home a half hour later. It had been all she could do to pull her hands away from the keys, and even now, her fingers stretched on the steering wheel, longing to blend notes for chords.

"So now you know how I spent much of my adolescence, practicing Bach's sonatas and perfecting my three-pointer," she said. "Neither were things Mom was particularly thrilled about."

"I can understand why basketball might not have been her favorite thing, but why not music?"

"It wasn't practical. She always paid for my lessons, but she never understood why music was so important to me. She was especially shocked when I decided to study music. It didn't make sense to her. She is an accountant, after all. It's hard for her not to see the world in terms of a W-2."

"I don't think parents are meant to understand their kids."

"Do you really believe that? I guess you did say you got into trouble, though you were a kid from a 'perfect' family. Didn't they at least try to stop you?"

"Oh, they tried, but there's no way you can slow down someone who's hell-bent on imploding. Too bad I had to take other people down with me."

Natalie couldn't help watching him out of the corner of her eye. "Are you going to tell me your story, or are you going to make me hunt down your secrets on the internet?"

"Juvenile records are sealed."

"Then you'll have to tell me."

For several long seconds, he said nothing. Without the radio on, the van was so quiet that the whir of the engine crowded the space. Would he pretend he didn't want her to know when he clearly needed to talk about it?

"There's an adrenaline rush that comes from getting away with something," he said finally. "I was addicted to it, and I surrounded myself with friends who craved it as much as I did."

"What did you get away with?"

"Little things at first, like pranks at school and then vandalism to the play structure in our subdivision. Stealing a couple of beers from an open garage. Letting the air out of a teacher's tires."

"So small-time stuff?" Out of the corner of her eyes, she saw his nod.

"Then in eighth grade, we upped the stakes. We experimented with drugs. But raising hell was still my favorite rush. That was why it was my idea to have the competition that night. The four of us were to go out on our own, steal the craziest things we could think of and meet up the next day to show our trophies. A perfect plan."

At Shane's foreboding words, Natalie's hands tightened on the steering wheel. "So not so perfect?"

"I was determined to win, so I stole a pair of Kevlar vests right from the backseat of a police car."

"You didn't!"

"The officer had parked his take-home vehicle near his house in the subdivision next to mine. But too bad for me, he was watching his own neighborhood more closely that night. I landed in jail."

Natalie let out the breath she'd been holding and grinned into the darkness as she continued down the dark road. "So you rode in the back of a police car instead of the front one time. I was expecting something worse."

"It was worse. My friend Connor wanted to take his game to a new level, too. At least we suspect that's what he'd planned to do. We'll never know for sure."

She swallowed. This was going to be bad. But she had to ask. "What happened?"

"He'd been huffing from a can of compressed-air computer cleaner to get high before he went out." Shane gripped his hands in his lap. "He never made it out of his bedroom. His parents found him dead the next morning. Cardiac arrest."

"It wasn't your fault," she blurted. "You know that, right?"

"But I wasn't exactly guilt-free, was I?"

Even if he had a point, she wished she could say something that might assuage his guilt. "How do you know he had plans to go out that night?"

"He was wearing dark clothes and had a dark pillowcase, a roll of duct tape and some nylon rope waiting on his bed."

"Whatever he did that night or intended to do, those were *his* decisions," she said. "You weren't responsible for them."

He didn't argue the point this time, but it was clear that he disagreed.

"It wasn't until three days later when I learned that Connor had died."

"But you were in jail, right?"

"Not the whole time—my parents put me under house arrest and took my phone. By the time my brother let me know what had happened, they'd already scheduled Connor's funeral. My parents wouldn't let me go, which was a good thing, since his family didn't want me there."

"They needed someone to blame."

"They weren't the only ones. My other friends told everyone about my dare, so…"

"So you were an unpopular guy."

"They didn't need to hate me. I hated myself enough for all of them."

"How did you go back to school?"

"I didn't. At least not there. My parents had to move so my brother and I could go to a different school. Stephen never forgave me for that."

"I've heard of kids moving to new schools and then just raising hell at the new school. Is that what you did?"

"I probably would have, if Kent Sawyer hadn't planted himself in my corner and refused to budge."

"Who's that?"

"The officer I stole the vests from."

"Are you kidding?" She peeked at him with her side vision, relieved that he was finally smiling.

"Yeah. No accounting for good sense. After Kent found out about my connection to the boy who died, he convinced the judge to assign him to mentor me as part of my juvenile sentence."

"I bet you weren't happy about that."

He nodded into the darkness. "And no matter how hard I tried to convince him that I was a bad bet, he refused to give up on me. He took me to the gym and taught me how to pound weights instead of fists. He even convinced me to go out for football."

For several seconds, he was quiet as if remembering. "He's been like a father to me. He saved my life. If not for him, I might have turned out just like Connor. Sometimes I—"

He stopped himself then, but Natalie couldn't help but to fill in the blank. Sometimes he wished he'd died instead.

Natalie parked the van in front of Shane's house, watching his profile in the light coming from the floods on both sides of his garage doors. A pickup she didn't recognize was parked out front, indicating that one of his friends was already there.

So much made sense now. Shane had become a police officer to atone for his mistakes and to repay the police officer who'd taken a chance on him. Once again he'd proven himself heroic, and it made her feel like a heel for all the things she'd decided about him without even knowing him.

"I'm sorry."

He turned his head to face her. "For what?"

"For judging you based on my prejudices."

He surprised her by chuckling. "Well, thanks. That means a lot."

"What ever happened to your other two friends who were there the night of the dare?" she couldn't help asking.

"I guess Mark straightened up after that. He's an accountant in Boston now. Nate wasn't so lucky. He got hooked on drugs. He's been in out and out of prison for the past fifteen years."

"And what about the officer who mentored you? Where is he now?"

Immediately, Shane's shoulders lowered. He stared out the windshield a few seconds before responding. "Kent had to take early retirement last July. Cancer."

"Is he okay?"

His shoulder lifted and lowered. "They thought he'd beat it. He was in remission, but now...not so much."

"Has he been given long?"

He shook his head.

"I'm sorry. Have you been able to visit him since...?" She let her words trail away without filling in the rest. They both knew what Shane had been dealing with the past few months.

"My coworkers take me to see him as often as they can. He's supposed to be coming to my commendation ceremony, but I don't know if—"

She nodded. Shane had a lot riding on that ceremony. He'd already said he wanted to be walking by this artificial deadline, and now there was another inexact deadline—a much less flexible date.

"Will your parents be able to attend...as well?" The last sounded awkward to her, but she was searching for something comforting to say, and she was coming up empty. She might as well have said *instead*.

"They both passed away several years ago. First Mom and then Dad a year later. They were older. A lot of health problems."

"I'm so sorry."

"Thanks." He shifted higher in his seat now. "At least they had the chance to see that I turned out okay. They even forgave me for the hell I put them through."

"What about your brother?"

He shrugged. "One of these days."

And hopefully one day Shane would be able to forgive himself, she thought as she opened her door. She pushed the button that opened the van's side door and lowered the exit ramp. Neither spoke as the automated system moved his chair from the passenger position and lowered him to the ground.

"Well, that was a downer of a way to end the night when we were supposed to be celebrating our first victory," he said as his chair rolled out onto the still-frozen ground.

"Thanks for sharing your story with me," she said simply.

"Now aren't you glad you decided to have my case reassigned? You never know what kind of lowlifes you'll have to work with."

When she didn't laugh at his joke, he finally nodded. He'd taken a risk to share his story with her tonight, and she couldn't have felt more honored that he'd trusted her with it.

"You know something, Shane?"

He stared at her, waiting.

"Someday you're going to have to forgive yourself. Hopefully someday soon."

He nodded. "I hope so, too."

Strange, they'd seemed so different when she'd first met him: two sides of a law enforcement story with no way to bridge that disconnect. But now she recognized that they weren't so different after all. They'd both experienced tragedy. Him more than once. And they both carried around survivor's guilt, questioning why they'd walked away when others hadn't been so lucky.

Maybe it was that shared experience or something more basic, like the need to connect with another human who understood pain and loss, but something urged Natalie to reach for Shane's hand and lace their fingers together. His hand was cold—they should have been wearing gloves—but warmth immediately spread where their skin touched.

For several seconds, Shane only stared at their hands as if surprised by the fingers entwined with his, and then he looked up at her. Natalie stilled, her muscles and joints frozen into place, as she fell completely and willingly into the magic of his mesmerizing eyes.

More intimate than any kiss, this one simple look touched her everywhere and nowhere, a promise filled to bursting with absolute trust. Just as she started to bend forward for another taste of those lips she'd sworn off forever only two days before, Shane untangled their fingers. A protest slipped from her lungs as he broke the connection, but then he only turned her hand so it was palm up, fitted their fingertips together and then traced down the length of her fingers and then across the hills and valleys of her palm.

Her breath caught. Like a guitar strummed only once, her body reverberated in the aftermath of his touch. She wanted… Oh, she didn't even know what she wanted, but she was convinced that she would die if he didn't touch her again. If he didn't do it soon, she would take matters into her own hands.

At the rumble of a garage door opening, Natalie jumped back, the stark garage light catching her in the act of wanting. Nearly catching her doing something about it.

"I thought you'd never get here," Jamie Donovan said as he strolled through the garage, clearly missing that he'd interrupted something.

"Busy night," Shane said simply.

"Thanks for the text to let me know you were still out gallivanting. Otherwise I would have called the police by now." He paused for dramatic effect. "Oh, I forgot. We *are*—"

"The police," Shane chimed with him as if they'd all delivered that particular punch line before.

Natalie didn't even bother trying to laugh. It would only have sounded flat. She should have been grateful for the interruption. He'd probably saved her from doing something she might regret.

So why did she feel annoyed enough to consider assaulting a police officer?

Jamie's arms crossed, and he started rubbing his upper arms. "It's freezing out here. Aren't you two cold?"

"Not too bad," Shane said.

The look he shot Natalie was so heated that she no longer needed a coat at all.

"Sorry to be the hovering help here, but you should really get inside before you get sick," Jamie told Shane before turning to Natalie. "Would you like to come inside, too? I can make coffee."

She shook her head. "No, thanks. I have to get home."

Straight to a cold shower, if she knew what was best for her. But that ship had long since sailed, and she wasn't waving frantically for it to return to shore.

"Yeah, I should be getting to bed, anyway," Shane said.

He leveled a look at Natalie that would make her coat unnecessary for the whole drive home.

"We'll continue our conversation later. Okay, Natalie?"

She cleared her throat. "Sure. Fine."

"I'll be in the clinic tomorrow."

"Great," Jamie answered for her then crossed to the back of Shane's wheelchair. Though he'd exited through the garage, he guided the chair up the ramp to the front door.

From the slightly higher slant, Shane glanced over at Natalie and smiled. Nervous tension and anticipation filled her.

Oh, they would continue that conversation, all right. She suspected, however, that when they did, there wouldn't be a whole lot of talking.

CHAPTER TWELVE

"YOU DID IT!"

At the shrill sound of Deborah's voice, Natalie started and this time turned fully to look at them. Immediately, she was disappointed. As many times as she'd sneaked glances at Shane this morning, she couldn't believe she'd managed to miss seeing him take those first few hard-fought steps as he held his own weight using the parallel bars.

"Good for you," she called out as applause filled the room. She didn't even care that she hadn't been the PT working with him when he'd done it.

The veins in his neck were visible from the exertion, and the hair at his temples appeared damp, but he grinned, clearly pleased with himself. He had every right to be. He'd worked hard for this. There was more work ahead for him, but he deserved the chance to enjoy this moment.

"You go, Shane!" Anne-Marie called from the hallway leading to the front office.

Even their boss, Meg Story, who'd emerged from her office and her spreadsheets for a rare walk through the gym, paused to clap against the file she held. She turned and caught Natalie's gaze, giving her a knowing look. At least Meg didn't know the whole story. She probably thought she'd failed in her attempt to help Natalie push through a personal fear, but that was better than knowing that her PT had been making out with a client.

Every look she'd exchanged with Shane today had been potent enough to make her blush. A dance. That was the only way she could describe the images those looks inspired. A slow dance with his arms drawing her close as they shared his chair, the music soft and carrying a beat so sensual, its rhythm full of its own promises. Each rock of her hip. Each gentle sway. It all felt like a prelude to a—

She stopped herself and looked away as she'd been forced to do so many times today, just to catch her breath. She jotted down notes on her new client, a seventy-seven-year-old female, post-op from a meniscus repair. With so much electricity in the room, was there any chance that other PTs or clients could have missed it?

After Deborah helped him return to his chair, Shane waved at everyone and even pressed his hand to his belly, leaning forward in an exaggerated bow.

"All right, Mr. Performer. Let's get back to work," Deborah told him.

Natalie turned her back on them to finish updating her patient's file. Maybe it was a good thing that she had no more clients today and could leave when she finished. Since last night she'd been unable to get Shane off her mind. With him only thirty feet away in the gym, she would never be able to stop thinking about him. She realized with a shock that she didn't even want to.

After Shane left the clinic, Natalie could finally breathe again, but the space felt empty without him there. She moved to one of the laptop stands and input the rest of her notes, her work moving more quickly than it had all day. Minutes later, she was bundled in her coat and hat, ready to brave the cold again.

Skipping the elevator, she took the stairs from the third floor, emerging near the building's east waiting area. Other patients waited near the exit for their drivers to pull into the circular drive outside the revolving door, but she only noticed one of them.

Although Shane was parked next to the bench just inside the door, his coat was unbuttoned, and he wasn't wearing a hat, as if he expected to be there for a while.

"Fancy meeting you here," he said.

As a sexy smile lifted Shane's lips, Natalie swallowed. Would she ever just be able to see him without feeling that immediate jolt to her system?

"Didn't you leave a while ago?" she asked,

though she knew exactly when he'd left. Probably to the minute. "What are you still doing here?"

"The downside to having state police troopers providing your free transportation is that emergency calls trump your taxi service. There's a three-car pileup on US-23. Can you believe they picked something like that over time with me?"

She shook her head, smiling. "What's wrong with them? So… I guess you'll be here awhile then?" She shoved her hands in her pockets, stalling when she should have waved and hurried out the door.

"Looks like it."

"Who's picking you up this time?"

Her thoughts flashed to the night before, when Jamie Donovan opened the door, either clueless about the moment he'd interrupted or the owner of an amazing poker face. She hoped he wouldn't be the one arriving today and announcing that he'd just won at cards.

"Delia Morgan. You haven't met her." He glanced to the window and then back to her. "Oh, I keep forgetting to call her by her married name. Peterson."

Her gaze met his. Had he added that last part just for her? She cleared her throat. "You did great earlier."

He grinned again. "I was sure I was going to fall again, and I did so much of the work with my arms and shoulders that they're killing me now."

"Nothing like bench-pressing your whole body weight."

"More like doing dips."

"Whatever you say, but you were moving your feet, as well. You should be proud of yourself."

"I guess."

He sat higher in his chair now, as if with those few steps he'd restored some of his confidence. That would help with his recovery, as well.

She glanced out into the parking lot, filled with snow-covered cars. "Do you have any idea how long it's going to be before they can pick you up?"

He looked from the parking lot to her. "Well, I was wondering…"

Shane didn't finish, but the question hung between them anyway. And his gaze, just as it had been earlier when the broad expanse of the gym had separated them, was warm and direct. She looked down at her boots, her tongue darting out to moisten her lips.

"I mean…it's okay if—" he began again.

Her head lifted, and she waved away his suggestion with a brush of her hand. "Sure. No problem. I have the van today. I can take you home."

"Great. I'll let Delia know she's off the hook." He bent to send the text and then pulled on his hat and buttoned his coat.

"You're lucky I got off early. I mean, that I didn't have any more clients today. You could have been waiting for a ride all afternoon."

She was talking too fast, but she couldn't slow her words. Her cheeks burned as she pressed the square button with the wheelchair symbol. The handicap-accessible door next to the revolving one opened wide.

"Yeah. Lucky. I really appreciate the ride."

Natalie had to smile over his effort. She wasn't the only one pretending a ride was the only thing he'd asked for. The only thing she'd just agreed to.

Outside, she helped him settle his chair onto the lift before rounding the back end of the van and climbing in the driver's side.

Shane didn't speak as she turned the ignition. And to ensure he remained silent, Natalie turned on the radio, selecting an oldies station. If either of them said a word out loud about what they had in mind, she would probably chicken out and drop him off at his house, leaving all of the *what if*s in the snowy tire tracks on his driveway.

But she didn't want to back down now. She didn't want to run or hide or second-guess. Each traffic light drew her closer to Shane's house. To Shane's bed.

She'd never wanted anything more.

NATALIE COULDN'T HAVE looked more nervous as she hung up their coats in the front closet. Shane had to smile at that. At least she was as nervous as he was.

"Do you want me to make you some tea before I—"

She stopped herself before she said *go*. They both knew she wasn't going anywhere for a while. At least he hoped they'd agreed on where they would be and what they would be doing. He'd thought of little else during that whole ride home as the radio had blared with some surfer's search for a perfect wave.

"It's freezing in here." Natalie rubbed her upper arms over her navy scrub top even though her white base layer covered her arms to her wrists. "Where's your thermostat? Let me check the temperature."

She shot past him though the heat control was in the front hall, where she'd just been.

"The temperature's fine. Natalie, stop."

She did. In the doorway between the foyer and the living room, she stood, but she didn't turn back to him.

"Come here."

The command sounded strange in his ears. She must have thought so, too, because she only turned and stared without moving closer to him or backing away. What was he doing? That wasn't him. Or at least if he'd ever been that guy, he wasn't anymore.

"Please," he said in a lower voice.

This time she did move.

Toward him.

When she finally stood in front of him, her arms pressed tightly at her sides, her gaze on the door as if she might bolt, he reached for her hand. She allowed him to lift it, but she didn't step closer. Didn't rush to him. She simply stared down at their hands and waited. Shane swallowed as he realized she was leaving whatever happened next in his hands, and even if everything else about him was different now, he still remembered how to use those.

With a gentle tug, he pulled her toward him until her leg pressed against the side of his footplate. His next move might have gone better if he'd remembered to lock down his wheels, but as it was, when he pulled again, the chair spun to the right, and she landed across his lap in an unceremonious plop.

"Umph." He cleared his throat. "Now, in my mind that was going to be a really smooth move."

As if to emphasize how far it was from that, Natalie chuckled. "Are you trying to kill me?"

She reached behind her and pushed down the lock on one of the wheels. He locked the other one himself.

When she turned to face him, he shook his head. "No, I had something far more pleasant in mind."

Her laughter died, and she watched for another cue from him. He didn't make her wait long.

Shane lifted his hand to her mouth and traced

his thumb over that tiny, delicious line at the center of her lower lip. The way her mouth softened and opened for him was almost his undoing. He squeezed his eyes shut and sank his front teeth into his own lip to regain control. Taking a deep breath, he opened his eyes and continued his exploration. He skimmed his fingertip over the soft curves of her lips until he brushed the dampness just inside.

He couldn't wait any longer, and judging from the impatient little moan that escaped from her throat, he wasn't the only one. Removing his hand, he replaced it with his mouth in a move more desperate than smooth. He'd tasted her before, and yet her silky lips still came as a surprise. So pliant. Sweet. And she wasn't pulling away. Instead, she was sinking into him, her fingers sliding over his biceps and shoulders to link behind his neck. His arms wrapped around her, and he tugged her closer still, as much as the chair would allow.

He shifted his hand over the curve of her shoulder and down her side, brushing his fingertips along the rounded underside of her breast. He wanted to call out in frustration when she lowered her arm, but she only turned to offer him better access and kept on kissing him. Spreading his fingers wide, he filled his hand with her soft feminine flesh. Her breaths came in short, delicious puffs.

Oh, he remembered this, the amazing feel of

a woman in his arms. But had it ever been *this* good? Had every moment been a precious discovery like the ones he was savoring now? Had he experienced this same desire to know a woman's body in intimate detail, to coax sweet sighs from her rather than worrying about his own pleasure? He didn't even have to answer those questions, because it was obvious that *everything* was different with Natalie Keaton.

Shane slid his hand beneath the hem of her scrub shirt and base layer. He knew he shouldn't rush, but her skin was too soft, her curves too enticing. When, at last, his fingers slipped beneath her lacy bra, she cried out into his mouth. He tasted her desire while trying to ignore his body's response. He leaned his head back and watched her until her eyes opened, the caramel cheeks stained pink.

"We'll be more comfortable in there." He gestured with his thumb to the hall that led to his bedroom.

"Do you need me to…?"

He shook his head. Maybe he couldn't lift her into his arms right now like some hero in a chick flick, but he could do this. If he moved really slowly.

"Are you sure this is a good idea?"

She was asking only about hitching a ride in his wheelchair, but a seed of doubt about the bigger picture tiptoed inside his thoughts, as well. Was wanting this to happen with every cell of his being enough to overcome such obvious obstacles?

"Of course it is," he said anyway.

"I mean, it's probably not safe." As if to emphasize her point, her foot tapped the hallway wall. "And you're working your arms twice as hard."

"Twice?"

"You know what I mean."

"I need the workout."

He smiled. This was about her insecurities rather than his. But because his were just as real and building, he focused on working his way down the hall.

"Your arms already have to be sore from your session earlier."

"That was nothing."

After what felt like an hour, he reached his bedroom doorway.

"Better duck."

She shifted closer, drawing in her legs and head. Her throaty laughter rumbled against his chest. He chuckled with her as they made it past the doorjamb and into the room without calamity. But when his chair reached the foot of the bed, he stopped. The rare afternoon sunshine filtering in through the window and stretching across the covers only added a stark spotlight to his dilemma.

Why hadn't he thought of this before? This wasn't as easy as getting from the living room to the bedroom. How was he supposed to move her from the chair onto the bed without both of them landing on the floor? Or without having to ask her for help. Now. At a time like this.

No matter how much he wanted her, maybe this was a bad idea. He wasn't ready. Maybe he never would be. Just when he needed to draw from a well of raw masculinity and years of experience, he felt uncertain, ill equipped.

What happened to that invincibility he'd felt after taking his first steps today? Why did she even want him when he couldn't— No, she deserved better than this. Better than a broken cop who might never put all of his pieces back together. His gaze lowered to the floor.

"So…what's going on, Shane?"

At Natalie's question, he blinked, drawn back from the dark cave of his thoughts.

"What do you mean?" he asked, looking up again.

"Well, I didn't expect that here would be the place where the magic…stopped."

"Sorry." He looked past her to the bare wall beside his dresser. "Maybe we shouldn't—"

"Shouldn't?" She shifted, lifted her arm from around him and clasped her hands in her lap. "I need to know one thing."

"Okay."

Natalie had said *one thing*, but she was a medical professional, so Shane braced himself for a litany of technical, humiliating questions.

"Are you going to reject me again?" Then she stared at her hands, asking in a small voice, "Don't you want me?"

His jaw went slack. He was shocked that she could even think he didn't want her. But what was she supposed to think? He'd been so caught up in his own insecurity that he'd been insensitive to hers. Her father had left her, and that loser of a boyfriend had bailed the moment things got rough. Of course she would see this as rejection when he was really just a coward.

"I know. It was more than just one question. I just…it's that—"

She was rambling, her talking hands telegraphing her distress, and then she started to lift herself away from him.

"Wait."

She stood anyway, stepping just outside his reach and turning away from him. Hands that had been so animated before were gripped in front of her now.

"Natalie, you have to know I want you. Right?"

For a long time, she didn't answer, but when she did, she still didn't look up from her hands. "I thought I knew."

"I do. Really. It's just that I'm so out of my element here." Was there any way to explain this without humiliating himself? "I used to know… well…uh, I was pretty good with women before.

But ever since the shooting, you know, I just can't trust… I mean, so many things have changed."

He shook his head and finally spoke the truth. "I just don't have a clue what I'm doing."

"And you think I *do*?"

"That's not what I meant."

"I think I know what you meant."

That she'd seen his medical record and probably *did* know only humiliated him more. His chest felt tight as she stepped farther away from him. But instead of leaving the room, she crossed to the bedside table, collected his transfer board that was next to it and returned to hand it to him.

Shane swallowed. He hadn't even asked for her help, and yet she was providing it. Then she settled on the end of the bed and patted the spot on the comforter next to her.

"Let's figure it out together."

She didn't appear as confident as her words, but then, she wasn't the one running from her fear like he was. Natalie knew more about his weaknesses, including medical ones, than any of the women he'd shared a bed with in the past, and here she sat, waiting. He'd told her about the biggest mistakes of his life, about the people he'd hurt, the things he could never take back, and yet she was still here, accepting him for the way he was physically. The way he might always be.

"You might want to turn off the lights," he said. "This may not be pretty."

He was only talking about his transition from the chair to the bed, but he realized his words might offer an apt description of the event—or nonevent—that might happen once he'd settled on the mattress. Instead of answering, Natalie sat quietly as he locked his wheels and shifted to the spot she'd patted next to her.

Once he was seated, Natalie reached for his hand. "No way that I'm turning out the lights. I don't want to miss any of this."

CHAPTER THIRTEEN

NATALIE WAS RELIEVED that she managed not to tremble when Shane brushed his thumb along her jawline. *Let's figure it out together.* She didn't know where she'd come up with those words. If he didn't know what he was doing, she wouldn't be much help. Her experience was limited at best, and so long ago that she could barely recall any of her awkward moves.

Either Shane didn't notice how distracted she was, or he wanted to bring her back to the moment with a jolt, but he leaned close and pressed his lips to the sensitive spot just behind her ear. Then he blew lightly on the dampened skin. She did shiver this time. Though the heat inside her had cooled when Shane had experienced his hiccup of misgivings, she warmed again now like candle wax, already softened and ready to puddle with the next spark.

"We'll probably be more comfortable if we can make it up to the pillows," he told her. "I would lift you, but—"

"But you know that I am capable of lifting myself."

She rolled to her hands and knees and crawled up the length of the bed and then propped a pillow and lay back on it. For Shane, the process was more challenging. He shifted his hands behind him, using his triceps to move backward. Natalie was tempted to help him, but she sensed that he needed to do this for himself.

"Sorry," he said with a strained chuckle. "This went a lot faster in my mind."

"Why? Do you have somewhere to be?"

"No."

"Good. Then we have all afternoon."

Where was she getting this stuff? If she kept talking like this, he would think she knew what she was doing.

"And I want to use every minute of it," he said.

Because that sounded more like the Shane from her fantasies, she grinned. When he reached the pillow next to her, Natalie propped it behind his head. He'd shifted his upper body to face her, so she turned, as well.

"I wish you'd been there to prop my pillows when I was still in the hospital."

"I'm sure there were plenty of pretty young nurses willing to do that for you."

"Jealous?"

"Absolutely."

He shook his head. "None as pretty as you. Not even close."

She stared into his eyes, so close now that she

could see specks of charcoal in their blue-gray depths, and she almost believed him. Almost.

"I'm sure we were all wearing the same sexy outfits," she said because it was easier to joke than to swoon. She brushed her hand down the front of her scrub top for effect.

"You're the only one I've dreamed about, and in those dreams you were wearing nothing at all."

Natalie swallowed. She wasn't the only one who'd awakened after a long night of sweaty thoughts.

"With all those painkillers you were on in the hospital, you probably didn't dream at all."

"Maybe."

Instead of saying more, he pulled her hand between them. He turned it over and brushed the backs of his fingers from her palm to her fingertips. At the top, he flipped his wrist and followed that same path back down. Her breath caught. He'd touched only her hand, and a delicious ache was already spreading in her most private places. What other tricks did the magician have up his sleeve?

When he tugged her forearm gently, she scooted forward until she was lying face-to-face with him and pressed to the length of his body. Her skin tingled at every point of contact. She wanted more. Strange how she'd never felt this dizzying need when she'd shared a bed with Paul. She'd never wanted a man this way before, craving him the way the lungs of an underwater swimmer cried out for air.

Was it that Shane had been off-limits that made her want him so much? The lure of the forbidden fruit. But that premise didn't ring true. There was just something about Shane Warner. What he did for a living had nothing to do with it. He could have been an archaeologist on a dig outside Cairo or a painter using his fingertips as a brush and she still would have been lying right here, hoping he would put his hands on her.

Finally, he did, though she would have chosen more interesting places than just her hips. But the way his fingers pressed into her backside, bracing her against him, was a wonderful start. He returned his mouth to hers then, kissing her with the thorough attention of a man with no deadline and a singular focus. He slowly seduced her mouth until she was sure she would explode if he didn't do more.

"I'm going to need you to do something for me," he whispered against her lips.

"Anything," she breathed. Her eyes flicked open with the realization that she meant it. She'd never trusted a man this way before. Never needed anyone like this.

His sharp intake of breath made her smile. He slid his arms up from her hips until they clasped behind her back.

"Now on the count of three, I need you to roll with me. One…two…three."

They rolled until Natalie landed on top, her legs resting on either side of him. For a few seconds, she stared down at his self-satisfied grin, but then the pull of that sexy smile proved too much for her. She brushed her lips over his. Her fantasies about him had been good, but they were just an out-of-focus photo when compared to the delicious reality. She didn't care that he'd had dozens of women in his arms before and probably just as many in his bed. He was with her now. That was all that mattered.

As if to put an exclamation point on that fortunate reality, he traced a line of kisses from her lips, over her chin and to the sensitive skin of her neck. She braced her hands on the mattress on either side of him and shifted to give him better access. His rough stubble would undoubtedly leave marks on her chin and neck, but, again, she didn't care. Each taste, each touch, only made her greedier for more.

When Shane's fingers skimmed the skin between the hem of her shirt and the waistband of her pants, she stopped and waited. Slowly, he shifted his hand up, bunching the material in his fists as he moved higher up her back.

"Mind if I help with that?" Would he be as offended as he'd been that first time when she'd tried to help him in the clinic?

"You kidding? In this particular activity, you can help all you want."

Sitting up, she straddled him and yanked her shirt over her head. Then, feeling suddenly bashful, she leaned close to him to cover herself.

"Wait." He braced a hand between them. "I want to see you."

Drawing in a long breath, she lifted up again, somehow holding herself still. For a few seconds, he touched her only with his warm gaze, tracing down her neck and over the outline of body. His lips lifted in a slow smile.

"You're beautiful," he breathed as he lifted a hand to follow the path his eyes had blazed.

Her skin awakened at each spot his fingertips skimmed. From chin to collarbone. From the inside swell of her cleavage and over the lacy barrier. When his fingers slipped beneath the lace, she gasped and leaned into the sensation. Closer to him. But before she rested her body against his, he reached both hands between them until they met at the center of her bra.

"This part I can do myself." His nimble fingers undid the front clasp, and the contents fell into his waiting hands. "Perfect," he crooned. "Just like I knew you'd be."

Her eyes drifted closed as she reveled in the rush of sensations. She'd been touched before, but never like this. Never with the skills of a master, the reverence of a worshipper.

But it still wasn't enough. Shifting back until she was seated just below his hips, she reached for the bottom of his T-shirt and slid it up over his belly to expose his broad chest, nearly smooth but for a dusting of light brown hair.

"Sorry you have to do this," he said, indicating his clothes.

"You kidding? I've been dying to take your clothes off."

"You probably say that to all your patients."

"I can honestly say you're the first." She pulled his shirt over his head. "But then, remember, you're not my client anymore."

She placed both hands on his chest, splaying her fingers over his heated skin and enjoying the way his muscles bunched in response to her touch. Her hips instinctively swayed over his.

Shane drew in a breath through his teeth. "You might want to remember that it's been a really long time, so…"

"So, I think we need to get rid of these." She settled next to him and untied the strings at his waistband.

"And those." He pointed to her scrub pants.

She lifted off the bed to do both tasks. Soon all of their clothes had been tossed in a single pile next to the bed. Natalie could only stare down at him as he lay there, his body so perfect and so thoroughly male.

"Are you going to just leave me here?" he asked after several seconds.

"Oh. Right." She cleared her throat. Some sex kitten she was turning out to be. "You want me up there again?"

His chuckle was low and so sensual that she felt it all the way to her womb.

"Sweetheart, I want you everywhere, but there is a good start."

She grinned as she slid over him again. Slowly, she fitted herself to him, skin to skin, their curves and planes perfectly aligned as if they'd each been built with the other in mind.

Shane dipped his head and found her mouth, kissing her again and again in a slow dance as sweet as the tiny rock of his hips against hers. Without pausing in the dance, he skimmed the back of his hand along the side of her body, over curve and dip and yet another curve until his hand rested at her hip bone.

"Do you have any…uh…?" she asked.

He gestured toward his bedside table. She reached across him and opened the drawer. The large box of condoms she found inside was half-empty, but she couldn't think about that now. Instead, she pulled one out and handed it to him. He didn't look at her as he ripped it open with his teeth, and she tried not to notice how efficiently he put it on.

But as she shifted back to their prior position,

Shane suddenly froze beneath her. She looked down to find him with his eyes squeezed shut, his lips rolled inward.

"Is something wrong?" she whispered.

But he didn't answer, didn't reassure her. When he finally opened his eyes, he looked as lost and uncertain as she felt. What was going on in his mind? He wasn't about to back out again, was he? She shook her head though he couldn't know the question she'd answered. She couldn't let him retreat now. Not when they were this close.

"I need you." Her voice sounded strange in her ears. She'd never spoken those particular words to another person in her life. They were too intimate. Too risky. They made her vulnerable, and she couldn't be vulnerable.

But if something inside him had been locking him in place, her words appeared to be the key. His arms slid around her again, pulling her close, his lips crushing hers in a desperate kiss. He moved against her until she thought she couldn't take any more and then brought them fully together with an effortless shift.

He waited several seconds, allowing their bodies to adjust. Then he began to lift and lower her hips in a dance so sensual, so excruciatingly slow that she couldn't breathe. But she let him lead, through each step, each twirl, the momentum building with the tempo of music played just for them.

The whimper that escaped her when she finally reached home sounded like it had come from someone else. She didn't make sounds like that. She didn't even *want* to make sounds that hinted she was out of control, though that's exactly what she'd been from the moment he'd come into her clinic and thrown her well-ordered life into chaos.

"You okay?" he asked in a tight voice.

"I'm fine." Her voice gave her away, but it was the best she could do. "What about you?"

"So far, so good, anyway."

What did that mean? When she would have asked him to explain, he shifted slightly beneath her, and that new, delicious angle made her forget her question as a new fire started to build within her. But just as the blaze was good and hot, he pressed his fingers at her waist, causing her to stop.

"Sorry." He leaned his forehead to hers and took several deep breaths. "Feels too good. Need to…slow down."

Again, she tried to make sense of his words, but her mind was too fogged with the sweet sensations. She wanted him, needed to connect with him in a way that went beyond just bodies. She sensed with a feminine awareness that he needed her just as much. And so they swayed together.

Natalie was the first to slip over the edge, tremors of ecstasy radiating to her limbs as she fell. But Shane chased her all the way down in his own release, their hearts pounding out a frenetic tempo and their bodies entwining as sweetly as their sighs.

"THAT WAS NICE," Shane breathed against Natalie's temple.

She swallowed as her head lay against his damp chest where she'd come to rest when her languid arms could no longer support her. Nice? He'd spoken about what they'd just done with the casualness someone might use to describe the weather instead of something that had rocked his world.

Or maybe it had only rocked *hers*.

Nice. Was that something he said to all of those other women *after*? She couldn't think about that. She wanted to bask in the afterglow the way that a beach bum soaked up the rays on a perfect day. Still, she couldn't escape the needling thought that their lovemaking might matter as little to him as any of those nights with other women had. It probably mattered less, since he'd nearly backed out of it.

"Yes. Nice." She nearly choked on the word. Because she suddenly felt uncomfortable sprawled across him like an afghan, she slid off to his side and pulled the comforter over her.

He didn't tell her to wait or try to prevent her retreat. Now that they'd had sex, would Shane want to escape from her and from this moment that he'd described with such a bland term? Would he leave her behind just like—

She squeezed her eyes closed to push away the thoughts. She sounded so paranoid. But the shoots of doubt had already taken root in all directions. She crossed her arms over her chest as if she could still protect herself.

He cleared his throat. "I'm sorry about…uh… putting on the brakes earlier."

"You don't have to talk about it." She hoped he wouldn't. The only thing worse than wondering why he'd nearly backed out of making love to her might be hearing his answer. "I have to get home to Mom, anyway."

She really was a lousy daughter. Even though her mother had been safe in her caregiver's protection, Natalie hadn't thought of her all afternoon until she needed an excuse to escape.

"No. I *want* to talk about it," he said.

He pushed himself into a seated position, using his arms to settle against the headboard. He didn't object when she propped a pillow behind him and pulled the sheet up to cover him.

"I said I didn't know what I was doing with the whole sex and the chair thing."

"But we…uh…figured it out," she said, her face heating.

"There was more to it, though." He paused, as if searching for the right words. "I haven't been worried only that I might never walk again. I was scared that I wouldn't be able to…you know…have sex again. To perform."

She glanced sidelong at him. No wonder he'd tried to back out earlier. Concerns about sexual performance were common with spinal injuries. She might have realized what had been bothering him if she hadn't failed to keep a clinical distance from him from the beginning.

"Didn't your doctors say you would be fine on that end?"

"I couldn't believe them without proof."

He had proof and then some now. She found a square on the blue-and-black-checked comforter to look at instead of at him. "Well, you know now, right?"

"I guess I do."

He brushed his fingers along her bare arm. Like earlier, his touch made her shiver, but instead of an awakening of desire, this time something just didn't feel right.

"So… I guess you'll be spreading your new-found answers around now."

Shane's hand stopped moving. "What are you talking about?"

Although she could feel his gaze on her, she couldn't look at him. She crossed her arms and the blanket slipped down in front of her. Snatching it up again, she tucked it under her armpits.

"You haven't answered my question," he pressed.

"It sounds like you get around. That maybe you're a womanizer. Your friends keep bringing it up."

He shifted on the bed. "I guess I'm guilty of that. But that was before—"

Natalie only shook her head to cut him off. "Now you know that everything is in working order, you won't have anything to hold you back."

"Except maybe that." He gestured toward the chair still parked at the end of the bed.

"You're not going to start using that chair as an excuse, are you?"

He stared at it for several seconds and then looked back to her. "No, I'm not. But you're right. I've dated a lot of women, and I wouldn't earn any awards over how I treated them. I've probably hurt more of them than I realize. But I'm not that guy anymore. I've changed."

She wanted to believe him, and not only because *her* heart might be the vulnerable one this time. But she knew from her psychology classes how motivated a person had to be to make a deep and lasting change. Yes, Shane had made changes in his life after his friend's death, but he'd been determined then. How much incentive would he have to alter the way he treated women when they'd flocked to him even while he'd treated them like dirt?

"For all the women in your future, I sure hope so."

Her sudden realization that she didn't want

other women in Shane's future only made her more uncomfortable. She had no hold over him. He hadn't offered a commitment, and she hadn't asked for one. She had no right to change the rules now.

"How about for the woman who's here right now?"

He stretched out a hand to her, and for several seconds, she stared at it, questions and misgivings holding her in place more effectively than restraints ever could. He was asking for her trust. How could she risk giving him that? She knew his track record and understood the odds.

But Shane didn't pull his hand back. He simply waited, his gaze steady as always.

And suddenly she found herself placing her hand in his, her better judgment losing the battle with her need for him. Her skin tingled with the anticipation of another round of his tender ministrations, but he only settled his arm around her, cradling her to his side. The gesture touched her more deeply than even his best caresses had.

She rested her head against his chest, his heartbeat thrumming a steady beat near her ear. It was probably a mistake, but she couldn't resist the temptation to trust someone, just this once.

"You know," she said to break the silence, "if you were able to prove to yourself that one of your fears was unfounded, then maybe you don't need to worry about walking again, either."

"Maybe you're right. If the doctors were right about one thing, then maybe I can believe them when they say I'll walk when I'm ready."

"You already took your first steps. You'll be running in no time."

"I hope so."

But as he settled back against his pillow, appearing content, Natalie only felt more unsettled. An image of Shane standing upright filtered through her thoughts. It was definitely him, but she could only see the back of his head as his form grew smaller and then disappeared entirely.

Maybe her worries hadn't been over his history with other women after all. At least not entirely. Something deep inside her had already concluded that when Shane walked again, it would be away from her. The whole time she'd known him, he'd needed her, even if he'd been reluctant to accept her help. To encourage him. To develop his therapy plan. Even today, she'd helped him prove that he had no worries in the bedroom. Of course he would leave her when he no longer needed her.

It wouldn't do for her to make something more out of this afternoon than was really there. She couldn't allow herself to have feelings for Shane Warner. He'd even admitted that there were heart carcasses strewn behind him in his dating history. She couldn't risk that her heart would join the others on that path of destruction. But was it already too late?

Shane had been staring out the window, but suddenly he turned back to her and kissed her forehead as gently as he might have a sleeping child.

"I still can't believe we're here."

She shifted next to him, his hold on her suddenly too constraining. "You've got that right."

"I bet that first day you met me at the clinic, you never would have guessed that we'd end up here."

"Not in a million years," she managed, though his words hit harder than a punch to the gut. When she'd met him, she'd known that she should stay away from Shane Warner, a cop who represented everything she'd lost the day of the accident. At least then she'd understood that letting a man with a badge into her heart would be a sign of disloyalty to her mother.

She glanced at the clock. It was almost five thirty. Her mother didn't know that she'd left work early, but even for a regular day, she would get home late. She scanned the floor for her cell phone but didn't know why she bothered. It was still in her purse near the front door, still on silent, the way she kept it at work.

"Oh, my gosh. I've got to get home."

She sat up on the edge of the bed with her back to him. Why was she trying to cover her nakedness now? He'd already seen all. Knew all. She grabbed her clothes from the floor and pulled them on. After sliding her feet into her work shoes, she retrieved his clothes and sat them next to him.

"Do you need me to help…?"

Somehow she glanced back long enough to see him shake his head, an unreadable look in his eyes.

"No, I can get it."

She nodded and stood. She couldn't worry that one of his friends might have to help him dress and would know exactly what they'd been up to. She just had to leave. Now.

With a quick wave, she rushed from his room. She was out the front door, down the ramp and back in her van before she could breathe again. No, she'd never expected to end up in Shane's bed, but she'd never anticipated that she would be tempted to care too much about him, either. She should have kept her distance. Hell, she should have walked away the moment her boss had insisted that she work with him.

Now here she was, leaving but still wanting him, rationalizing her choices today and still needing him. Aware she should run for her life and yet tempted to fall in love with him. Didn't she understand that loving him would be the biggest betrayal of all?

CHAPTER FOURTEEN

AT THE SOUND of the engine starting, Shane let go of the breath he'd been holding. At least she'd made it safely to her car. As fast as she'd raced from his room and as quickly as her footfalls had traced her path through the house, he'd worried that she might hit a patch of ice and fall. He cursed his broken body, not for the first time today, knowing that even if he hurried, he wouldn't be able to get his boxers on and make it to his chair and to the window before her taillights disappeared down the road.

A woman had never run away from him so fast. Or ever. He was usually the one running. Well, walking fast, with a phone number scribbled on his palm that he planned to wash off as soon as he got home. So this was what karma felt like. The first time he wanted to stay with a woman, wanted *her* to stay, she was running for her life. And he'd thought getting shot had hurt.

If this was what love felt like—as if someone had tried to gut him while still alive and sat with a fist pressed into his heart—then count him out. But worse than being in love with Natalie Keaton—which he could no longer deny—was realizing that she didn't share his feelings. She'd barely been able to look at him as she'd dressed for the walk of shame back to her car.

He shook his head as he yanked his sweatshirt over his head and, shifting to a seated position on the side of the bed, he began the exhausting process of pulling on his boxers and sweatpants. One of his friends would be stopping by soon, and the last thing he needed was to be found naked in his bed on a lazy afternoon.

That thought made him smile. Six months ago, he would have been sharing this afternoon's juicy details with any of them who would listen. But he wasn't that guy anymore, whether Natalie believed him or not. She was the one who'd made him want to change. He'd wanted to tell her that, too, but he didn't have the guts.

He didn't recall removing his socks—Natalie must have done that—but he didn't bother putting them back on. It was enough of a pain using that sock-aid gadget to put them on each morning without having to do it again now.

Using the transfer board, he shifted himself back into his chair. It wouldn't have been a big deal if one of his pals found him in bed. He was convalescing, after all. But he didn't want them anywhere near his room, which still smelled of that floral scent she always wore. He didn't want their questions, didn't want to explain that after having the most amazing physical experience with a woman he'd wanted desperately, he felt sad instead of sated.

How could he have misread her so completely? No, he couldn't have been that wrong about her. That hooded look of passion in her eyes, her encouraging sounds and the feel of her enticing moves against him—he couldn't have imagined all of that. He was certain that she'd wanted him. She'd even encouraged him when he'd been ready to chicken out. She'd said he was rejecting *her*. That was the biggest irony.

Had it been just sex to her? Just an afternoon activity to scratch the itch that had been developing between them since they'd met? Or had she given herself to him out of pity? After he'd spent a lifetime sharing meaningless sex with women, the one time that Shane had hoped it would mean something more, she could have just felt sorry for him and wanted to help him.

The problem was that Natalie saw him only as someone in need of it. The whole time she'd known him, he had needed something from her. Her professional expertise. Her support. He'd even needed her body to help him prove that all of his parts still worked.

For Natalie, it was different. She'd never needed him for anything, and even if she'd said she did while they were making love, that had only been to push him past his fears. Yes, he'd helped her with the basketball team, but she hadn't really needed his help or asked for it. If he ever hoped to be with her—and he did hope for that as much as he longed to walk again—he couldn't risk letting her choose him because she pitied him. So that she could be a long-suffering caregiver for him just like she was for her mother. That would be worse than never walking again, worse than giving up the career that defined his life.

He rolled his chair across the room, past the dresser, where he could see himself in the mirror. His overgrown hair was standing up in all directions after their time in bed. But even after he patted it into decent order, he couldn't stop staring at the man looking back at him.

"You need to be strong for her, in or out of the chair," he told that man.

She needed to know she could count on him to take care of her and not just the other way around. But how could he prove to her that he was strong when she'd already seen him at his most vulnerable? She'd been there when he was too nervous to even attempt walking. She knew about his fears over his sexual performance. She knew his ugly stories that suggested he was weak, even as a child. So how could he show her that there was more to him?

He needed to do something for *her*. It was as simple and as complicated as that. But what? As he started down the hall, passing the family room on his way to the kitchen, he considered it. He opened the refrigerator door, staring at the over-stuffed contents and then closing it again. Why was he looking there? He wasn't even hungry. But as the door clicked closed, he glanced up at the freezer.

Their night at the ice-cream shop and her mother's "emergency" call stole into his thoughts. Meeting her mother had explained so much about Natalie. The fierce love. The resentment. The dimming hope. Besides offering a warning about what his life could be like if he didn't choose to live it, Elaine Keaton presented him with a perfect opportunity to do something for Natalie. Elaine was stuck in a cycle of simply existing instead of really living, but maybe she just needed someone else, someone with some of the same challenges she faced, to show her how. He was just the man to do it.

As loud radio music and the sound of a powerful V-8 engine filtered from outside his house, Shane rolled back to the family room. He was acting like a kid caught sipping from his dad's nasty bottle of sloe gin, but he couldn't help himself. He had secrets now, and his friends were trained in knowing when someone was keeping those.

"Shane, you in here?" Vinnie called out just after the garage door opened.

"Family room." He flipped on the TV before his friend made it into the room.

Of course, it would be Vinnie taking extra

shifts and stopping by on his dinner break again. If only he could convince him that the shooting wasn't his fault. Shane schooled his features, hoping he could look as if he'd just been interrupted from an afternoon of bad television.

"Hey." Vinnie stood in the doorway, wearing his uniform. "You said you didn't need a ride back from the clinic. Everything okay?"

"Yeah. I already had a ride and figured I could save one of you guys the headache of carting me around."

"You know it's not a head—"

"You know what I mean."

Vinnie shrugged and then sauntered into the room. "So, who gave you the ride?"

The question seemed almost too casual to Shane, but then he was probably just hypersensitive today.

"Natalie," he said just as casually. "She had the afternoon off."

"Oh, really." Vinnie's eyebrow disappeared completely under his hair. "Did she bring you home to play doctor?"

"Nothing like that." He forced himself to look right at Vinnie as he answered the question. It was unfair that Vinnie had more experience than he did at ferreting out the truth from lying suspects. "She just happened to be finished with all of her appointments, so she could help me out when Delia took a call. Natalie usually drives me to basketball, anyway, so she already knows where I live."

"I'll bet she does."

"Cool it, Vinnie."

It couldn't have been clearer that Vinnie didn't buy his convenient-ride story, but he didn't press for more. Usually, he wouldn't have had to. But today was different for so many reasons.

Shane turned back to the television he wasn't really watching. Maybe that was best when all he could think about was flawless mocha skin and lips sweeter than any candy he'd tasted.

"Do you often watch police dramas?"

The strange question bringing him back from yet another tangent, Shane shifted his head to look at his friend.

Vinnie pointed to the show Shane had been pretending to watch. On the screen, a pair of TV detectives were investigating a grisly murder scene and making critical errors like moving the body and lifting a possible murder weapon with their bare hands.

"Got a problem with them?"

"Other than that you always hated them, no."

Shane couldn't help but grin. "Never know what I'll do lately to stay close to police work."

Vinnie made a sound like a wrong-answer buzzer. "I don't buy it. You're just watching because of the hot detectives."

Shane glanced at the screen, where a female detective bent over a body. She wore a tight blouse and badge pinned at the waist of her formfitting slacks.

"Maybe," he said, though he doubted it. Lately, he couldn't think about any woman other than a certain physical therapist who had the cutest freckles and a problem with her height.

"You'll be back at the post in no time." Vinnie glanced at the TV and shook his head. "But, sorry, I can't promise you'll get to work with any hot babes. At least any dressed like that."

He couldn't promise a quick return to work or even an eventual one, either, but neither mentioned that.

"Can I get you something from the kitchen?" Vinnie asked as he jumped up and strode toward it.

"I could eat something." Actually, he was so hungry he could finally empty out his refrigerator, but he wasn't about to say that. How was he supposed to explain how he'd worked up that appetite? Were his few steps at the clinic today enough to justify that?

Soon there was a veritable feast of leftovers on the tray in front of him. A little chicken, some pasta, half an enchilada. A big old glass of milk to wash it all down.

Between bites Shane said, "Should I be nervous that you're trying to fatten me up like a Thanksgiving turkey?"

"Just making sure you keep your strength up," Vinnie said with a grin. "Anything else I can do before I go?"

Shane shook his head. "Several others have offered to stop by. You don't have to take all the shifts."

"I know. I just miss seeing your ugly face at the post."

Shane dragged his teeth across his bottom lip. "Eventually, you're going to have to forgive yourself for not getting there fast enough." He didn't bother mentioning *where*. They both knew what he was talking about.

Vinnie shook his head. "I should have been there. I should have—"

"No. *I* should have waited for backup."

"You know you couldn't wait."

Shane crossed his arms. "So you can admit that I had no choice but to go in, but you can't accept that without teleporting yourself, you couldn't have made it to the scene any faster? You're just going to have to let it go."

Vinnie shook his head, refusing to be let off so easily.

"Remember, we're both getting commendations," Shane said. "You saved my life that night."

"Wait," Vinnie said with a grin. "Then maybe you should be bringing *me* dinner. I like sushi. *Homemade* sushi."

"I'll get right on it."

Vinnie chuckled and then became serious again. "I just wish there was something more I could do now."

"Actually, there is something. Are you off tomorrow?" He waited for Vinnie's nod before continuing. "I need you to take me to visit Kent and then take me to my game later on. Me and a friend of mine."

"Do you and this PT of yours need a chauffeur or something? Can I watch in the rearview mirror?"

This PT of yours. Shane frowned. If he'd thought he'd pulled one over on Vinnie, he knew better now. "The other person will be Natalie's mother."

"Sounds kinky, but you do you."

"Vinnie…"

"Fine. Just tell me where and when."

Vinnie pulled his notebook from his uniform pocket and took down the address. He agreed to drive his SUV since they would be bringing along two wheelchairs.

"What is it about this chick?" Vinnie said as he tucked away the notebook.

"You mean Natalie's mom?" he said with a grin.

Vinnie only waited, using those interview skills that helped him to regularly get confessions from suspects.

Finally, Shane couldn't help but answer. "Natalie's just had a rough time since her mother was paralyzed in a high-speed police chase."

"Oh, man. That stinks."

"Anyway, her mom hasn't bounced back the way anyone would have hoped, so I thought that someone like me—" he paused, gesturing broadly to his wheelchair "—might be able to reach her. Help her move forward."

"It might make a difference."

"I just want to help out. That's all."

Vinnie's skeptical look told him he didn't buy that this was *all*. But Vinnie didn't call him on it. That was at least one of the reasons they were friends. They might push each other on certain subjects, but they also knew when to pull back. When to just let the other one work it out for himself.

Sure, Shane hoped Vinnie would eventually forgive himself for a situation over which he'd had no control. Unlike Shane, he bore no culpability for the incident that kept him up at night. But like Shane, Vinnie had done his best afterward to make things as right as he could in the new reality that followed. Shane had suggested that Vinnie should forgive himself. Let it go. Maybe one of these days, he would follow his own advice.

SHANE PUSHED OPEN the door to Kent's room at Clearview Hospital and peered inside. It looked the same. Stark. Antiseptic. Not a good place at all for a person to die. Kent's wife, Tammy, was reading in a chair next to the bed, but she noticed him, smiled and stood, moving the chair out of the way.

"It's good to see you again, Shane," she whispered and then lifted her chin to kiss him on the cheek. "He's resting now."

"How's he doing today?" Shane asked in a low voice.

"Why don't you ask me yourself?" Kent whispered.

The other two turned back to him, and they all laughed. How his friend hadn't lost his sense of humor by now, Shane couldn't begin to understand. Kent looked worse every time Shane visited, his body thin and frail, his cheeks sunken and his eyes bugging out from his face.

With a wave, Tammy excused herself from the room for a much-needed break. Shane moved his chair into the empty spot where the guest chair had been.

"Okay, she's gone now. How bad is it?"

"Take the worst day of your life…and multiply it…by a thousand," Kent told him.

He laughed when he said it, but his laugh deteriorated into a long round of hacking. Shane braced himself, wanting to call for the nurse and yet realizing that this was part of it and would be until the end.

"Now don't worry about talking," Shane said. "We can just stay quiet."

But Kent only shook his head, cleared his throat. "You talk. About the girl."

Shane could only smile. He'd shared more details about Natalie with Kent than he'd told anyone else, but then he knew Kent never shared his secrets.

"Natalie's great. I saw her again yesterday."

"How much of her?" Kent managed.

This time, Shane only shrugged.

"So that's how…it is."

Shane lifted a brow. "What do you mean?"

"Details become…private…when she's special."

He nodded. "Oh, she's special. I can't believe she's paying attention at all to my sorry butt, but she is. She doesn't treat me like I'm broken, either. I really like that about her."

"Think you like…everything about her." Kent broke off in another series of coughs.

"I do."

"Did you…tell her…your stuff?"

Shane nodded. "And she's still around."

"She's…a good one."

"You're right. She is."

"You're a…good one, too. Always…have been."

Emotion clogged Shane's throat then, and he had to wait a few seconds before he could speak again. "You know, I owe you so much."

Kent only shook his head. "Best investment…"

"You ever made," he finished for him. He'd heard it dozens of times before. If only he could believe his friend's words.

"You need to…forgive yourself," Kent told him. "It's been…too long."

Kent might have said more, but he started coughing again, and this time he couldn't stop. A couple of nurses rushed into the room, and Shane found himself in the hall, waiting and hoping now wouldn't be the time.

A few minutes later, Tammy reemerged from the room.

"They gave him something so he can rest now," she said. "Maybe you can come back tomorrow. He loves your visits."

Shane rolled forward to hug Tammy and then turned and headed down the hall. He would come back tomorrow and every tomorrow after that if Kent wanted him to. He wasn't sure he was strong enough to do this, to watch Kent die, but he would do whatever was necessary. Kent had been there for him when no one else had. And Shane would be there for him until the end.

CHAPTER FIFTEEN

NATALIE FROWNED AT the gymnasium door as the Junior Cats lined up their chairs on one end of the court to practice free throws. Players from the Lansing Lightning repeated a similar drill on the opposite end. But at least that other team had more than one coach to catch the rebounds that bounced off the rim and rolled every which way.

Where was Shane? He was supposed to be here in time for the warm-up. Did he think she could coach this team alone? The last question deepened her frown. When had Shane become so indispensable to the team and to her? She'd coached without an assistant for two seasons before he'd come along, but now it didn't seem right without him.

Natalie glanced at the door again, though she doubted he could have made an entrance since she'd last checked thirty seconds ago. Was it just that she was annoyed that he was late after he'd told her he would meet her at the gym, or was she coming out of her skin over seeing him after yesterday? After he'd seen every inch of her and vice versa. Was she just supposed to pretend everything was normal after they'd shared the most

intimate thing two people could and then she'd
sprinted from his house?

She blinked several times to push away the del-
uge of images that filled her mind and caused heat
to crawl up her neck. Those pictures had been
following her around for the past day, but she especially shouldn't be thinking those things here.
There were children around, for goodness' sake.
To keep her mind more appropriately occupied,
she chased a few more basketballs, tossing them
back to the players.

"Great job, Kendall," she called out when the
girl's basket sank home.

Lucas stopped his chair next to Natalie.
"When's Coach Shane going to get here?"

Her gaze flitted to the door again, and then
she glanced down at the boy. "I'm sure he's on
his way."

But she wasn't sure. Had he been in a car accident? He already had a serious injury. Had
something acerbated his physical issues, like, for
instance, an afternoon of great sex? She couldn't
allow herself to wonder if it had been truly good
for him, a guy who'd had many women before
her and would continue to that habit after she was
gone.

Only a few minutes remained until tip-off. Her
jaw tightened. Was Shane missing because the
game was on Saturday this time, and it messed
with his social life? She had no time to worry

about that now. Whether Shane was there or not, these kids needed *her*. Now that they'd learned what it felt like to win, she needed to help them repeat that joy. Of all the teams in the league, the Lightning was the only team with a record almost as bad as the Cats', and they needed to capitalize on that vulnerability.

"Go, Junior Cats!"

At the familiar voice, Natalie jerked up from where she'd bent to collect a ball. Sure enough, Shane was coming through the doorway, his friend Vinnie behind him.

"Coach Shane's here!" one of the players called.

Their balls forgotten, the players started toward Shane, who was wheeling their way, as well. He caught them before they reached half-court.

"You're here, Coach Shane." Chase squeezed in to claim a high five.

"You're late," Lucas pointed out.

"Why are you late?" another asked.

That's what Natalie wanted to know. At least he was safe. With one of the balls still in her arms, she strode over to them and stood in the circle forming around Shane.

"About time," she mouthed when he glanced her way. She pointed to the game clock, where valuable minutes of warm-up time were slipping away.

"I was just apologizing to the kids," Shane said to Natalie instead. "My errand took longer than I expected."

Natalie nodded, disappointed with his excuse. Even after all the time he'd put into his work with the team, he wasn't taking his responsibility as assistant coach seriously. Just like he didn't take the time he and she had spent together seriously.

"I hope it was an important errand," she couldn't help saying.

"Oh, I think so."

At his vague comment, she frowned. Shane only grinned like a kid with a secret.

"I brought a surprise. For you."

His gaze caught with Natalie's, letting her know that he was referring to her.

At his nod, Vinnie stepped to the door again and leaned outside. When he backed away again, the foot-plate of another wheelchair appeared in the doorway, two feet on top of that peeked out from beneath a plaid throw that looked vaguely familiar. Natalie continued her visual path up, past a bulky parka to a face peeking out from beneath an oversize stocking cap.

Her mother's face.

Natalie dropped the basketball. She didn't even try to retrieve it. Elaine waved as if surprising her daughter at a basketball game was something she did daily and twice on Thursdays. That only made her appearance there tonight seem like more of a slap in the face. Natalie could count the times her mother had watched her play basketball on no hands whatsoever. And as for the number of times Elaine had been a spectator at a game she coached, well, including today, that would be... one.

Natalie would have rubbed her eyes, but her hands seemed to be glued to her sides. What was her mother doing there? Finally, she managed to return the wave, but a smile was just too much to expect.

Laura, Elaine's caregiver, appeared in the doorway behind her chair and reached down to pluck the cap off her head. A few electrified strands stood at attention, but the rest of her hair stayed in place, suggesting that Elaine had taken special care with her appearance. For Shane.

"Who's that, Coach Natalie?"

She started as Chase took hold of her hand. She hadn't even noticed the child's approach.

"That's my...mom." She hated how those words stuck in her throat. If only she'd been able to point out her mother to her teammates even once while she was actually playing.

"Your mom has a wheelchair like us?" Kendall asked.

"You have a lot of friends who drive wheelchairs," Lucas noted.

She managed a smile and ruffled his hair. "Yes, I do."

One too many right now, she decided. She turned her head to find that superfluous friend watching her. Shane was so pleased with himself that her hard look seemed to surprise him. Had he really expected her to turn cartwheels over his orchestrating her mother's appearance? How dare he get involved in something he didn't understand.

The buzzer sounded then, indicating that warm-up time had ended. Great. Now he'd messed up the warm-up, too. They were going to lose, and it would be all his fault. A rumble of fury slid through her, anger that was probably an over-the-top reaction to Shane's naive intrusion, but she couldn't stop herself. She felt trapped, this moment playing with an audience when she wasn't prepared to talk about it even in the privacy of her home.

But, like in so many other areas of her life, she had a job to do. An obligation. She owed these kids to be a strong coach, even if she might fall into a jumbled mess of emotions as soon as her players were all safely in their cars and headed home.

"All right, everybody," she called out. "Huddle in." She wished she could say *everybody but Coach Shane*, but she didn't need to draw more attention to the situation. The parents probably already knew something was up, anyway, with an assistant coach who arrived halfway through the warm-up and a coach who let precious warm-up time slip away while staring at fans.

"I'm so proud of each and every one of you for all you've accomplished so far this season."

She refused to look toward the woman parked on the far end of the bleachers. The woman who'd seldom praised her over any of her accomplishments, let alone those on the basketball court. Though she could feel Shane watching her, his gaze as heavy as a touch, she didn't look his way, either. He'd forced her to face some of her life's biggest resentments in front of a crowd, like she was on some reality TV show but without a clever script.

"You've worked hard," she told her players. "You've learned to work as a team. Now I just want you to play your best and have a great time out there."

In the few games he'd attended as assistant coach, Shane had sat back and let her give the pregame and postgame speeches, but this time he rolled forward from his place in the circle.

"You've also learned what victory tastes like. And it tastes sweet, doesn't it?" He grinned as he glanced around the circle, waiting for a nod from each player. "So play together, have fun and, if you get the chance, kick some butt, too."

Their eyes wide over the fact that their coach had said "butt" in front of them, they all nodded again. Natalie was the only one not smiling.

"Everybody ready?" She waited until all the players had their hands poised in front of them.

"Break," they all said in unison, clapping their hands just once.

The five starters rolled onto the court for the tip-off. Natalie held her breath until after the toss that put the ball into play. She'd done that every game since her first few seasons in elementary school, one of those strange traditions that players develop and superstitiously continue for fear of impact on their game if they don't. Everything felt different about it this time. The flat thuds of the ball bouncing on the court as if it was low on air. The uncharacteristic brightness of the old fluorescent gymnasium lights.

"Let's go, Junior Cats!" Shane called out.

At least that should have sounded normal to her. He'd repeated those same words at every game he'd attended, even before he became her assistant. But the response that came from the stands— now that was different.

"Yeah, go Cats!"

The voice was unmistakable. The voice she'd longed to hear with every basket she'd made, when she'd received her first varsity letter and her scholar-athlete award.

The voice that had always been silent...until now.

Natalie couldn't decide whether to be thrilled for the now or resentful for the past, and she couldn't hold her feet still, either. Though she'd been standing in one place next to the bench, she jogged along now, following the play up and down to half-court in the regulated area for coaches.

"Let's go, Cats," she repeated several times under her breath and then called it out louder. The crowd responded, cheering louder than she'd ever heard them before. This team had finally experienced victory, and there was something invigorating about watching a team with at least the possibility of winning.

She held her breath as Lucas set up his first shot. It swished through the net so smoothly that she didn't even mind that he didn't look to see if he should pass first.

As the opposing team started down the floor toward their basket, Kendall reached in and claimed the ball, her first steal of the season. The cheering pounded in Natalie's ears, though she couldn't take her eyes off the court. Couldn't breathe normally. Couldn't relax. But the game on the court before her wasn't the one playing in her thoughts. Instead her own highlight reel replayed in vibrant color. Each shot. Each rebound. Each steal. Even the three-pointers she'd made occasionally.

She knew it was selfish to be reminiscing about those games right now. Tonight was about this ragtag group of athletes who'd overcome so much more than just one deserting parent and another who couldn't have spelled the word *support* if a spelling-bee championship trophy were on the line. But she couldn't help herself. Her mother was watching her team tonight, even if she wasn't actually the one in uniform taking the shots. And she desperately wanted the Cats to win this game.

As the buzzer marked the Junior Cats' second victory of the season, Natalie leaped up from the team bench and waited on the sideline of the court for the players rushing toward her. Though Shane had been parked on the other end of the bench past the row of sub players, he reached her first.

"What was that all about?"

"I don't know what you're talking about." But she didn't look at him.

"That's the best answer you've got?"

The crush of wheels, cheers and sweaty basketball players shielded her from having to answer immediately, but she knew Shane too well to think he would let his question go unanswered.

Sure enough, they'd barely finished their team meeting before he was next to her again.

"Meet me in the hall."

She shook her head, her gaze sliding to her mother, still parked at the end of the bleachers with Laura on one side and Vinnie on the other. Natalie's tongue darted out to dampen her dry lips, a move Shane didn't miss if his blink gave any indication.

"Okay, then," he said. "We'll have this conversation right here. Don't worry about the ladies. Vinnie's over there entertaining them. He'll keep them laughing until we're finished talking."

"Fine. The hall."

She started that way herself, glancing back only once to see if he'd followed. This wasn't the way she would have imagined their first conversation since their afternoon in bed. Discomfort she'd expected. Even warmth that would spread up her neck and face over the sweet images that would replay in her thoughts. But she wasn't prepared to be called out to the hall for a lecture. She wasn't the one who'd done anything wrong.

As soon as they'd passed the heavy double gymnasium doors, she whirled to face him. "Why did you bring her here?"

Shane stared back at her, his mouth open. "Are you kidding? You should be thanking me for getting your mom out of the house. When is the last time you convinced her to leave when it wasn't for a doctor's appointment?"

A hell of a long time. "But you shouldn't have brought her *here*. It's none of your business. And it's certainly nothing you can fix by flirting with a lonely, fragile woman."

"I wasn't…flirting—"

"That's not the point. You shouldn't have gotten involved in something you don't understand."

"Wait." He studied her as if trying to decipher all that she'd said. "What am I not getting here?"

"She…never…came." The words sounded flat in her ears, childish even, and yet a mix of emotions tightened her throat.

"To watch the games you coach?"

"To watch me." Her voice broke on the last, so she stared at the ground. "Ever."

"Not even when you were little?"

"She dropped me off and picked me up." Long-buried humiliation resurfaced over being *that girl*, the one whose parent was never in the crowd, whose mother never volunteered to bring the team bagels for after a game.

"Well, that's an awful thing to do to a kid."

Natalie blinked, but the corner of her mouth lifted. Shane had taken her side. "Remember, she said she didn't like basketball."

"That's no excuse."

"But she had other reasons."

"You didn't know that then."

He was right. Why was she defending her mother now when she'd carried that anger with her all these years? Was it because Shane was critical of her, too?

"I'm sorry," he said finally. "I shouldn't have brought her here."

"That's okay. You didn't know." But then she couldn't help asking, "Why did you bring her here, anyway?"

"You were here," he said with an eye roll. "I wanted to surprise you."

"It was a surprise, all right."

He shrugged, his silly grin back in place. "You said you wanted her to finally start living again. I thought I could help her get started. You know.

Because of this." He patted the armrests of his chair.

Natalie cleared her throat. He'd convinced his friend to drive, talked her mother *and* her caregiver into coming, and brought the whole merry band to a basketball game, and he'd done it all for her. And she'd been furious at him for it. What kind of ungrateful person was she?

"How *did* you talk her into it?"

He brushed off the question with a wave of his hand. "It wasn't that hard. Really. She was more concerned that her hair wasn't done."

Natalie couldn't help but grin at that. She'd seen how her mother reacted to Shane when they'd met. Of course he'd been able to convince her to go with him. Even now, looking through the gym doors, Natalie saw her mother reach up to pat her hair as she continued talking to Vinnie on the other side of the gym.

"It looks like she fixed that."

"I gave her and her nurse a few minutes to primp."

She nodded. Besides having her hair neatly combed instead of the messy way she usually wore it, Elaine was wearing lipstick. Natalie couldn't remember the last time she'd seen her mother wearing any. She was surprised Laura had found a tube that wasn't dried up.

"I think she has a little crush on you."

Natalie glanced over to find Shane watching her instead of her mother.

"I do have a way with women. Especially the Keaton ladies."

He was kidding with her, telling of two very different ways she and her mother had been susceptible to his charms. But his gaze was so warm that she wasn't certain if all the heat on her face had come from the inside. Even in the hallway, where anyone could have walked in and interrupted them, he allowed his gaze to linger indecently on her.

If only the full meaning of his words hadn't settled heavily on her chest then, stealing her breath and cooling her skin quicker than an ice pack. *A way with women.* She'dguessed that about him. So why did it bother her so much? Why did she get the sense of a long hello and a short goodbye that would leave her more scarred than even the gunshot had left Shane and the accident had left her mother?

"Besides, it looks like I have some competition now."

He gestured toward her mother again. Either Vinnie had said something funny or Elaine was having a blast tonight—maybe both—but her mother was laughing in a way Natalie hadn't seen in years.

Signaling something to her mother's caregiver, Vinnie stepped behind Elaine's wheelchair and pushed it to the bench where some of the players were still meeting up with their parents. Elaine gripped each of their hands and must have congratulated them on their game because they all sat higher in their chairs as they continued past her.

Though Natalie smiled, her expression felt fragile, a happy image carved into the softest wood. But the children's joy was contagious, and she realized with a shock that her own mother had inspired it. More than that, she could see a spark of possibility in Elaine, as well. Hope filling the void of despair.

"Still think I shouldn't have brought her tonight?"

Shane was watching her when she glanced at him again, and he was grinning.

"It's a start," she admitted, not wanting to jinx anything by speaking too soon.

"The first step's the hardest, right? And then another and another."

Their gazes caught again and this time, held. They were talking about so much more than her mother's first outing in who knew how long. For Shane, one exhausting first step offered hope of the next. Promise of a reward just out of reach. Would his next step lead him closer to her or just stretch his shadow behind him as he walked away from her?

She couldn't worry about any of that now, she decided, as her mother noticed her standing in the doorway and started toward them. Elaine was grinning before she even reached them.

"Why didn't you ever tell me how fun this was?"

CHAPTER SIXTEEN

MAYBE SHE WASN'T ready for her mother's first step toward a new life. Natalie accepted that hard truth with a frown as she pushed Elaine through the front door, exhausted after a long ride while listening to her mother gush. Laura must have been tired of the conversation, too, as she'd slipped away to her car just after they'd parked in the drive.

"That's the most fun I've had in years," Elaine said as Natalie closed the front door.

"So you've said, Mom." She took both of their coats and hung them in the closet.

Having missed Natalie's snide comment, Elaine prattled on as she drove her electric wheelchair into the family room.

"That Shane is such a nice young man. You and the kids were so lucky to have him join you as a coach."

"Yeah, from the way the Livingston Community Center people talk about him volunteering with the Junior Cats, you'd swear he was a retired Detroit Pistons player and not just a cop on leave from his day job."

"Oh, that's right. Vinnie told me that Shane didn't know anything about basketball when he started volunteering."

Natalie could only stare at her mother. She'd expected her to have at least some reaction to her coaching with a police officer.

"I never realized how much fun it could be to cheer on those young athletes."

"Really?" Natalie snapped. She'd been itching for an argument all night. "You would have known it if you'd ever just once come to one of *my* games."

Elaine stopped and turned back to her. "What are you talking about? Of course I attended—"

"No, Mom," Natalie said. "You didn't."

Her mother blinked several times, shaking her head as if the delicate construction of her make-believe memories had just been rammed at their cornerstone.

"That's not possible. I wouldn't have—"

This time her daughter interrupted her with a fierce and final shake of her head. Then she posed the question she'd longed to ask after so many wins, losses and other moments no parent should have missed.

"Why not, Mom?"

Elaine turned her chair away so her daughter couldn't see her face. She stayed that way so long that Natalie wondered if she would get the answer to her question tonight. When she finally turned back, her cheeks were damp.

"Why not?" Elaine repeated the question.

Something gripped inside Natalie's chest. As much as she'd wanted answers and apologies, now she only longed to restore equilibrium, to balance the toxic cradle of secrets and lies they'd rocked in for so long. But as she opened her mouth to take back everything she'd said, her mother looked straight at her.

"It hurt too much."

For a few seconds, Natalie froze. Prior to the accident, she couldn't recall her mother ever admitting to weakness of any kind, let alone of actual pain. She sat on the love seat closest to her mother.

"What hurt?"

"I couldn't watch you play. It reminded me too much of *him*."

Her mother no longer needed to announce her pain. It was telegraphed in her eyes. Natalie might not have been able to understand her mother on so many issues, but she could relate to this.

"My father?" she asked, because the word needed to be said.

Elaine nodded and then studied Natalie's face for so long that she had to look away.

"You should have seen him play. It was like watching a perfectly choreographed but utterly masculine ballet with a basketball for a prop."

Natalie frowned. Somehow she couldn't connect the picture her mother painted to the man she'd been researching on the internet now that she actually had his name.

"He was so handsome. Like a fine black statue, but larger than life and a lot shinier."

Natalie could only stare at her mother, who never spoke in analogies. Who always wrote her world in the black-and-white columns of a spreadsheet. Except in that journal from long ago. And in the words she spoke about a man Natalie had never known. Someone who had no interest in ever knowing her.

"I'm sorry."

"For what, Mom? For never letting me know anything about the other half of my heritage? For not even telling me his *name*? For keeping my father to yourself so I would come to see him—and myself—like some dirty little secret?"

Elaine's eyes widened as if she only recognized now the damage she'd caused. "I should have told you."

"Yes, you should have." With that, Natalie stood and stalked from the room, pain propelling her forward.

"Natalie, wait," her mother called.

But she couldn't wait. She'd waited for far too long. Now she needed answers. All of them. Instead of heading to her own room, she stepped inside her mother's bedroom and pulled the item she needed from the second drawer in the bedside table. It was hidden all the way at the bottom, beneath the flannel pajamas.

In the same tight clip with which she'd marched from the room, she returned to where her mother sat. Instead of reacting, Elaine stared out the window at a cobalt night sky as stingy with light as she had been with details involving her daughter's birth.

Natalie lowered the book into her mother's hands.

"I found this."

Elaine stared at the journal and then traced her index finger over the embossed leather cover. She didn't complain about the violation of having her daughter go through her private things. Those boundaries had evaporated long ago when the child had been forced to become the parent.

"So you know," she said, not looking up.

"Some of it, yes. At least I know his last name now. Did you ever plan to tell me the truth about my father?"

Finally, her mother looked at her. She shook her head. "I never wanted you to know."

"That he left you instead of the other way around?"

Elaine's expression was stark, the pain still real, even after so many years.

"I wanted to protect you," she said in a small voice.

"Was it really for me, or were you just protecting yourself?"

"Both, I guess," she said with a sigh. "I was humiliated. Zeke Morris, hero power forward, and me, the bookworm. Even if we were opposites, I thought we had a future. So when I became pregnant with you, I thought it was just a wrinkle. He…didn't agree. He had big dreams of fame and fortune in a European league. He thought I was trying to steal money he didn't even have yet. He chose those dreams over me. Us."

"I read that in your journal. A kid just didn't fit in with his plans." She didn't need to have those words repeated in an ode to the fact that he'd seen *her* as an end to those dreams. A trap.

"You read the part where I said I always wanted you, right?"

Natalie could only nod. Her mother might have been a young woman at the time, and one who found out she was on her own rather quickly, but there was no doubt in those words that she'd wanted her baby.

"You weren't the only one who was a kink in his plans," she said with a sad smile. "There I'd been, thinking I would go along with him on this amazing ride, and I found he hadn't even planned to take me before the pregnancy. In fact, I wasn't even his only girlfriend whom he intended to leave later—out of sight, out of mind."

"Were there other…babies?" She had to choke

out the question. As if it hadn't hurt enough to find out that she was left behind. Now she might discover that she'd only filled one crib in a whole nursery.

"Not that I know of."

"Did you love him?"

As soon as the words were out of her mouth, Natalie regretted them. From the pain in Elaine's face, from the effort she'd made to keep her secrets, Natalie already knew the answer. Just as she knew that if she wasn't careful, she just might fall for Shane.

The Keaton women were unlucky in love. Both had taken a leap of faith—her mother with Zeke, and Natalie with Paul—and both had been burned. Just like her father, Paul had left the woman he was supposed to love when she needed him most. As if Natalie's life hadn't been dark enough in the aftermath of the accident, while her mother was still hospitalized, Paul left a note on her apartment door, saying he couldn't be with someone who had so many problems. She didn't need more proof than that. Love was too dangerous. Not worth the risk, no matter how tempted she was to let herself fall.

"Yes, I did." There was a faraway look in Elaine's eyes as she stared out the window into the darkness, but then she turned back to Natalie. "I was a naive kid. I didn't even know what love was…until I became a mother. So instead of wasting my time crying about my situation, I put all of my energy into building a career so I could support the two of us and make a home for you."

A lump formed in Natalie's throat. Why had she held her own secret for so long, waiting for the right moment to spring it on Elaine? She'd wanted to hurt her mother, of course, just as her mother's secrets had hurt her, but now it just seemed cruel. Even her frustration over being the center of her mother's life seemed petty and selfish now. Still, there had been secrets between them for far too long. It was time for the whole truth to be told.

"Did you ever hear from Zeke again?"

Elaine shook her head. "Since I wasn't going after him for child support, there wasn't even a paternity suit. I assume he had some glamorous career in pro basketball and then went on to be a coach or something."

"That wasn't exactly how it happened."

Though her mother had been staring down at her folded hands, she jerked her head to look up again.

"What do you mean?"

Natalie reached for the journal that she'd set aside and produced a dated photo of a handsome African-American man in a basketball uniform. The name Zeke Morris was printed at the bottom.

Automatically, Elaine reached for the photo, staring at it for several seconds before looking up again. "How did you get this?"

"After the accident, the hospital people told me I should look for the documents containing your advance directives and life insurance policy, just in case. I found your journal instead. Then I had more questions, so I just kept looking." She hadn't really answered her mother's question, but she wasn't ready. Wasn't sure she could make herself say it.

Though Elaine appeared to be trying to listen, her attention kept returning to the photo in her hands. It was probably a reflex that had her tracing her thumb over the photo's glossy surface.

"I don't look a lot like him," Natalie said to make her stop.

"What?" Elaine asked, startled. She pulled her hand back. "Oh. I guess not. You look more like me."

Natalie leaned in for a closer look and then shook her head. "He doesn't look much like that photo anymore, either."

She pulled a second photo from the journal, this one on printer paper instead of glossy photo stock. It was a portrait of a man in a business suit, his head shaved, a paunch causing his suit jacket to pull slightly. If not for the same wide-toothed grin, he might not have been recognizable at all.

"Are you sure that's him?" Elaine stared at the more recent photo, her expression bewildered as if she couldn't reconcile that man with the one from her memories.

"It's him. He did play in Europe like he said he would, but his pro career was short-lived. Just two seasons in Italy, and much of that riding the bench. Then he retired and moved back to the States."

"Were you trying to find out what happened to him after that?"

Natalie had to smile at the way her mother posed the question, trying not to sound too interested.

"He's a Realtor in Cleveland now and is married to, from what I can gather, his third wife."

Natalie paused as Elaine shifted and set the photo on a side table as if it was too painful to look at it now. He'd been married, after all. Just not to her, any of those three times. Would she say she didn't want to hear any more? Would she refuse to talk about it now just as she'd hidden from it all of those years?

But Elaine didn't say anything. Instead, she tilted her head to meet her daughter's gaze, folded her hands across her belly and waited.

"From his bio on the real estate company's website, he likes to work on his classic Mustangs and plays an above-average game of golf."

"How did you find out so much about him?"

"You can find anything online. In fact, I'm surprised you didn't look him up yourself."

"I wanted to know, but I was afraid of what I would find."

Natalie nodded. She understood that dilemma

because she'd lived it. "He also has three kids. Three *sons*."

The word tasted sour on her tongue. Of course, her father hadn't known her gender when he'd left her mother. He'd only known that she existed. But it still hurt that he'd acknowledged *those* children. Welcomed them. Loved them. *If* a man who denied his own child was even capable of love.

"They're probably jerks just like their father," Elaine ground out.

Natalie couldn't help grinning. "Hey, that's my father you're talking about. And, apparently, those are my half siblings."

"I'm sorry," Elaine said for the second time.

"That you called him a jerk?"

"That I kept it from you and forced you to hunt down your own history. That you don't have a better dad. He's the one missing out on the chance to know his amazing daughter."

"He doesn't seem that concerned."

"What do you mean?"

Elaine lifted a brow and then turned and picked up the portrait that she'd set aside. She must not have noticed them before, but now she pointed to the words written in marker in the right bottom corner. It read, "All best, Zeke."

"Why do you have an autographed photo of your father?"

"He must have thought I needed one. It's what he sent to me when I wrote him after the accident." At her mother's narrowed gaze, she explained, "Just to let him know."

Elaine pressed her lips together, the pain obvious, even if hidden beneath callused layers she'd formed for her own survival.

"What did you expect him to do, send a welcoming party?"

Natalie shook her head. "I don't know what I expected. That he would have some regrets for what he did to you. Or maybe he would recognize me now that I'm an adult and he wouldn't have to pay child support."

She pointed to the photo in her mother's hands. "But, hey, I got an autographed photo out of it."

"And I was even luckier. I got you."

The loving words only made Natalie feel lousy. Had her mother really been lucky to have a daughter like her? One who ambushed her over the discovery of her secrets? Who cared for her physical needs but resented her for it? Who'd betrayed her by becoming involved with a police officer when cops were the very reason she would never walk again? Who still wanted the cop and had let him befriend her mother when he would just leave them both the moment he was steady on his feet?

She couldn't let that happen. Her mother had already experienced enough hurt to last a lifetime. Now that she finally appeared ready to live in the world again, the last thing she needed was to experience more pain and another setback when her volunteer life coach grew bored of this project and moved on to fix someone else.

Like before, Natalie would be left to pick up the broken pieces and restore her life and her mother's to their comfortable norm. She wasn't sure she had it in her to do that again. So to assure against that possibility, she had to back away from the man whom she wanted more than she'd ever wanted anything. And she had to guide her mother to step back from her new best friend. It was for the best, she told herself. Some sacrifices needed to be made for the greater good, and for all the sacrifices her mother had made for her, she could do this one thing in return. If only she could convince her heart she was doing the right thing.

NATALIE CAUGHT HER mother yawning a week later as she pushed her through the power-assisted door and out into the movie theater's patio area. As had become her habit lately, she immediately turned back to assist Shane through the doorway. And, as usual, he was already right behind her, requiring no help.

"I told you that you were doing too much this week, Mom," Natalie said, shaking her head. "You're going to wear yourself out if you don't watch it."

"I'm fine, you worrywart. It was just one yawn. Anyway, that movie was amazing." Elaine lifted her hands for emphasis. "Don't you just love movies about law enforcement?"

"They do get your heart pumping," Shane agreed. "I'll give you that."

"Come on." Natalie frowned. "That movie might have been the worst one I've seen in three years."

Shane grinned when she shot a look back at him. There was no way he could have liked that film with its awkward police dialogue about perps and dirtbags. Having missed that he hadn't exactly said he'd enjoyed the movie, Elaine prattled on about justice and the "war on crime."

How could her mother say she loved that movie, anyway? In the high-speed-chase sequence near the end, the police cruiser had narrowly missed a mother pushing a baby in a stroller *and* a puppy on a leash. Had she forgotten what it was like to be on the other end of those squealing tires? But then her mother loved everything this week, particularly everything to do with a certain state trooper.

"What did you think about it, Laura?" Natalie asked, looking for an ally.

Laura, who'd finally agreed to come on one of their outings, shrugged. "It had interesting cinematography."

"That's like saying a book had good margins," Natalie said with a frown.

"We definitely had the best seats in the house," Shane chimed.

"Yes, the view was perfect," Elaine agreed.

If they could call Natalie being sandwiched in the wheelchair section between the chairs, with Laura on the other side, then they were the best seats. Unfortunately, they were also too close for Natalie to avoid breathing in the spicy scent of Shane's cologne and to miss when his tongue darted out to lick the popcorn salt off his lips.

So much for her grand plan to put some distance between the Keaton women and one Shane Warner. Elaine had outmaneuvered Natalie on every attempt she made to avoid Shane this week, calling him before Natalie even got home from work and scheduling plans with him instead of allowing her to serve as coordinator.

Shane hadn't been much help, either, and had even been intentionally obtuse when she'd suggested that her mother needed more rest instead of more activities. Still, more often than not, she would find Elaine and her new best friend waiting in the living room for her when she arrived home from work. Usually, there wasn't even a patrol car in the drive to give her a heads-up to expect him there—nothing to prepare her for the tingly reaction she had every time she came near him.

Once they reached the lobby, Elaine spun around to face her. "I need to use the facilities before we go."

Natalie scanned the hall for the ladies' room. "Let's go."

"Why don't you stay here?" her mother said. "Laura can take me."

Natalie watched after her, feeling summarily dismissed and highly aware that she and Shane were alone again—well, as alone as one could be surrounded by about thirty other moviegoers.

"Hey, could you give me a hand with this?" he said from behind her.

When she turned back to him, he held out his hat to her.

Her gaze narrowed. Since when did he accept any kind of help from her, let alone with dressing? Now, *undressing*, he'd been especially grateful for that kind of assistance. When she reached down to take the hat from him, their fingers brushed in a move that didn't appear accidental, and a shiver began at the tips of her fingers and stretched all the way to her baby toes inside her snow boots. She pretended to feel nothing. She'd done a lot of pretending lately.

She pointed as his hands. "You should be wearing gloves."

"You're not wearing yours," he retorted, but his smile suggested he knew exactly what his touch did to her.

He pointed to the mini marquee outside the theater they'd just exited.

"Wow. That movie really was terrible."

"Why didn't you say that before?"

"It seemed so important to Elaine that I would

like it. And, anyway, I never said I did. Only that it got the heart pumping." Then he shrugged. "But it just might have been the company."

Natalie's jaw tightened. "Why do you keep doing this?"

"Doing what?"

How could she answer that when his very presence had all of her senses on high alert? When even when she wasn't looking at him, which she admitted was rare, she could feel his gaze on her, heating her skin with its caress? "Why do you keep accepting my mother's invitations?"

"Because she keeps making them, and I don't want to be rude."

Was he also trying not to be *rude* when he sat so close to her at the restaurant the other night that their knees kept brushing, or when she caught him staring every time she flipped her hair out from her coat? *Every single time.* Had he realized that she was trying to pull back from him and had decided to make it impossible?

"How do I know you're not the one inviting her on outings just to—" She stopped herself before saying he was trying to get to her, but he had to know what she'd meant.

"I guess you don't know."

"Then stop."

He shrugged. "But I like the company."

"You like *our* company? The guy who admitted to making the rounds with women wants to hang out with a former recluse and her overly tired daughter?" He'd already had her in his bed. She was no longer an enticing mystery to him, so why wasn't he off in search of his next conquest?

"I said I like the company. A lot."

"Is this because I'm not pining over you?" she asked when he didn't answer the first question. "Is that why I still present a challenge to you? Is that part of the game?" Why was he making it so hard for her to shield herself—and her mother—from the hurt he would leave behind when he decided it wasn't fun anymore?

Where laughter lit his eyes before, Shane suddenly looked serious, hurt even.

"If one of us is playing a game here, it's not me."

Natalie's eyes widened, and she licked her lips. What could she say to that?

Her mother and Laura saved her from having to answer by finally returning from the ladies' room. Natalie shot a glance at Shane, but this time he wasn't looking.

"I think we should go get coffee," Elaine announced as if she'd just come up with a brilliant idea.

"But it's getting late, Mom. And we've been out every night this week. You haven't been this active in a long time. You have to be exhausted. I know I am."

"It's not even eight o'clock yet," Elaine said with a pout.

"I could drink coffee," Shane said to her mother instead of her. "There's that new place on Grand River."

Natalie turned back to her mother. "You definitely don't need coffee this late. You know you have trouble sleeping."

"I'll make it decaf," Elaine said.

She glanced at Laura, again looking for support, but the middle-aged caregiver only shrugged. "I like coffee."

"Come on," her mother said. "It's just coffee."

The grin won Natalie over. Her mother had smiled more this week than she had in the last *year*. That it had everything to do with Shane was as frustrating as it was undeniable. She couldn't blame her mother. There weren't many women who could deny Shane's charms. But it was more than just his charm that Shane had invested in her mother. He'd been genuinely kind to her, acting as if he truly wanted to be her friend.

As if Natalie hadn't already found too many things attractive about him, the way he treated her mother made him nearly irresistible. That kindness, and her mother's smiles, she would miss most of all when he moved on.

She blew out a frustrated breath. "Fine. It's three on one. We'll get coffee. But we're getting it to go."

CHAPTER SEVENTEEN

THE SYRUPY SWEETNESS of the specialty coffee drink still sat uncomfortably in Natalie's stomach as she helped her mother pull the nightgown over her head an hour later. Somehow she'd managed to make it all the way to Shane's house without any of them spilling coffee inside the van. She hadn't been so lucky in her attempt to avoid his touch—and all the aftershocks that went with it—as she'd helped him inside. She could still feel the brush of his lips on her cheek from the kiss he'd given her while she was helping him out of his coat.

A platonic thank-you kiss, not so different from the one he'd given her mother earlier in the evening, but Natalie had felt it everywhere and had craved more than she had any business wanting.

"Tonight was fun," her mother said as they shifted her body into the bed.

"Yes, it was." Natalie propped two pillows behind Elaine's head that she would need to remove before lights out. "I just wish—" She stopped herself, realizing that the things she really desired would never be the ones she would mention now.

Obligations were more important than desires, anyway.

"What do you wish?" her mother prompted.

"I know you're enjoying going out lately, and I think that's great. We should definitely continue doing that, though maybe once a week instead of *every night*." She inserted a smile, both to make her words more palatable and to give herself a chance to form them. "But I was thinking that maybe we shouldn't invite Shane to go with us."

Her mom's arms automatically crossed over the pink flowers and lace near the top of her nightgown. "Why not? I like Shane."

So do I. More than she had any right. So she used the one excuse that might convince her mother to step away from him.

"He's a great guy, and he's been so kind to share all of these activities with us. But I know you wouldn't want him to feel *obligated* to do things with us. He's already donated so much time to helping out with the team, so..."

She let her words trail away and waited. She hated making her mother feel like a charity project, but that was better than allowing her mother to be hurt later, when Shane left them and Elaine realized that he wasn't her friend, after all.

For a few seconds, Elaine sat there, staring down at her crossed arms. Were her feelings more hurt than Natalie had predicted? But finally her mother looked up at her with the same incisive stare she'd used when Natalie had sneaked out after basketball practice. That too smart look of a woman who Natalie had once believed could read minds.

"Why don't you want to spend time with Shane?"

Natalie blinked. "This isn't about me."

"Isn't it?"

"Of course not," she said, though it had always been useless for her to lie to her mother. Before the accident, anyway. "I just don't think it's a good idea—"

"I would think you'd want to spend more time—not less—with the man you're in love with."

Natalie started shaking her head. "I don't know where you got that idea, but you're wrong."

"Am I?" She smiled. "I don't think so."

Natalie's throat tightened, and she stuffed her hands in the back pockets of her jeans to keep from fidgeting because she didn't think her mother was wrong, either. Now that someone had spoken the truth aloud, something shifted inside her. Why had she bothered denying it to herself, let alone to the one person who'd known her all of her life?

"You should see the way you look at him, like he has all the answers to every question you've ever asked," her mother said.

Again, Natalie shook her head, not because it wasn't true, but because it would be easier and safer for her heart if it weren't.

Her mother only smiled the knowing smile of someone who'd been there, even if her love story hadn't come with a happy ending.

"He looks at you the same way, you know." Elaine rolled her lips inward and looked toward the ceiling as if considering, and then she shook her head. "No, it's not quite the same. He looks at you as if you scare him to death."

Then they should look exactly alike, Natalie decided, though just the thought of him staring at her at all squeezed her chest with possibilities. Could there be something real between them? Something that could last?

"You have such a great imagination, Mom. But this isn't one of your shows. This is real life. *My* life."

"So, live it."

Natalie could only stare at her. Even though she'd been serious only seconds before, she couldn't help grinning now.

Elaine held her hands wide as she smiled back at her. "Okay, I know I'm not the best role model for doing that. I just don't want you to repeat my mistakes. Some of them were even before the accident."

"You did the best you could."

"I could have done better," she said with a shrug. "I could have searched for happiness for myself again instead of burying my heart to protect it from being hurt. I think I would have been a better mother to you if I'd been happier."

"But you were—are—a good mother."

"And I could have tried to make the best of it and realized I was lucky to be alive after the accident. I guess I was just angry. I'd already had so much taken from me, and I kept asking myself how this could happen, too. I got caught up in my own pity party, and I couldn't get out."

"You're getting out now. And that's a good thing, right?"

"Because of your young man."

"Mom, please." Natalie squeezed her eyes shut and then opened them again. "But...you know he's a cop."

"And you want to blame him and every other person wearing a badge for the accident that put me here." Elaine waved her hand toward her chair, parked in the corner of the room.

"You don't blame all cops for it?"

She shook her head. "In the beginning, I did. In fact, I blamed the whole world, including you, for what happened to me. It wasn't fair. I didn't deserve it. But I guess I've mellowed with time. I don't even blame the two officers in the accident anymore."

"You don't?"

"Well, if you remember, those two officers performed first aid on the both of us though they were injured in the accident, as well. One of them even had a broken ankle."

Natalie nodded. "I guess I had forgotten that. But even now I can't see someone in a police uniform without thinking about the accident."

"I'm not likely to forget it, either," Elaine said with a smile. "I doubt I'll ever be able to hear any kind of emergency vehicle siren without thinking about it. But I can see police officers now and recognize the good they do. And when I think of Shane and the other officers he's introduced us to, I remember what good people they are."

Natalie stared at her hands for several seconds. When she finally looked up, her mother was watching her.

"Did you think that letting Shane into your life would somehow be betraying me?"

"No, Mom. That's not it." Natalie stopped and considered. "Well, at least not all of it." After all they'd discussed, how could she tell her mother that her misgivings were far more about the risk to her own heart than worries over what her mother would think?

"Well, that's not acceptable to me."

Natalie blinked. It was as if her mother had sneaked into her private thoughts and had responded to them. "What do you mean?"

"You can't use me as an excuse."

"I'm not. It's just—"

"That you worry that loving Shane somehow

hurts me though he wasn't in the car that night? Though he wasn't involved in any of the decisions about whether to call off the high-speed chase."

"Well, when you put it that way…"

"It sounds ridiculous, doesn't it? That's like blaming me for Eve eating that apple. I am a woman, after all."

Natalie nodded. It did sound silly.

"I was trying to tell you this earlier, but you weren't listening."

"What? When?"

Her mother rolled her eyes. "Tonight. At the movies. Why do you think I chose that awful police flick?"

"Because you have lousy taste in movies?"

"Possibly true as well, but I also wanted you to know that I don't hold a grudge against law enforcement."

Natalie only shook her head. "It's still difficult for me to see how you don't."

"That's because you never accepted that it was just an accident. Why was it so hard for you to accept that?"

Natalie shook her head. "I don't know. Guilt. For being born and making your life so hard. For being the one who walked away from the accident."

"And I'm grateful for that every day." She took her daughter's hand. "I know I've been selfish, but

I have always believed if one of us had to be hurt, it should have been me."

Elaine brushed her hands together as if to say that the topic was closed. "Now back to Shane."

"Mom, can we just talk about him another day?"

"Are you looking for an excuse?"

"What do you mean?" Then she shook her head. "No."

"Good. I just can't let you use Shane's career, the accident or even me as an excuse not to take a risk on someone. Because love is always a risk."

"You, of all people, have to know that the risk doesn't always pay off."

Elaine nodded. "I guess I do, but I also know that there are worse things."

"Like what?"

"Like always wondering what you missed and wishing you hadn't been too much of a coward to try."

"KELLY, IS THAT you?"

At the sound of Shane's voice filtering in from the other room, Natalie stopped and leaned against the door to the garage. Her pulse pounded in her ears, and her coat felt too warm though she'd been freezing moments before. She hadn't stopped or even slowed since the moment her mother had finally fallen asleep. A cacophony of sounds playing in her head—her mother's words tonight overlaying bits of the conversations and intimate echoes she'd shared with Shane—she'd rushed out into the night.

She'd had to get here. To him.

But now that she was here, so close that she could hear his voice, her feet were frozen to the welcome mat. She'd planned on throwing herself into his arms, holding nothing back, and now she couldn't even make it past the garage. What was she supposed to tell him when she finally peeled herself away from the door? That she'd only now recognized that she loved him, so he should get started immediately with breaking her heart? She hauled in a breath, as she'd had no time to think or breathe until now. Or to stop herself. To tuck all of those feelings back inside while she could still shield her heart.

Natalie swallowed, but she still couldn't move. This was like taking a step forward on a swinging bridge where each of the planks she crossed dropped away behind her. And she wasn't ready to have no path for retreat. She really was that coward her mother had spoken of, too afraid to reach out for the one thing she wanted more than anything. Shane.

"Kelly?" he called again, voice sounding closer.

Taking a deep breath, she toed off her boots and pushed herself away from the mat. She padded down the hall in her socks, and just before she rounded the doorway into the family room, he rolled into the hall.

"Oh. It's you."

He couldn't have looked more surprised.

"It's me," she confirmed.

He backed his chair through the doorway again and then moved out of the way, gesturing for her to follow him into the family room. He parked near a TV tray in the middle of the room. It was covered with half-empty dishes. He'd been watching basketball highlights on some sports show, something he pointed to with a grin before clicking off the power. He gestured for her to sit on the recliner closest to him, but she remained where she was, her hand gripping the white-painted door frame.

"What are you doing here? Did you forget something?"

She was grateful that he didn't point out that if she'd forgotten anything, he could easily return it Monday when she picked him up for the game. Clearly, she had no good excuse to be here at this time of night, and they both knew it.

"Sorry I interrupted your late-night dinner," she said to fill the long pause. She had no clue how to answer his question.

If he noticed that she hadn't, he didn't mention it. "No, I'm done. Guess I wasn't hungry, after all. All that popcorn your mom and I ate at the movies wasn't such a good idea."

"You'll have to tell her that. She refuses to give it up."

"Everything in moderation."

Everything except him, a voice inside her suggested, making her grip the frame tighter. A little of Shane would never be enough for her. She would always crave more. All.

She blinked away the thought. Why couldn't she do this? She had so much to say to him, so many feelings to reveal, and yet the words wouldn't come. Was that a sign that maybe this leap of faith she was tempted to take would end in a crushing fall? Could she survive if she put her trust in him and he walked away like the others had? Was that kind of pain worth the risk she was taking to let him in?

The silence having stretched too long, Shane cleared his throat. "When I heard the door, I thought you were Kelly because she's my on-call person tonight," he explained unnecessarily.

Still, Natalie's jaw automatically tightened over the truth being spoken aloud. Good thing he was looking at the screen of his cell phone and missed it.

He pointed to the digital time on the screen. "But it's too early for her to be here, anyway."

"She's still coming?" Glancing behind her, she checked to see if the other woman had magically appeared since she'd come inside.

"Later. After her shift."

She nodded. She would have preferred that he not have female officers as overnight guests, even on the sofa, but she had no hold over him, and she would have to accept that if she told him what she came to say tonight.

"So what's going on, Natalie? You're making me nervous."

"That makes two of us." She licked her lips. So much for her grand gesture.

"Did something happen?"

"I guess you could say that." How could she begin to describe a realization that had changed everything? Like giving birth to possibility when only a barren womb had existed there before.

Shane gripped the armrests of his chair. "Well, are you going to tell me what it is, or do you need to me to keep guessing?"

She had to smile at that, as he would do just what he said. In fact, his follow-through was one of the things she loved about him, whether with coaching the youth basketball team, helping her mother to get out in the world again or making patient love to her. Yes, just one of the things she loved about him.

"I've been fighting it since the moment I met you at the clinic," she said finally. The weight that lifted off her right then confirmed that it was true.

"Your hatred of cops?"

She frowned at him, and he shrugged his apology. If he wanted her to answer his question, then he just needed to be patient and let her talk.

"No. My...uh...attraction to one."

"Oh."

He said it as if her words had knocked the wind out of him. Maybe it surprised him as much as it had her.

"I had all of these preconceptions about what you would be like, and, let's admit it, some of them weren't so far off the mark." She paused, waiting for his nod before she continued. "But a lot of them were wrong. Dead wrong."

"I surprise people that way."

She crossed her arms and frowned at him. "Would you let me get this out?"

He gestured with his hand for her to proceed.

"You're this mass of contradictions. A good-looking guy who turns out to be nice. Cocky yet vulnerable. A big, burly police officer who's impossibly kind to kids and senior citizens."

"But...?"

Her head had bent and her gaze had lowered to her gray cotton socks as she'd touted all of Shane's qualities, but at his question, she jerked her chin up again.

"What do you mean, *but*?"

"*But* you want me to stop coaching and stop hanging out with your mom so you can get back to focusing on what's important. *But* you can't see yourself with someone whose past is as checkered as mine. *But* you don't want someone who'll never really be whole whether I can shake this piece of metal or not."

He slammed his hands on the armrests of his chair. Instead of looking to her for confirmation, he shoved his hands back through his hair and stared out the window, where dark smudges of night had overwhelmed the sheet of drab gray that had passed for Michigan daylight earlier. Did he still feel that way? That he wasn't good enough?

"There isn't a *but*."

"There has to be one."

Now his insecurities were beginning to annoy her. "Can you ever, just once, accept that you might deserve to have people who care about you? Can you just forgive yourself and get over what happened when you were a kid? You've paid your debts. When are you going to stop lying prostrate and wearing sackcloth? Even most of the people you arrest who are convicted eventually serve their sentences and get out of prison. Are you ever going to stop punishing yourself?"

Her words had grown louder with each sentence until the last came out as almost a shriek. Like a stone rolling downhill, she hadn't been able to stop until it was all out, but when she glanced back to him, he was staring at her with wide eyes.

"Um, do you want me to answer each question individually? If so, you'll need to repeat them slowly."

Natalie shook her head and shoved her fingers through her hair. Then she met his gaze. "I just want you to know that you are worthy. You've always been worthy. The only one who can't see it is you."

His licked his lips, his gaze lowering to the floor and then lifting again. "I'm trying." He paused for several seconds and then asked, "Is that what you came here to say?"

"No, it wasn't."

"Then what was it?"

She cleared her throat. "What I'm trying to say is…well…I want you."

For what seemed like hours rather than only a brief gathering of heartbeats, neither spoke. Neither moved. Shane simply stared back at her with those same piercing eyes that had seen through her all along. What was he thinking? He didn't give her any clues. He didn't roll closer, but he didn't reverse the chair and retreat, either.

Finally, Natalie couldn't wait any longer. Whether he planned to reject her now or later, this was her time to be honest with him and with herself. Her first, slow step away from that doorway and toward him felt like stepping out on faith, no pausing for the future to be written in indelible ink, no stalling for the safety nets to be properly hung. She took that first step. And then another. And then another.

Still she'd made it only halfway across the floor

when Shane did one thing that probably shocked him as much as it stunned her.

He stood up.

CHAPTER EIGHTEEN

SHANE DIDN'T KNOW when he'd made the decision—or even if it was an actual decision and not the most perfect reaction to her belief in him—but he was walking. Well, stepping, anyway. He took one painfully awkward step, and his other foot must have remembered what it was supposed to do as it shifted forward to restore balance.

A step and a second one. And a third. He couldn't believe it. This was happening. He was doing this on his own, something he'd wondered if he would ever do again. Natalie looked as shocked as he was, her eyes wide, her jaw slack. He needed to get to her now and give her every bit of the loving she'd just asked for, but his legs weren't quite as ready as he was. After that third step, he waited for the other leg to do its job and shift his weight forward on the other side again, but the message must have been relayed wrong because it stopped instead.

The rest felt like a slow-motion movie sequence with him cast as the schmuck whose knees buckled and whose body twisted wildly on its way down. Only this time when the floor reached up to grab him, Natalie was there with her competent arms wrapped around his waist.

"Sorry about this." He sagged against her, trying not to take her down with him. This was not how this was supposed to go. He'd needed to make a grand gesture like that one she'd just made, not this reel of romantic-scene bloopers.

"You walked, Shane!"

"Not far, but I guess I did."

Her arms tightened around him. "Don't worry. I've got you."

He squeezed her shoulders slightly tighter until it felt more like a hug than a rescue.

"Yes," he said, pausing before he added, "you do."

Natalie had already backed him up one step toward his chair, but now she tilted her head up so she could look at him. Her wide eyes told him everything he needed to know. She'd understood what he was really trying to say. She did have him. He was hers.

She smiled, and he could think of nothing but her sweet lips. So close. So tempting.

That he dipped his head to kiss them then must have been one movement too many. It disturbed the delicate balance they'd established, and, for the second time in five minutes, he nearly hit the floor. And this time he almost took her with him.

Natalie's laughter rumbled against his chest, and he couldn't help joining in as she backed him up the two remaining steps and helped lower him into the chair.

"I was going to say, 'But not for long,' when I said I had you, but you probably don't need me to clarify that now."

"Yeah, I got the idea." He chuckled again, reaching for her hand and lacing their fingers together. "My plan wasn't so great. Trying to make the grand gesture. Epic fail."

"I happened to like it. No, that's wrong. I *loved* it. You came to me. You...*walked* to me."

When Natalie's voice broke, Shane had to swallow several times to push back the emotion clogging his throat. "Tried to, anyway."

This time she frowned. "Are you trying to ruin this moment for me?"

He grinned and shook his head. "Wouldn't dream of it."

"Good. Because I'm trying to make a gesture of my own."

She leaned in close and lifted one of the side panels from his wheelchair.

"Did this statement of yours involve knocking me to the floor? If so, you could have saved yourself some time by just letting me fall a few minutes ago."

"Hush." She pressed her index finger to his lips, but when she lifted it away, she reached down to trace her hand over his mouth.

He might have had another joke lined up after

that, was almost sure he did, but he forgot what it was. When she lifted her hand away, he moaned in protest.

Natalie only grinned at him and removed the second side panel. Pushing aside the foot plates, she stepped between them, slid one of her legs up and over his lap and then settled over him.

Shane couldn't help himself. He drew her so close that he wasn't sure where each of their halting breaths began, inside his chest or hers. Still, she wasn't close enough. He wanted more. He realized now that he would always want more. With Natalie, it would never be enough.

Again, his gaze lowered to her lips, so close that her breath feathered over his cheek. He had only to dip his head to capture them, but he held back. Natalie had come to *him* tonight. It was her night, and he would wait for her to make the next move, even if it killed him.

And if she didn't do something soon, it just might.

Finally, when he was certain he would die in just this position—on the cusp of ecstasy but never quite getting there—she tilted her lips to his.

Her kiss was almost unbearably light. A whisper when he longed for a siren. Because he was tempted to take over, to yank her to him and make this about his needs rather than hers, he slid his hands to the wheels of his chair to hold back.

"Still holding on?"

She asked the question as her lips slid away from his, but she didn't wait for an answer before tracing a line of kisses down his throat, up his jaw and back to his lips. Hell, yeah, he was holding on. To a desire that was barreling out of control. To a need more visceral than anything he'd ever experienced.

But this was Natalie, tasting and touching him at her leisure, eliciting responses from every nerve ending in his body and then expanding her range to reach his soul. This was the woman he loved. His first. His last as well, the clench in his gut told him. Sex was different with her, a glimpse of paradise instead of a brush of bodies. *He* was different with her, and he wanted to be different.

He was hers. But was she his?

"Still worried that I'm going to hurt you?"

Shane blinked. There was a sparkle in her eyes that suggested she was kidding, but it was as if she'd read his mind and had spoken aloud the thoughts he didn't want to admit, even to himself.

She leaned her head back so she could study him. "Are you?" she asked again, this time glancing down at his arms that still gripped the wheels.

He pasted on a grin. "Absolutely."

"Well, I won't."

If her words before had been in jest, she seemed suddenly serious. It was a promise that everyone made and no one ever should. Yet he wanted to take her at her word. So when she kissed him again, he encircled her in his arms and drank in her kisses with the desperation of a wino, meeting her touch for touch, taste for taste.

As they peeled away each other's clothes, he cherished her smooth skin and perfect curves with his gaze, his hands, his mouth. He closed his eyes, memorizing her body with his hands and drinking in each precious moment. He refused to rush her. This wasn't a high-speed chase, after all. This was a leisurely drive, and he intended to relish each sight, each sound, each taste. He might have been certain of little else, but of this he was sure. The journey to Natalie had been a long one, but it led him home.

"I LOVE YOU."

The words slipped from Natalie's lips on a drowsy sigh, her liquid limbs draped over him, but she jerked when she realized she'd spoken them aloud. Though she'd been snuggled against him, her head resting on the pillow of his bicep, she shifted carefully now, turning so that her back was to him.

When Shane's hand came to rest on her shoulder, she started again.

"What is it?" he asked. "Did you hear something?"

She blinked several times, adjusting her eyes to the low light coming in from the partially open blind slats. "No. Nothing." The question was, what had *he* heard? She swallowed, her pulse pounding in her ears. What would he say if he had heard? Would he get up and roll right out there even though it was *his* house?

It wasn't that she didn't want him to know how she felt. She would have told him…eventually. As in after he'd said the words *first*. If he ever planned to say them. But, now, with her admission hanging out there in the room, she felt like a player at a poker table who'd just turned all of her cards faceup without having any idea which cards her opponents held. Of course, after the way she'd come here to make her big statement, he might have already guessed that she loved him. But she'd said *want*, which wasn't necessarily the same thing. He'd wanted her, too. He'd proven that a few times now, but could that have been all it was? And, if so, would she be able to accept that truth? Was what he had to offer enough for her?

She blinked several times to push away the questions. When Natalie opened her eyes again, her gaze came to rest on the wheelchair parked at the side of the bed, its side panels reattached. Exactly when they'd relocated their party from the family room to his bedroom she couldn't recall, but from the series of steamy images now etched into her memory, she could only guess that it had been hours ago. Nothing had mattered to her except showing Shane how much she wanted him, and his chair must have proven to be just another obstacle on her path to that goal.

She refused to second-guess her decision to come here now that she lay sated in his bed, but she was surprised by how chilly it had become in his room. She pulled the sheet and the comforter higher to cover her because she was cold. Not because she suddenly felt a little more naked than she'd been a few minutes before.

"What time is it?" He reached up to rub his eyes. "How long was I asleep?"

"Not long."

That she could have told him precisely how long he'd been asleep made her pull the sheet higher again. She'd found it strangely comforting lying there listening him breathe and then noting the change when he'd drifted off to sleep. It felt different now. And no longer soothing.

Shane was looking toward the spot on his nightstand where a digital clock had been earlier, but it wasn't there anymore. She bit her lip, remembering how her foot had connected with it at some point.

"I'll get it." She sat up, drawing the sheet up with her, and then searched the carpet next to the bed with her toes. Where the heck were her clothes?

"Everything's still in the family room," he said, answering her unspoken question.

Then, as if he understood far more than just

the question she hadn't asked, he reached under the comforter and yanked out the top sheet on his side. "Here."

"Thanks."

Natalie wrapped the sheet tightly around her, tucking in the end at the top. She didn't know what she was trying to hide when he'd already seen every inch of her nakedness. A few times now. Most of it he'd also cataloged by taste and touch.

But somehow this was different. She'd bared her soul to him, even before speaking the words that she prayed he hadn't heard. She felt exposed. More vulnerable in a way she never had before. She'd handed him her heart and could only brace herself for him to crush it.

In her toga of sorts, she hobbled to his side of the bed and got down on her hands and knees to pat around under the bed for the missing clock. When her hand connected with its power cord, she grabbed it and pulled until it tumbled out. As she set it back on the nightstand, she noted that it was already close to midnight.

"It's getting late. I'd better get home. Mom's probably wondering where I am." She scrambled to climb up from the floor, holding on to the sheet at the top.

"You don't think she could have guessed?"

Natalie shrugged and licked her lips as she lifted her hand away from the clock. She took a step back, but Shane reached out to catch her hand before she could take a second one.

"I don't know," she said, staring down at their hands.

"Well, I think she could have."

"How do you know that?"

He tugged her a little closer to the side of the bed. "She asked me."

"Are you kidding?" She jerked her hand back, and Shane released it. "What did she ask you? What did you tell her?"

He answered only one of the questions. "I didn't see any point in lying, so I told her there's something between us, but we haven't defined it. Yet."

Us. We. Yet. The words played inside her mind, making it difficult for her to hear the rest of what he'd said. Did that mean there was an *us*?

"Whether she knows or not, it's nearly midnight and—"

"And you're twenty-eight years old. Do you still have a curfew?"

She shook her head. He didn't understand. "You know how she relies on me."

"You said she was asleep, right? So, she's fine. I'm not telling you to abandon your responsibilities. You have your cell phone, right? If she needs you, you can be there in minutes. Just like the last time."

Immediately, Natalie glanced toward the door. She would have reached into her pocket for her cell, but it was still in the living room among her discarded clothes. When Natalie turned back to him, Shane was grinning.

"So, okay, you don't technically have your phone on your person right now, but I'm still sure everything's fine."

She nodded, but because she couldn't believe him without proof, she hobbled from the room and reclaimed her phone from the family room. She found it in her coat pocket. Clicking the button to awaken the screen, she found that he was right, after all. No calls. No texts. Nothing.

When she finally returned to the bedroom, having retrieved her clothes, and his, from the family room floor, she found him sitting up in the bed, with the lamp switched on and both pillows propped behind him. He'd pulled the cover up to his hip bones, but it hung loosely there, like a sexy photo shoot all for her. He wasn't being fair.

"You see? Everything's fine, isn't it?"

After a few seconds, she nodded. "Fine. You're right. But I still need to get going."

"You mean you won't stay and cuddle for a little while. What kind of player are you?"

"Player?" She was already struggling to slip on her panties beneath the bedsheet, but his comment made her miss the leg hole, so she had to start over again. "Why are you calling me that?"

"If the toga fits, sweetheart. You're in and out

of here like… I don't know. Wham. Whir. Thank you, sir."

She'd made a second attempt at slipping her panties on, and this time, she got one foot in and missed the other, ending up toppling backward onto the end of the bed. A giggle began deep in her chest and bubbled out. Shane laughed out loud. Natalie dropped back on the end of the bed, rolling back and forth and not even caring that the top of her sheet wasn't wrapped as tightly anymore.

"Wham, whir?" she couldn't help asking when her chuckle died down.

"The best I could do on short notice."

"Strong words altogether, coming from you."

She waited for his answer. They could go on like this for a while, trading barbs and slowly backing away to soften the evening-after awkwardness. But when she realized he wasn't going to answer, she popped up and spoke to him over her shoulder.

"You're not seriously upset that I'm leaving, are you?"

He grinned back at her to suggest that he was joking, but usually his laughter reached his eyes. This time it stopped short.

"Nobody likes to be the one left behind when the other creeps out the door. I've just learned that."

"Sorry," she began, not really knowing what else she could say. She didn't want to be the one

to leave, but it was the only way she could protect herself. She turned away from him again and
started slipping on her clothes, this time from a
safe, seated position.

"Do you think it's really possible for a person
to change?"

Natalie stopped just as she'd settled her panties into place. She wasn't sure what he was really
asking. Were they still talking about sex, or was
he back to the subject of his childhood mistakes
that he couldn't forgive?

"*You* have to believe it. Isn't the whole crimi-
nal justice system based on the idea of second
chances?"

"Depends on who you ask. But that isn't what
I asked you. I want to know what you believe."

His expression didn't give away what he was
thinking no matter how hard she stared at him.
Why was it so important for him to know what she
thought? She'd proven to him from the day she'd
met him that she could be unforgiving no matter
what changes someone else had made.

"It's rare for people to change," she said after
a few seconds. "But do I think it's possible? Yes.
Otherwise, there would never be hope for any of
us."

Slowly, he nodded. "Then I want to tell you
again that I've changed. I'm not the ladies' man I
used to be. Maybe not even the hotshot teen who
screwed up his life." He stared right at her then.

"That guy is dead. I think he died the minute the shot didn't kill me."

Natalie could only stare at him. What could she say to that? So many times she'd judged him, first on his career, and then on his past with women. Why had she worried about him leaving her when she'd done nothing to make him feel good about staying?

"I'm sorry—"

He shook his head to stop her. "There's one more thing I need to tell you."

She pressed her lips together, staring at her hands, but finally, she looked up at him.

"I love you, too."

Natalie blinked, not sure she'd heard him right. "You're saying that you love me?"

"That's what I said." This time there was no doubting that his smile was real.

"But—" She stopped herself as the rest of what he'd said settled in her thoughts. "Too? You love me, *too*. Do you mean to tell me you heard what I said all along? You let me try to hide it when you heard everything I said?"

Shane shrugged, still smiling. "You didn't seem to want me to know, so I didn't want to disappoint you."

"Oh, man. I can't believe it." She buried her face in her hands, shaking her head.

"What? That I'm in love with you or that you were backing away from confessing how you feel about me as fast as your toga-tied feet could carry you?"

"Both," she answered automatically and then realized she'd spoken the truth. Only one of those things felt like a miracle, while the other shamed her. She was a coward, and now he knew it, too. She lowered her hands to her sides and turned back to him, scrambling for something to say.

"Do you want to run away and pretend all of this isn't real?"

She shook her head as she stood up from the bed and turned back to face him.

Shane continued as if he didn't recognize her attempt to respond. "Because it would be easier for the both of us if you ran. No harm, no foul, you know. Nobody gets hurt."

She shook her head again. "I don't want to. I don't care if it would be easier."

He was wrong that no one would get hurt, either, but she didn't add that. Their feelings were involved now. Even if they walked away today and never turned back, they couldn't shield themselves from pain. At least she couldn't.

"I don't believe you," he said.

He glanced over at the window and then turned back to her. "Are you going to keep using your mother's condition as an excuse to hide from the things that scare you?"

"No." She paused, realizing that she'd done just that in the past twenty minutes. "Not anymore."

"Think about it, Natalie. You won't get any guarantees from me or from anyone else. It doesn't work like that."

She shook her head as she rounded the end of the bed and started up the side where he was seated. "I don't want guarantees."

He lifted a brow, clearly not believing her. "What do you want, Natalie?"

This time she didn't even hesitate. "You." Then recalling what she'd said before, she took another step forward, both figuratively and literally. "I love you."

It wasn't a whisper this time, and she didn't want to take it back. No matter what happened now, she was all in.

Instead of repeating those words back to her, Shane smiled. "I have one more question for you."

"Haven't you asked enough already?" She frowned, but finally she nodded.

"Are you ever going to climb back in this bed with me?"

Her gaze flicked to the clock, responsibility at odds again with her personal desires. This time desire won out.

"I guess I can stay a little while longer."

"Now that's an answer I like to hear."

Tossing back the comforter that had barely covered him before, he lay there unashamedly nude. A way she would never be. When he reached for her, she stared at his hand for a few shaky breaths.

"Come here," he said as he curled his four fingers inward on his extended hand.

Instead of taking his hand, she crossed to the other side of the bed and slid in next to him. When she scooted close to him, he curved his arm around her.

For several seconds, she simply lay there and snuggled against his chest. She breathed in the scent that was uniquely his and felt the rise and fall of his chest against her ear. Oh, she could do this. It was amazing. *Maybe too amazing to last*, an unwelcome voice inside her suggested.

Just as she considered pulling back the way she always did, Shane shifted, making it necessary for her to lift her head.

"Is everything okay? Is there something I can help you with?"

"No. I've got this." He sank his teeth into his bottom lip with the effort as he rocked and shifted his body, but finally he settled next to her on his side, his head propped up with his hand. "Now that's better."

"You never let me help with anything," she said.

He leaned so close that his breath feathered over her lips. "I'll always let you help with this."

Dipping his head, he brushed his lips over hers once, then again and again.

When he pulled his head back, Natalie stared back at him. "Always?"

He pressed his lips to hers again, his free hand

sliding up her neck so he could cradle her face. "Always."

Shane kissed each of her eyelids and her nose, but he stopped just short of her lips. "I love you, Natalie Keaton."

"You do?" She searched his face, wanting to believe it this time, wanting to trust in a way she never had before.

"Oh, yeah."

His words were deep and sensual, but in his eyes, that vulnerability he tried so hard to hide remained. It was that nakedness that went so far beyond any lack of clothes that inspired her to take the leap into complete trust. Her heart was his alone.

His eyes closed as he went in for another kiss, touching his tongue to the seam of her lips until she opened for him. He'd said he loved her, and it was just too easy to let him in. So she gave herself to him and to the moment, letting him peel away her clothes a second time and show her how much.

CHAPTER NINETEEN

SHANE ROLLED HIS chair through the Clearview Hospital entrance, rotating the wheels so quickly his arms ached. But he didn't care. He had to get to Kent before it was too late.

"Do you know which way you're going?" Kelly called as she jogged behind him.

"Yeah, I've been here a few times," he said without slowing down. In fact, Kelly might have been the only one of his driver friends who hadn't taken him to visit Kent in the past few weeks.

He turned down the hall toward the bank of elevators and jammed the button when he reached it.

"Did you just get the call from the hospital?"

"I told you when I called you." He wished he didn't sound so terse, but she was asking too many questions, and he couldn't focus on willing the elevator door to open.

"Well, you didn't tell me much of anything."

He shrugged. That was probably true. He hadn't really said anything since he'd called and asked her to pick him up as soon as possible. Of course, he'd received his own distressing call twenty minutes after Natalie had left. Since Natalie should have already been home by then and Kelly could get to him faster, he'd called her instead.

It seemed like days rather than just an hour or so since Natalie had awakened in his arms and had nearly taken flight as she'd raced from his house. It couldn't matter that he needed her with him now as he faced all of this. It wasn't about him.

And there was no time.

After the elevator door opened, he rolled in with Kelly close behind him.

"They called right before I called you. They just said that he was asking for me. I don't know anything else."

"I'm sorry—"

"Don't," he said, lifting his hand to freeze her condolences. "Not yet."

"Okay."

They stood in silence until the doors opened, and Shane hurried out again.

Just one more hall. One incredibly long hall.

But just as Kent's room came into view, the door opened, and a haggard-looking man stepped outside. In the few seconds it took Shane to place the man as Kent's younger brother, whom he'd met only once, Shane had already come to another conclusion.

He was too late.

Even the fire from the piercing of that bullet felt like nothing compared to the stab to his heart now. His chest squeezed in an unforgiving grip.

He was glad he was already seated, sure his knees would have buckled if he were standing.

Shane stopped several rooms down from Kent's and waited, his heart too heavy to approach, and yet he was incapable of leaving. The barrel-chested man bent over at the waist and buried his ruddy face in his hands. Sobs rattled his body, but he didn't make a sound.

Not so for the family members left in the room. Muffled sobs in varying pitches escaped through the open door, each shaking Shane as if they'd come from his own body. There were so many people who loved Kent. More than just those crowded inside that room.

"I'm sorry, Shane," Kelly repeated from behind him.

This time, he nodded, and gooseflesh appeared on his arms. Acknowledging her condolences seemed to make it true.

His friend was dead.

This was the man who'd believed in him. Sometimes the only one. He'd loved him more unconditionally than even his parents could. And he'd fought for him, even when he hadn't come close to deserving it.

As emotion crammed inside his throat and heat built behind his eyes, predicting tears that he couldn't let himself shed here, Shane realized something that had eluded him all these years. Some debts were never meant to be repaid. The breadth of those gifts was too large, too far-reaching, for the figure ever to balance in the ledger of someone's life.

As a half-dozen relatives spilled from the hospital room, Shane sat frozen, an eyewitness to their grief, not really a part of it, yet intrinsically connected. Among them were Kent's son and daughter, only preschoolers when Shane first met them, now teenagers. Their faces were red and swollen from tears. They'd lost more than he had, and yet his loss still felt as significant as a missing limb. Things he should have said, good deeds he should have done, pinged in his head with no hope for relief.

The last to emerge from the room was Tammy, who'd stood strong through the whole ordeal of her husband's illness. But, unlike the others, too encased in their cocoon of grief to even glance down the hall, she looked up from the floor, and their gazes connected. Her normally peachy skin was blotchy, and the streaks of mascara attested to the tears she'd already shed, but she still was every bit that elegant beauty Kent had taken Shane to meet when he was still a kid.

Instead of looking away, she rushed down the hall toward him. He lifted his arms, and she leaned down to hug him. For a long time, neither let go.

"Oh, Shane," she said when she finally straightened again. "I'm so sorry we didn't reach you in time. After all this time, it happened so fast. He couldn't…wait."

When her voice broke, he reached for her a second time. She bent to let him hold her.

"I know," he soothed. "It's okay."

He didn't even know why he was saying that. What did it matter whether he was okay with his friend letting go of life at that moment? And nothing was okay for Tammy, nor would it be for a long time.

When she straightened again, she glanced behind him to where Kelly had been standing. She extended her arm. "Is this—"

He shook his head to interrupt her and turned his chair back to find Kelly, leaning against the wall and giving herself a nervous self-hug. If she'd picked up anything from the other woman's question, she didn't let on. But just as he gestured toward Kelly to introduce her, Kelly stepped forward, reaching out a hand to Tammy.

"Mrs. Sawyer, as a fellow law enforcement officer, I just wanted to thank you for your husband's service to the community." She shook her hand and released it. "Please accept my condolences."

Though her eyes filled with tears again, Tammy nodded and managed a smile. "That's very kind." She glanced over her shoulder. "I'd better get back to my children."

Down the hall, family members still gathered,

talking in low tones and holding each other for physical support.

Tammy turned back to Shane. "Do you want to go in there? I'm sure he wouldn't mind."

Shane licked his lips and then shook his head, his insides shakier than they'd been the whole way to the hospital. No, he couldn't see Kent this way, in the stark aftermath of a life stolen too soon. This moment was private, to be shared only with Kent's real family. The funeral would be soon enough.

"I'll be there for the calling hours and the funeral." He took hold of her hand and pressed the back of it to his cheek. "But if you need anything before then—or after—just call. Any time."

Tammy nodded and returned to her family.

Shane turned back to Kelly. "You ready?"

"Yeah. Are you okay?"

"I guess so." As he started down the hall toward the elevators, he glanced back, but his wheelchair handles obstructed his view. "It's worse for them."

He continued rolling forward, the click of Kelly's dressy boots behind him adding to the low buzz of his spinning wheels. "But you've lost someone, too. Someone who meant a great deal to you."

Because his eyes immediately filled like one of those clogged gutters on the front of his house, he kept moving, away from that hospital room, away from all that concentrated grief. He needed to get back to his house, where he could spend some time alone, digesting the many changes that had taken place in his life in the past twelve hours.

What had begun as the best day of his life had just become the worst.

NATALIE CLIMBED OUT of bed and padded to the wall switch only a few hours after she'd crawled into bed. Light flooded the room, but nothing could clear the fog that clouded her vision. She didn't bother trying to tell herself she'd slept more than a few minutes, and even those were so peppered with chaotic dreams that they didn't count. What had she been thinking coming home so late? Even though her mother had been perfectly fine when she'd arrived home, that didn't make her dereliction of duty seem any less…derelict.

It would have helped if she hadn't fallen asleep next to Shane in what had felt like the middle of the night and had awakened truly in the middle of the night. It wasn't even a good excuse that he'd just told her he loved her. Words and events that seemed perfectly clear last night were fuzzier now, but maybe her gritty, sleep-starved eyes were causing the problem.

Had it been too soon to tell him she loved him? Sure, he'd said it back, more than once even, but would he have said it at all if she hadn't spoken those words first? She shivered as she pulled on her robe and slid her feet in her slippers. She wouldn't go there. She wouldn't second-guess her decision to go to him. She wouldn't wonder if she should have planned her route like she always did instead of going off-road.

She squeezed her eyes closed and shook her head, trying to shake away the temptation to worry about those things. Crossing to the bedside table, she unplugged her phone from the charger and pressed the button to awaken the screen. When the digital time popped up, she frowned. It was nearly seven thirty. Her mother would usually have been calling for her for a half hour by now.

Curious, she started down the hall and knocked on her mother's door. "Hey, sleepyhead. It's time to get up."

She waited for the snarky comment from the other side of the door. It didn't come.

"Mom...?"

Nothing.

Her mother was a light sleeper. In fact, it had shocked her that Elaine hadn't awakened when she'd slipped in this morning.

Natalie considered all of two seconds before shoving open the door. When she flipped on the light, her mother blinked several times and then squeezed her eyes closed again in obvious pain.

"What is it, Mom?" She rushed over to the bed and bent over her.

"It hurts."

Natalie stiffened. This wasn't the first time she'd dealt with her mother's physical complaints in the past eight years, but something about her voice and the strain in her jaw told her this was different. Was she unusually pale, or had Natalie just never noticed?

"Where does it hurt?"

Elaine grabbed fistfuls of the quilt covering her and squeezed her eyes shut again.

"Where, Mom?"

"Back. Side. Stomach. Head." She paused between each word, closing her eyes again and gritting her teeth. "I don't know. Everywhere. I think I'm dying."

Natalie shook her head, refusing to hear that. "You're going to be okay."

It must have been a memory from her childhood that made her check her mother's forehead when she'd complained of pain, but as soon as she touched her, she jerked her hand back.

"Holy crap, Mom. You're burning up."

Elaine thrashed her head back and forth and ground her fists deeper in the quilt. "I can't take this. It hurts so much."

"What's your pain level?"

"Ten," she said through gritted teeth, tears leaking from the corners of her eyes.

Natalie swallowed. Her mother might have complained of pain before, even cried wolf on occasion, but Natalie would bet her life that this time the pain was real.

"Here, let me see." She carefully rolled her

mother onto her side and slid her nightgown up so she could examine her back. "I don't see anything."

Carefully, she patted fingers across her mother's back, not even sure what she was supposed to be looking for. But when Natalie came to a spot low on her mother's back, Elaine called out in agony.

"Don't touch it. It burns. It burns." She buried the side of her face in her pillow.

"I'm sorry, Mom. I don't know what it is." She watched her for several seconds longer as she writhed in pain as much as someone without the use of her legs could, and then Natalie came to a decision.

"Let's get you to a hospital."

She braced herself for an argument. Since the accident, Elaine hated hospitals and doctors equally. Usually she complained from the moment they loaded her into the van to go to an appointment.

Elaine only nodded. "Okay."

Her mother was anything *but* okay, and Natalie knew it. The worst part was knowing that Elaine could have been suffering all night long. Sure, she'd checked on her when she'd gotten in this morning, but she hadn't studied her that closely. Just enough to be sure she was breathing and sleeping. Had something been wrong last night? Maybe even before?

"I'll be right back, sweetie," she told her.

She hadn't even reached the stairs before she yanked out her phone to text Shane. She didn't care that misgivings had kept her going in and out of sleep all night. Or even that their relationship was beyond new. Just this once she needed someone, too, and she knew in her heart that Shane would be there, not just for her mother but for her, as well.

She jogged upstairs, threw on yoga pants, a sweatshirt and tennis shoes and then reached for her phone again to stuff it in her sweatshirt pocket. Only a few hours before, she'd thought of that little piece of electronics as her protector. As long as she had her phone and her mother didn't call, everything would be fine. But everything hadn't been fine. She shuddered with realization that while she'd selfishly been experiencing ecstasy in Shane's arms, her mother had been alone and in pain.

The thought hurrying her steps, she jogged down the stairs, stopping at the coat closet for her mother's maxi-length dress coat and her own parka. With loaded arms, she returned to her mother's room and looked back and forth between the woman in agony in the bed and the chair she would need to be in before Natalie could get her out of the house.

"I'm sorry about this. It's going to hurt, but I have to get you in that chair." She rolled her from one side to the other so she could put the coat over her long nightgown and placed the wheel-chair in position. Finally, she moved the hydraulic lift, which they seldom used anymore, closer and slipped the sling beneath her mother's bottom. As the lift did all the work of hoisting her mother, Natalie tried to ignore Elaine's hisses of pain.

She released the breath she'd been holding when her mother was finally seated. She slipped on Elaine's boots, hat and gloves and then grabbed her own coat and phone and headed for the door.

"Now we can get you to the hospital, where they'll figure out what's going on."

Once they were inside the van, she hurried as much as the slippery roads would allow. Every few seconds, she glanced at her mother, who was strangely quiet. It didn't seem fair. Why did this have to happen now, just when her mother was finally embracing life again and getting out to enjoy activities? But as soon as she asked the question, the answer appeared in her thoughts. Maybe whatever was ravaging Elaine's body wasn't just some unlucky coincidence but rather a direct consequence of all the gallivanting she'd been doing. All the things Shane had been encouraging her to do.

Natalie didn't want to believe it, but circumstantial evidence was building in the argument's favor. Elaine had been out too late too often lately—all at Shane's insistence—and she'd possibly been exposed to who knew what. Now there was something wrong with her. Really wrong. And only one person might be to blame: Shane.

CHAPTER TWENTY

THE NEON EMERGENCY Room sign didn't look as bright as it had in the dark, Shane decided as he opened the patrol car door and waited for his driver to bring his chair around. But then a good five hours had passed since his earlier visit to Clearview Hospital, and that had brought daylight with it, even if it was the grayest day he could remember.

It would have been okay with him if he'd never visited this hospital again. Ever. That he had to come back again today felt like a cruel joke where even the comedian wasn't laughing. But Natalie had needed him, and there was no way he wouldn't be there for her. She would have done the same for him this morning if she'd only known that Kent had passed away.

Trevor Cole rounded the car and parked Shane's chair in the space of the open door and handed him the transfer board. "Are you sure you don't need me to stay? I can probably hang out here until I get a call."

Shane shook his head. "No, it's okay. Really.

I'm going to be here awhile, waiting. After that, if I need a ride, I'll call for one."

"You do that."

"You know how willing I am to use a free taxi service."

Trevor nodded but didn't add to Shane's sorry attempt at a joke. Nothing about today had been even a little funny.

Shane had already rolled onto the mat that activated the sliding doors when Trevor called out to him from the car's open window.

"Hope Natalie's mother is okay."

Shane glanced back and nodded. Sure, he'd let Trevor know what was going on in the vaguest terms when he'd asked for the ride, but from the officer's knowing expression, he could only guess that Trevor had been putting together some puzzle pieces. His friends were good cops. Had he really thought he would be able to keep something from any of them for long? But because it really wasn't anyone's business, he didn't go into detail why he would be visiting his former PT's mother in the hospital.

Trevor didn't ask. Instead, he waved, rolled up the window and pulled away.

Shane continued into the ER waiting room, looking around at what should have been familiar territory after this morning. But this time he didn't have a specific room to go to, a place he'd visited several times before. He could only hang out in the waiting room and hope Natalie would come looking for him.

He crossed to the far wall, where several seating groups were separated by end tables with piles of magazines on them. It must have been a slow day in the ER, as only a few people were scattered around the room, some watching TV and munching on snacks, a few others sleeping in uncomfortable positions in the chairs. Where was Natalie? Had she and Elaine already been called back to one of the examination rooms? Had Elaine been admitted? Had Natalie even said *this* hospital?

He yanked his phone from his pocket and opened his texts once more.

Something is wrong with Mom. Taking her to ER at Clearview. Can you meet me there?

Shane let out a breath as he read her words. At least he was at the right place, especially when he'd made that promise that appeared in the text bubble beneath hers.

I'll be there.

He'd promised it, and he wanted to believe he would have made it to the hospital, even if he'd been forced to roll his chair the five miles there all by himself. But he'd thought he would be there when the time came for Kent as well, and he'd been too late.

Something squeezed inside his gut, making him shift in his seat. What was happening with Elaine? Natalie hadn't offered any details, and it was killing him. Had she fallen from her chair? Was there a problem with her medication? Was it bad? Was he too late to help? He shook his head, refusing to accept that idea. Other than being a little tired lately from too many late nights, Elaine was the healthiest paraplegic he knew, and he was getting to know a lot of them.

But no matter how hard he tried to push away the negative thoughts, a shiver scaled his spine all the same. Natalie had never said what had happened to her mother. She hadn't texted again to update him on her condition. What did that mean?

Immediately, he reopened the texting app and typed a second message to her.

In waiting room. Come find me when you can. Let me know how I can help.

Of course, she wouldn't come find him if she didn't know he was there yet. He held the phone between his hands, waiting, but other than a delivery notification, he received no response. He checked the screen every few seconds, but that didn't change.

What was he supposed to do now? She was

the one who'd asked *him* to come. He rubbed his gritty eyes and then shook his head. Obviously, it had been a long night and an even longer morning. For the both of them. She probably had more important things to do right now than to be staring at her phone and waiting for texts from him. Maybe she was talking to her mother's doctors, grabbing something to eat in the cafeteria or even taking a much-needed nap at Elaine's bedside.

He'd never been needy before, and he didn't intend to start today, no matter how tempted he'd been to call Natalie this morning from the moment he'd left the hospital, lost and alone.

Leaning his head forward, he massaged his temples. He could use a nap himself. He closed his eyes, just to rest them, but when he opened them again, what could only be seconds later, Natalie was marching straight toward him. Her expression was too odd, her movements stiff. He took hold of his chair's armrests and steadied himself for bad news.

"Good of you to at least show up here, since this is all your fault."

Shane shifted his head back reflexively, as if she'd hit him. It felt as if she had. "What are you talking about, Natalie? Is your mom all right?"

"No! She's not all right!"

Her voice was so sharp that the couple watching a morning talk show on the flat screen on the wall turned back to look.

He leaned forward and spoke in low tones. "Can you quiet down? Whatever it is, we'll—"

"We'll do *nothing*. Haven't you done enough to her?"

"To Elaine?" He held his hands wide. "I would never do anything to hurt your mother."

"You wouldn't? You already did!" Her voice was louder instead of quieter, and she shook her index finger at him. "You took her everywhere. Our games. The park. The movies. Restaurants."

"So?" He shook his head. "Those are all good things. She's happy. She's living, just like you said you—"

"You made her *sick*!" She shoved her hands back through her hair. "The doctor thinks she has shingles. She's going to have agonizing pain and an awful rash, and because of her other health issues, they're going to admit her…"

"I'm sorry. That stinks, but she'll be better before you know it." He reached for her hands, but she jerked them away, crossing them over her chest.

"You took her all those places, and it kept her from sleeping right and eating right." Her words came faster, as if she couldn't stop them.

"Come on, Natalie. I'm sorry she's hurting. I would never want her to hurt, but I couldn't—"

"You made her do too much. You lowered her resistance, and then you took her to all of those places where she was exposed to more illnesses. She couldn't fight it off."

"Fight it off? Shingles? That virus already had to be inside her since she had chicken pox as a kid."

She shook her head. "Illness or stress can re-awaken it. And you put her in that position—"

"So let me get this straight. You're saying that I made her sick. That it's all *my* fault." Shane knew he should be trying to defuse this situation. Hell, he knew the steps of de-escalation like the back of his hand from his work on the force. But he didn't want to de-escalate. She didn't deserve this to go away so easily.

He shook his head hard. "No. I refuse to accept that. Do you have any idea how ridiculous that sounds?"

"I don't care."

"Well, I'm sorry your mother is sick. I love your mother. I'm worried about her, too, but it's ridiculous for you to hold me responsible for her illness."

"Why couldn't you just leave her alone? She would have been fine if you'd just left her at home where she was safe and where she had proper care."

"Who would it have been better for, Natalie? Your mother or you?"

"How dare you!" She waved her index finger so close to his face that she nearly hit him with it. "You know nothing about me or my mother."

"I know that you need your mom to stay a patient because if she ever gets her own life, you'll no longer be able to play the sanctimonious, longsuffering daughter who sacrificed everything to care for her poor, injured mother."

"I can't believe you just said that. And Mom thought the two of you were friends."

"I thought you and I were, too, and for that reason I'm telling you this. You should take your own advice and forgive yourself. You were right about me. It was time for me to forgive myself and move on," he said. "You need to do the same, whether it's with me or not."

He knew he should stop. He'd already said too much. But his words frothed over like a beer poured hot. He couldn't stop himself any more than she could have slowed her diatribe since marching into the waiting room.

"Why does it bother you how I treat your mother?" he asked. "You're worse than I am. You blame her for your having to leave college and changing your major, when you're the one who made those decisions. In fact, you blame everyone other than yourself for your choices."

"You don't know anything about my choices. Unlike you, I didn't have any choice."

"We always have choices, Natalie, and you *chose* to stay mad at the two police officers from the accident. Those guys were just doing their job, and you know it. Did they make the right call in that split second? Who knows? But at least they made a decision, and they stood by it. You just look for someone else to blame for yours.

"You blame them and the accident for stealing your future in music instead of admitting that you didn't fight for that future because you were a coward," he said. "Your mom wasn't a fan of your choice to study music. It made no sense to her. But after the accident, instead of telling her it was something you still had to do, you allowed her to guilt you into making a more practical choice. And then you blamed *her* for it. Are none of your choices your fault?"

She planted her hands on her hips and faced off with him. "I'm so glad that one of us has all the answers. Those are rich comments coming from a guy who's still trying to make up for a mistake he made when he was just a kid. It's been fifteen years, and you're still trying to prove that you're good enough. You still question whether you were worthy of what your mentor did for you."

The conversation had been heated until then, and loud enough for a few people to shush them already, but now fury blanketed Shane faster than a heavy snow on the ground. He gritted his teeth so hard his jaws ached.

"You don't get to say anything about Kent," he said. "You don't know anything about him or the things he's done for me." He would have thrown it in her face that she'd denigrated him on the day of his death, but the truth was still too new, too raw. Saying it out loud would be making it true, and he wasn't ready for that kind of honesty.

"I know what you've told me."

"Which was almost none of it." He brushed his hands over each other, palms down, to demonstrate that the topic was closed. "And if I'm still chasing redemption, what business is it of yours? At least I took responsibility for my decisions instead of blaming them on someone else. At least I'm not too much of a coward to take control of my own life."

"Not a coward?"

She might have quieted for a few minutes, but these words she nearly shouted. Or was it only that they reverberated in his ears? He hoped she would stop there. They'd both said too much already. Things they couldn't take back. But he knew she would say more just as surely as he recognized there was so much more she could say.

"If you aren't a coward, then when are you going to walk again?"

Shane shoved the foot plates of his chair aside and came to his feet so fast that he nearly barreled over her, but he managed to stop himself. As it was, he stood so close that she had to tilt her chin up to even see his face. She looked as shellshocked as an accident victim, and the ruddy color of her anger drained from her face, but he was too furious to care. His hands were fisted at his sides, and he had to unclench his jaw just to speak.

"Whether or not I *ever* walk again, at least I'm not blaming it on anyone else that my legs don't move. And, unlike you, I actually have someone I could blame."

With that he lowered himself into his chair. It was more of a fall, really, since he'd neglected to lock down his chair's wheels, but the row of chairs stopped him from a full spinout. He landed on the seat with both of his forearms smacking the armrests with twin thuds.

Natalie's hands went to her face, cupping together to cover her nose and mouth. Slowly, she turned her head back and forth as if for the first time noticing that they had an audience and she'd just berated a man in a wheelchair for his inability to walk. He almost couldn't believe it himself. That was just the worst of the things she'd said—the things they both had.

Like they had been all along, the other waiting room guests pretended not to have been watching and listening. Shane didn't believe them for a second. He would have listened to every word if he'd been in one of those other chairs. And he would have been ready to intervene in case there appeared to be a moment when the verbal exchange would turn violent. Though not a hair on either of their heads had even received a split end in this one, it felt worse. He wished she'd slugged him instead.

As a signal that other guests hadn't been the only ones watching, a uniformed security guard stood at the far side of the room, appearing ready to pounce. Before the guard could start their way, Natalie turned back to him and spoke in a low voice.

"Look, Shane. I didn't mean—"

He shook his head to interrupt her. "I just can't figure you out, Natalie. What are you so scared of? Is it being alone? Or maybe you're just terrified that someone will leave you again. Is that why you started pushing me away right after we... you know. No, before that. You had my case reassigned. You accused me of being a womanizer when you were the one running away. You even told your mother to avoid me. Now you're going to desperate lengths to push me away."

"You're wrong." Still, she crossed her arms over her chest in a move more self-protective than defiant. "Anyway, I'm not pushing—"

"You blamed me for your mother's *shingles*," he supplied to interrupt her.

"You've got to understand," she began, her voice rising again. But when she glanced over at the guard, she lowered it. "It's just that Mom hasn't been in pain like that since— I was scared."

"And upset," he finished for her. "But I also know that if you didn't have a strange virus to blame me for, you would have found something else. Some other reason to push me away."

This time she just shook her head.

He should have stopped then. He'd already made his point, had certainly revealed more about himself than she had any right to know, but he couldn't stop himself.

"And even knowing you would eventually find that reason, I probably would have just hung around and waited for you to do so. What does that say about me?"

His dry laugh sounded strange, and it didn't make him feel any better. "You need to ask yourself something."

She stared at the floor for several seconds, but finally she looked up at him from under her lashes. "What's that?"

"Ask yourself if this is the first time. You know, that other guy who left you. I bet you pushed him away, too."

As soon as the words were out, he clamped his mouth shut. But the wide eyes looking back at him told him it was too late. She turned her head to look away from him just as the husky security guard from the corner suddenly appeared next to them.

"Sorry, folks, but there's been a complaint about the noise. This is a hospital. You either have to quiet down or you'll need to leave."

Natalie waved her hand to push away the suggestion. "Sorry. We'll quiet down."

Strangely, though, the man wasn't really looking at Natalie when she spoke. He was watching Shane instead.

"Sir, are *you* all right? Maybe we can step outside... I mean we can *go* outside. Take a breath."

Shane shook his head, words refusing to come. The security guard, and likely whoever had summoned him, was concerned about *his* safety. He'd thought he couldn't be more humiliated than he was having Natalie announce to anyone listening that he was too much of a coward to get out of his wheelchair. He'd been wrong.

The guard was surreptitiously checking out the exposed skin on his hands, neck and head as if looking for signs of abuse. From Natalie. And then the guy looked at his face again.

"Wait. Warner, is that you?"

His well of humiliation still hadn't bottomed out. "Yeah. It's me."

The man tapped his chest. "It's Lennie. Remember me?"

"Oh, yeah. Lennie," he said, though he didn't have a clue.

"Whew." The guard brushed his forehead in relief. "I thought—" He shook his head. "I don't know what I thought."

Shane glanced sidelong at Natalie, who was so ashen that she might need the wheelchair more than he did. She didn't deserve his pity any more than he deserved hers, but he couldn't help himself. Those feelings inside him wouldn't be that easy to just shut off.

"No. Really. Everything's fine here. We have everything under control now." Strange how the word *we* tasted sour on his tongue now. They'd barely become a *we*, and now they would never be more than a couple of *I*'s. "In fact, Miss Keaton needs to head back to her mother, who's being treated in there." He indicated the bowels of the ER with a tilt of his head. "And I'll be heading out. Just waiting for my ride."

Natalie's gaze shifted his way, and then she nodded. At least she understood that he couldn't stay with her now. If he did, he would actually *be* that vulnerable guy the guard wanted to protect. That wasn't going to happen.

She cleared her throat. "I'd better get back in there."

Lennie looked at her sternly. "Just keep it down, okay?"

Natalie nodded and started toward the door. The impulse to call her back was startling and unacceptable. Why did Shane want her to come back again? So she could criticize him more? Clearly, he needed that psychological evaluation he would have to pass before he could return to full-time patrol.

But as she pushed the silver button for the automatic door, he couldn't help calling after her, "Tell Elaine that I hope she feels better?"

"Yeah, hope she's doing better," Lennie said.

Shane's gaze shifted to the security guard, who was probably hanging around to ensure that they didn't start arguing again. When he turned back to Natalie, she was watching him, her gaze soft, sad. He knew just how she felt.

When she turned and disappeared through the opening, Shane felt like someone had parked a patrol car on his chest. This wasn't how everything was supposed to happen. Kent was supposed to still be fighting his cancer in the oncology ward upstairs and, this time, winning. Elaine should have been at home inviting him out on another fun outing. And he and Natalie should have been together. Always.

But that wasn't going to happen now, and it was as much his fault as hers. Nothing could change the things they'd said. Awful things. Cruel things. And they couldn't take them back.

Shane stayed parked where he was even after Lennie left him to return to the security office. Even after he'd texted Vinnie for a ride home. It was as if he expected her to come back through that door. What would they do then? Pretend she hadn't just called him a coward? And what would she say? That it was no big deal that he'd accused her of pushing all the men in her life away?

But she didn't come through that door again,

no matter how many times it swung open, with doctors and nurses and patients and their family members spilling through the opening each time.

Finally, when Vinnie texted to let him know that he was parked outside, Shane started toward the exit. Natalie might have figured it out first, but they'd come to the same conclusion. There was nothing left for them to say.

CHAPTER TWENTY-ONE

Natalie awoke to the sounds of muffled voices coming from behind the curtain on the opposite side of the room. Annoying beeping from another patient's IV stand filtered in through the open door. Her mother lay in the hospital bed, so close to where Natalie sat that her outstretched legs rested under it. Elaine's head was turned away from her, but at least she was finally getting some rest. Natalie peeked at the numbers on the monitor, just to be sure all was well.

Stretching, Natalie slid her hand down her aching neck. The chairs in this place didn't make for great beds, but since this had been one of the longest days of her life, her exhausted body was taking what it could get.

Too bad it couldn't have been a peaceful sleep. Or even just a dreamless one. But what had she expected when warring feelings had battled inside her all afternoon and had refused to stop slashing, even after she'd passed out from exhaustion? Sure, she was ashamed of many of the things she'd said to Shane. Calling him a coward for not walking yet definitely had not been one of her finest moments.

But she'd had every right to be furious. How could he say that she wasn't taking responsibility for her decisions when every choice she'd made over the past eight years had been *about* taking responsibility? She'd changed her whole life so she could care for her mother. Didn't that count for anything?

Emotion welled in her throat at just the thought of his cruel words. Could a person who loved someone still believe such awful things about her? Did Shane really love her at all?

Natalie shook her head, closing her eyes. She definitely couldn't use the words she'd spoken as some litmus test to prove her love. Yet she didn't doubt, even for a minute, that she was in love with Shane, and she'd said some awful things to him. Unforgivable things.

"At least one of us is getting some rest in this place."

Blinking, Natalie turned to sound of her mother's voice and found her watching from the bed.

"Oh, I thought you were asleep."

Elaine shook her head, smiling. "Oh, I dozed off and on."

And she didn't appear to be hurting right now, either. That was something. Natalie rubbed her eyes and pasted on her own smile. It probably didn't look natural, but it was the best she could do when she felt this numb. This lost.

"How long was I asleep?" Natalie shivered as her question reverberated in her head. Shane had asked her the same thing not twenty-four hours ago, when they were together in his bed, when her mother was still healthy and her own life was still filled with the giddy optimism of a roller coaster's first hill. Now she felt that end-of-ride letdown when the brakes squealed and the safety bars lifted.

But she couldn't dwell on mistakes she'd made and the things she would never have. Not if she hoped to be of any support to her mother. Or have any chance of making it through the day.

"Oh, you only slept a half hour or so."

"I'm surprised I slept that long in this thing." Natalie patted the arms of the chair, though the thoughts and self-recriminations pounding in her head all day might have had something to do with it, too. "Speaking of sleep." She paused to give her mother a pointed look. "Why aren't you getting any? What's your pain level? Is your head still hurting?"

Elaine pointed to the IV attached to her arm, the one that contained pain medication in addition to fluids. "That's definitely taking the edge off, but the doctor's more concerned with my blood pressure, since the pain was making it go up. As far as my sleep, I don't know. I'm just not tired."

"Maybe they'll give you something to help you sleep tonight."

"Maybe," Elaine agreed. "The nurse said she doesn't see any signs of the rash yet."

Natalie nodded. "It might still be a few days before you see it."

"They'll probably kick me out of here before that."

Natalie smiled again. "That's a good thing, right?"

"I guess so. I used to think your cooking was… *challenged*. But this place makes yours look like haute cuisine."

"Thanks, I think."

"After another day or so of eating it, I'll be ready to eat anything you put in front of me."

This time when Natalie grinned, she didn't have to fake it. "Now you see, there will be some good to come out of this little hospital visit. I'll have a less picky eater to work with."

"I wouldn't count on it."

"Thanks for helping me not get my hopes up."

Natalie shouldn't have done that with Shane, either. It had been a mistake to open up to him, to put her trust in him. If only she hadn't let him into her heart. If only—

She stopped herself as his words repeated in her thoughts. *What are you so scared of?* Was he right to believe that she'd pushed him away because she was afraid that he would leave her someday?

Had she pushed him away, and Paul before him? Well, whether it was a self-fulfilling prophecy or she'd just been right to be afraid, the result was the same. She had that same sense of desertion she'd known all her life, the feeling of being untethered in a wicked wind. But for the first time, she was convinced she deserved to be alone.

"Do you think Shane will visit me here, or will he wait until I get home?" Elaine asked. "You let him know I was here, didn't you?"

Natalie glanced up in surprise. She refused to acknowledge her mother's knowing look. What had she done to give herself away?

"Of course I did." She cleared her throat. "But I don't know when he'll be able to come." It was a coward's way out, but she didn't know what else to say. Shane was the one person her mother had connected with since the accident, and Natalie had sent him packing.

But instead of acting suspicious, Elaine only nodded. "That makes sense. He's probably really busy with his friend and all."

"What are you talking about?"

"He's probably visiting his friend in the hospital instead of me." She shrugged. "That's okay. I'm sure he needs the visit much more than I do."

"Are you talking about Kent?"

"Oh, right. That's his name. Shane's mentor." Elaine paused, shaking her head. "It didn't sound good last I talked with Shane. He was declining fast and had been admitted—here, I think—for some sort of treatment."

With each word her mother spoke, something stretched taut inside Natalie. Why had he shared those things with her mother instead of her? Had he avoided telling her because she'd been closing herself off to him? Had she been so caught up in her own dramas that she'd been unable to even *hear* his?

Elaine drew her brows together. "Oh, I was sure he would have told you. He mentioned it yesterday when we were planning to go to the movies."

Yesterday. It didn't seem possible that only a day had passed since the three of them had been together. Even less than that since she'd been so happy in Shane's arms.

"Maybe he just didn't get the chance to tell you about it while we were out."

There hadn't been much time later, either, Natalie noted, though she didn't think her mother needed to know that. Could it be that in addition to making some memories with her in his arms, Shane had also been trying to forget some of his own sadness? That she'd missed those signals in him was just further proof that in addition to being insecure, she was self-centered, as well.

"Maybe he just didn't want to think about it for a while." She shrugged, straightening in her seat as she moved on to the next difficult subject.

"Anyway, you might not want to count on Shane visiting at all."

"Why not?"

"He just won't be hanging around with...us... anymore."

"What did you do?"

Natalie swallowed. She wanted to be angry that her mother never questioned which one of them was at fault, but Elaine knew her better than anyone and was well aware of her relationship failures. Since she was bracing herself for a lecture, her mother's plea took her by surprise.

"Please, please don't make the kind of mistakes I did. Don't let your pride prevent you from being happy."

Natalie's eyes filled. "You don't know the things he said to me. The things I said to *him*."

Her mother only smiled. "But I do know how you look at him when you think no one's watching. How he looks at you. I know that Shane is a good man, not a self-centered one like your father. And I know that you deserve to be happy."

"But it's too late. Some things you just can't take back." She squeezed her eyes shut, trying to push away the image of her towering over a man in a wheelchair, calling him a coward.

"That might be true, but it's never too late to tell someone you're sorry." Elaine turned her head and stared at the cream-colored curtain that separated her side of the patient room from the other.

When she looked back, it was at Natalie's hands instead of her face. "And I am."

"What are you talking about?"

"I'm sorry." This time Elaine met her daughter's gaze. "I should never have pressured you into giving up your life to take care of me."

"No." Natalie shook her head for emphasis. "You didn't pressure me."

"But I didn't exactly insist that you get on with your life. I let you forget how to live your own life, how to grab on to happiness with both hands and never let go."

Natalie reached for her mother's hands. They felt so small and cold. "You can't blame yourself, Mom. I wasn't a child when I made those decisions. Those were *my* choices. You weren't the only one whose life changed the day of the accident. I wasn't the same after that. During that time afterward, I also learned how much I enjoyed helping people."

"Is that true?"

Her mother lifted a doubtful brow and studied her a little too carefully.

"Of course." Natalie was surprised to discover that she really meant it this time. "I still love music. I always will. But I also love working as a PT and knowing I've made a difference in people's lives."

"You've definitely made a difference in mine.

And I'm grateful for everything you've done for me."

Her mother shifted on the bed and then grimaced, reminding Natalie why they were there in the first place. Her mother's health was an issue and always would be. Natalie closed her eyes, but when she opened them again, Elaine was staring right at her.

"But it's time for me to fire you."

"What? Why?"

"I can't have you using me as an excuse not to live your life anymore."

"But I'm not."

"Really?"

For the second time today, her mother was questioning her honesty, and this time she'd caught her in a lie. So Natalie shrugged and stared at the floor.

"So when are you going to fix things with my friend Shane so he can visit me?"

"I already told you that I really messed things up. We both did. We can't go back to where we were."

"Do you love him? Is he worth it?"

Her mother had asked two separate questions, but Natalie could answer both with a nod.

"So make it right. Forgive him. And beg him to forgive you. And do it now."

"What if I can't forgive him? What if I decide that love is too much of a risk?"

"That's a choice, too. Just like I made when I had my heart broken and I chose to never take a risk again." Elaine studied her hands for a few seconds and then looked up at Natalie. "Please don't make that choice. Don't end up like me. Alone."

SHANE PROPELLED HIMSELF out his front door and started down the ramp the moment that Vinnie pulled his SUV into the driveway the next morning. After spending a whole day alone with his thoughts, he would have taken the chair on the road if Vinnie hadn't answered when he'd called him a half hour before.

He'd had every right to be angry, at Natalie for the awful things she'd said to push him away, at cancer for choosing one of the good guys when there were so many convicted child molesters and serial killers out there living with good health until their eighties. At the world for not being fair.

"So what's the rush?" Vinnie called as he jumped down from the driver's seat and barreled toward Shane, slipping on the ice. He caught himself against the ramp railing with a *thunk*. "Slow down. It's dangerous out here. You're going to get yourself killed."

"Look who's talking."

Vinnie reached him when he was halfway down the ramp. "Why'd you call so early anyway? Not that I mind, but this is my day off, and you know how much I need my beauty sleep."

"Kent's wife, Tammy, asked me over for coffee."

"This early?"

"I told her she could call me any time and I would be there," Shane said.

"Almost exactly what I told you." Vinnie waited until Shane was buckled into the truck's seat and then folded the wheelchair and loaded it in back. "Let's get this train rolling."

Soon they were on the road again, the scenery brushing by in a continual stream of white and dingy off-white images and an occasional stoplight. Not for the first time, Shane wished Natalie was with him on what would be an emotional visit. He didn't know why he bothered wishing that.

She'd said everything she could think of to sabotage them, and she'd been more successful than she knew. He didn't want to be with someone who couldn't put her trust in him. Certainly not someone who thought he was a coward—even if he was one. But Natalie was as much of a coward as he was. Only her fear had proven costly to them both. It had cost him *her*.

"I'm surprised that Kent's wife has time for coffee. Isn't she busy planning the funeral?"

Shane startled, his friend's words drawing him back from his painful thoughts. "She said it was something about Kent's papers."

"But this funk you're in is about more than

just your friend's death, isn't it?" Vinnie said in the calm, steady voice he used when questioning suspects.

"Is that not enough?"

"Sure," Vinnie said slowly. "But I'm thinking this is about Natalie."

Shane jerked his head to look at his friend's profile. "How'd you know?"

But Vinnie only smiled and kept driving.

"I thought we had something there for about a minute," Shane said finally.

"Sorry, buddy, but I don't think the minute's up."

He shook his head. "We had a huge blowout. She accused me of causing her mom to get shingles."

Vinnie glanced sidelong at him. "That's quite a trick, but you're a resourceful guy. I suppose you could do that if you wanted to."

Shane shifted as some of Natalie's other words replayed in his head. Was she right when she'd said he thought he was unworthy of all that Kent had done for him? Many of the decisions he'd made in the years since then supported her theory. His choice of career, for example. But if she couldn't understand why it was important for him to give something back for all the mistakes he'd made, then she didn't know him at all.

He squeezed his eyes shut, but her image refused to budge. He'd thought he'd finally found someone who understood him, who loved him for *him*, but she clearly didn't. He'd known it was too much of a risk to love her, to believe that he could have the kind of love that other people took for granted. Some people were meant to be alone, and apparently he was one of them.

"THANKS FOR COMING," Tammy said as she set steaming mugs of black coffee in front of Shane and Vinnie on her dining room table.

"As I said, any time," Shane told her.

Tammy stirred sugar into her coffee but didn't take a sip. Sure, she looked fragile today. Her eyes were puffy, and deep half-moons of exhaustion had formed beneath them. But Shane never doubted her strength for a minute. She would handle these next difficult months with a grace that would make Kent proud.

"You said something about papers," Shane prompted when the conversation stalled.

"Oh. Right." She turned to the sideboard behind her and lifted a stack of papers with a smaller pile of photos on top. Twisting back to the table, she set them in front of her.

Again, she stirred her coffee, and, again, she didn't drink.

"Kent loved it when you came over," she told Shane. "You reminded him why he became a police officer and why he still had work to do."

"He was a great guy," Shane said as he watched

the woman who loved his friend. "Great cop. An even better person."

He sipped his coffee and tried to ignore the heat building behind his eyes. How could he be of any help to Kent's widow if he couldn't hold his own grief in check? And he had to be there for her. He owed Kent that much.

"You have to know that you were one of my husband's best friends," she said. "You were on the list of guys he wanted me to ask to be his... pallbearers."

With a shaky hand, she lifted her mug to her lips, took a sip and set it aside. Then she shuffled through her pile. She withdrew a lined piece of paper, written in Kent's small block handwriting. Sure enough, on the list of possible pallbearers, Shane's name was listed in the first six.

"He thought you'd be farther along in your recovery when he passed." She cleared her throat. "He thought...he had more time."

She pulled a familiar photo out of the stack and handed it to Shane. It was from Shane's freshman football season, a photo of him in his uniform with Kent standing proudly next to him.

Vinnie, who'd been uncharacteristically quiet, leaned over to get a closer look. "Is that you?"

Shane nodded. "I was fourteen."

Vinnie pointed to the stack of photos. "May I look?"

Tammy nodded. As Vinnie flipped through the

pictures, Tammy reached into the stack of papers once more. She pulled out a small envelope with Shane's name on it, again in Kent's handwriting.

She pushed it across the table to Shane. "Here is the other thing. I hadn't seen this in his papers... before, but Kent wanted you to have this."

Trying to keep his hands from shaking, Shane lifted the envelope and pulled the letter from inside. His eyes filled as soon as he started reading. It was a question he'd always carried in his heart, and his friend had left the answer for him to read.

Shane,
  If you've ever wondered if I was right to reach out to that scrawny delinquent so long ago, I can tell you that I was. I saw something in you then. Something good. And I couldn't have been prouder as I've watched you prove me right.
Love,
Kent

Shane could picture Kent grinning back at him as he read the note, his hands wide in his trademark two thumbs-up. If only he could see him strong and healthy now, like the guy in Tammy's photos. The way Kent would want to be remembered. The way that Shane really hoped his friend was, wherever he was now.

Blinking several times, he lifted his chin to

fight back the emotion that seared at the back of his eyes and swelled in this throat. But the hurt won out, and tears seeped from the outside corners of his eyes. Shane brushed his fingers on the letter. He couldn't believe it. Even with pain that had never been fully under control and the nausea from an umpteenth round of chemo, Kent had been thinking of him and wanting to make sure he knew he was proud of him.

Per their unspoken guy agreement, Vinnie pretended not to notice Shane's tears and continued looking through the photos instead.

But Tammy, whose loss had been so much greater than Shane's, reached over and squeezed his hand.

"That husband of mine sure did like making a statement," she said with a wistful smile. "He always used to say he was glad you picked *his* patrol car for your little adventure in larceny."

He smiled back. "Yeah, I bet that just made his day."

"Knowing you changed his life as much as his mentoring changed yours."

He nodded, but he could never agree with what she'd just said. How could he ever find balance between two things so unequally weighted?

"He was really looking forward to attending your commendation ceremony." She paused, glancing toward the letter still in Shane's hands.

"And if it's all right with you, I'd like to attend in his place."

A lump forming in his throat, Shane nodded. "I'd like that." He turned and gestured toward Vinnie. "This guy here will also be receiving a commendation that day."

"Anything to avoid doing my job," Vinnie said.

But Tammy patted Vinnie's forearm. "My husband and I were grateful to you, too, for what you did for our Shane."

Vinnie thanked her and exchanged a look with Shane before returning to the photos.

Shane read the words in Kent's note once more. "I'd hoped that Kent would get the chance to see me *walk* across the stage to accept the award."

Again, she patted his hand. "Kent always said you would walk again…when you were ready. He fully expected you to return to active duty, too. He never doubted it. And as for *seeing* you walk on stage, I have to believe that he will see it when it happens."

After a few hugs and words of condolence, the two men returned to the vehicle. For the first few minutes of the drive, neither spoke, but at the first stoplight, Vinnie cleared his throat.

"Guess I'm not the only one who still feels indebted to another police officer."

"But our stories are completely different," Shane told him. "You never owed me anything for what happened in the shooting. You never did anything wrong."

"It only matters that I feel that I do, right?"

"Yeah, I guess so."

"Do you think it's possible that some debts are never meant to be repaid?" Vinnie asked, still staring at the road. "That maybe all we're meant to do is to pay it forward?"

"Good thing we have opportunities to do that every day on the job."

"Yep, we're lucky guys," Vinnie agreed.

Shane could only hope that Vinnie would forgive himself rather than carry his need for atonement like another layer of weighted clothing beneath his bulletproof vest. The way Shane had for so many years.

He bent his head to look down at the letter he held between his gloved hands. It was more than a parting gift from a friend who'd already given him too much. If he let it, the letter could serve as a tangible sign that his debt had finally been repaid.

CHAPTER TWENTY-TWO

THE HOUSE TOO quiet to even be able to sleep in on her first morning alone there in years, Natalie flitted around, straightening already straightened pillows, wiping down immaculate countertops. Finally, she settled with her smartphone and a cup of coffee in a chair near the TV tray where her mother usually took her meals. Used to, anyway. BS—*before Shane*. Everything before Shane came into their lives was different, and now that he wouldn't be in them anymore, she and her mother would never be the same. Her most of all.

If only she could find some way to occupy her mind so she could stop thinking about him. She couldn't even distract herself with worries about her mother's hospitalization when she'd already been assured it was only precautionary. And she couldn't go to work without either passing Shane in the gym or seeing him and his new PT in the hall and being reminded of how poorly she'd treated him when he'd first been assigned as *her* client. She'd had so many preconceived notions about him, and he'd dispelled each one of them.

On her phone, she launched the browser. Why

she bothered telling herself she was just wasting time internet surfing, she wasn't sure. She knew exactly what she was searching for.

It was so easy to find, just a simple search on the name Trooper Shane Warner. The articles she'd avoided reading until now appeared at the top of the hits.

Officer Shot During Domestic Call.

Suspect Dead After Police Shooting.

Trooper in Critical Condition After Shooting.

Wounded Officer Called Hero.

Before she hadn't wanted to know any of the details beyond what he'd told her. Now she was starved for details, no matter how small. She wanted to know about the dilemma Shane faced when the victim was in danger and he'd had no backup. Even though she already knew the outcome, she braced herself as she read about Shane's injuries. All of the stories pointed to a man who was self-sacrificing and inherently heroic.

This was the same man she'd resented on principle, just because he was a cop, and continued to hold at arm's length because of the job he did and the risk he represented to her heart. It sounded so ridiculous now, as nonsensical as hating all cops based on the choices of only two. Shane had said that even those officers had just been doing their jobs, just as he'd been doing his when he was shot. And for the first time, Natalie recognized that he was right. Both situations had involved risk but had been in the service of others.

Natalie clicked on one of the most recent follow-up articles. The victim had come forward to thank Shane several weeks after the shooting. The victim had called him "my guardian angel," saying that she would have been dead if the officer hadn't "risked his life for mine."

A guardian angel *and* a knight in shining armor. He'd been both of those things for Natalie as well, coming to rescue her from her well-insulated house of half-truths. He'd encouraged her to take charge of and responsibility for her own life—and she'd thought *she* was the one taking care of *him*.

It didn't seem possible that a man like Shane could still be running on a treadmill, trying to prove to others and himself that he was good enough. Well, he was good enough. He was worthy of every bit of help his mentor had given him and of all the respect he'd earned as a police officer. She needed to tell him that, too, even if he could never forgive her for the things she'd said. And she needed to tell him that she forgave him, but most of all she wanted to thank him for telling her the truth.

Natalie set her phone on the end table and stared at it for a few seconds before grabbing it again. Her mother had mentioned that Shane's mentor had been in declining health. Now she wanted to know more about the man who'd taken a chance on Shane. It took her a few seconds to recall his name, but once she did, she launched the browser and keyed in his name.

Several hits appeared, but when she read the one at the top, her breath caught. It read Obituary for Kent Sawyer. Her stomach dropped as she discovered that the same morning she'd accused Shane of making her mother ill, he'd been reeling from such tragic news.

He hadn't told her any of it. But had she really given him a chance? Just when he could have used the support of the woman who claimed to love him, she'd been shouting at him in front of a crowd of strangers. It was just one more thing that he would never be able to forgive. But it was also one more reason she had to try.

SHANE'S HOUSE WAS dark when Natalie pulled into the drive three days later, though the gunmetal sky would have required lights even in the middle of the day. She parked anyway and hurried up the ramp to his front door. That no one answered didn't surprise her, since he'd ignored her calls and messages for days.

She rapped several times, waiting for sounds between each series of knocks, but only a hollow noise emanated from inside. Her mother had suggested it would be harder for Shane to turn her away once she was standing on his front porch, and Natalie had agreed. Now she guessed that either Shane was more determined to avoid her than she'd thought or he really wasn't home.

Where could he be? Not at an appointment at the clinic. He'd already canceled one this week, and according to the schedule, he wasn't due in for another two days. If their basketball season hadn't ended, she could have counted on seeing him at practice or a game, but now she couldn't rely on that, either. If she couldn't see him, how would she ever apologize to him? Of course, there was the possibility that he was ignoring her, but she intended to make it as hard as possible.

"Wait a minute," she said and took her phone from her pocket. She pulled up Kent's funeral information again. Of course—he was there. The past few days while she'd been caught up with bringing her mother home from the hospital and figuring out a way to convince Shane to talk to her again, Shane must have been dealing with the business of saying a formal goodbye to his friend. She couldn't imagine how difficult that must have been for him.

Natalie glanced once more at the funeral details and noted that the service had started nearly an hour before and should be ending soon. She was down the ramp and back in her car before she'd even worked out the details of her plan. It was selfish for her to go to him today of all days when he had so much gratitude to bury along with his friend. But she needed Shane, and whether he realized it or not, he needed her, too.

Especially today. He needed someone who understood just how much he'd lost. Just how indebted he still felt, even after all of these years.

She tried not to speed as she drove toward the cemetery listed in the obituary. As she'd hoped, she arrived before the funeral processional did, and the pair of patrol cars parked near the cemetery entrance confirmed she was in the right place. She drove in a secondary entrance and parked off to the side, away from the area already marked with a tent.

She'd expected a larger funeral procession than normal behind the hearse and the limousine. But nothing could have prepared her for the line of patrol cars from different agencies that entered the cemetery gate, their lights flashing, sirens muted. They kept coming. And coming. And coming.

They parked in rows three deep like the starting line of the Belle Isle Grand Prix. There were probably personal cars in there somewhere as well, but they were hidden in a wash of red-and-blue flashing lights. Police officers in dress uniforms spilled from the cars and approached the burial site en masse.

In the past, the display would have made her so uncomfortable that she couldn't sit still, but now she watched them in awe. She'd never seen such brotherhood as the officers of different agencies stood shoulder to shoulder in a solemn display. Surrounded by all of these officers in blue, Natalie expected that disdain she'd long felt for all police officers to resurface, but she discovered that it was gone.

She couldn't look away as more of them passed by her, their posture rigid, their expressions somber. When finally there was a break in the line of heads, her gaze shifted to it and slid lower. At the center of the group, Shane looked devastatingly handsome in his dress uniform, his hat perched on his head. He sat straighter in his chair today than she'd ever seen him as he joined the others to honor his friend's service.

They all continued on to the grave site, none appearing to notice her as she climbed out of the car and joined them, remaining at the back of the crowd. The police chaplain used a microphone, but from where she stood, it was still difficult to hear.

The service was short, just a few comments, a few scriptures, and then it was over. As a bugler performed a haunting rendition of "Taps" at the back of the crowd, Natalie searched for Shane's face among the mourners, but the crowd was too dense.

But as everyone returned to their cars, several stragglers remained, lining up to file past the casket one last time. She finally located Shane near the back of the line, waiting for his turn to pay his respects. Only when it was his turn, Shane looked ahead as if judging whether the narrow aisle between the casket and the guest chairs would be wide enough for his chair. But then, instead of rolling past, he locked his wheels, moved aside the foot plates and stood.

Natalie's breath caught, but she took a few steps forward to get a better look. The officer behind Shane handed him a cane and stood close behind him for support, but Shane did all the work. Gripping that cane handle so tightly his arm shook, he took several small steps along the length of his casket. He paused to splay his hand on the top and then continued another few steps to the opposite side of the tent. Two officers there helped him back into his chair.

Her throat thick with emotion and her eyes filling, Natalie smiled over Shane's accomplishment. He'd told her that he hoped his friend would be healthy enough to attend his commendation ceremony, and he'd hoped to walk across that stage under his own power. Life had disagreed with his plans, though, so he'd taken this walk for his friend's sake. And his own.

She was already brushing tears away as she hurried back to her car. Coming to see him here hadn't been such a great idea after all. He didn't deserve to have her ambush him at such a private moment.

She was halfway to her car when Shane called

her name. She turned back to find him rolling up behind her. He stopped when she turned to face him.

"Why are you here?"

She'd expected him to be mad that she'd tracked him down, but he just looked drained, his face ruddy, his eyes red and swollen.

Natalie shook her head. "I'm so sorry for your loss, Shane. I didn't know..." She paused and shrugged. "I shouldn't have come today."

He glanced over his shoulder to the officers who'd helped him back to his chair. One of them pointed to let him know where they would be. Shane nodded and turned back to her.

"Maybe you shouldn't have. But you still haven't told me why you did."

"I wanted to say I'm sorry. For so many things. But you wouldn't give me a chance."

"In my defense, I have been a little busy." He gestured toward the scene where his friend's body had just been laid to rest.

"I didn't even give you the chance to tell me about Kent."

He smiled this time, even if it was a sad one. "I guess you didn't. But I didn't exactly answer your voice mails or texts, either."

"Oh, you noticed that."

"I wasn't ready." He licked his lips. "Maybe I'm still not ready."

She crossed her arms over her chest, suddenly

cold. He might never forgive her for the things she'd said, but she still owed him an apology.

"I just need to say a few things and I'll go." She waited for his nod before continuing. "I'm sorry for all the things I said to you."

"You were just worried and upset."

"That's no excuse."

"I guess not." He shrugged and then considered for a few seconds. "Even if some of the things you said were right?"

Natalie shook her head. "It was cruel and unprofessional for me to call you a coward over your recovery."

"I'm sorry, too. We both said a lot of cruel things. Things we didn't mean."

She rolled her lips. "I wish I could take back everything I said."

"Everything?"

She drew her brows together. "What?"

"I'm asking if you want to take back *everything* you said."

At once she understood what he was asking. She might have called him a coward, but she'd also said she loved him. Her heart squeezed with the memory that he'd said it, too. That he'd appeared to mean it as much as she had. She would never take those words back. She would carry them with her forever in her heart.

"You didn't answer me."

The pain in her chest squeezed tighter. She

couldn't answer him. Not now. Not when the pain in her heart was still so raw. She chose to answer some of the questions he hadn't asked instead. Something she hoped would show her love, even if she could no longer say those words aloud.

"I'm sure you made both your parents and your mentor proud through the man you've become," she said simply.

Shane's gaze narrowed, but he didn't point out that she hadn't answered the question.

She gestured toward his uniform with its navy jacket, lighter blue pants with a darker stripe and the silver tie knotted at his neck. His bright silver badge reflected the light, even on this gray day. It was the first time she'd seen him in uniform and the first time she could appreciate the significance of it.

"You should be proud as well of the honorable life you…have chosen."

Natalie hated that her voice broke on what should have been an innocuous comment. She turned and stalked away, running from impotent feelings and dashed hopes. It was she who'd wanted to come here. Now she would be the first to walk away, taking her broken heart with her.

CHAPTER TWENTY-THREE

TWO MONTHS LATER, Natalie took her seat in the high school auditorium, where Shane's commendation ceremony was about to begin. The event had been rescheduled a second time, perhaps to allow Shane to be further along in his recovery, but it was finally about to begin.

At least she wasn't the only nervous one, she decided as her mother sat next to her in the wheelchair section, gripping handfuls of her long skirt in her lap. It was hard enough for Natalie to not get her hopes up tonight without having to worry that her mother would be disappointed if Shane's invitation had only been a polite one.

The memory of when they'd first received it still made her smile. Natalie had planned a pity party when her mother had announced that Shane had invited *her*, only to discover that both of their names were on the envelope.

"Aren't the flowers nice?" Elaine gushed as they glanced around the auditorium, taking in the decorations and the table covered with framed certificates.

"Everything's beautiful."

But Natalie wasn't really looking. At least not at those things. She couldn't pull her gaze off the five rows of uniformed state troopers in their seats up front.

She didn't want to dampen her mother's enthusiasm, though. Elaine looked healthier than she had in months, her cheeks a pretty pink and even the sores from her shingles healing up nicely under her skirt and long sweater. Maybe their new living situation, with Natalie in her own apartment and her mother living on her own with full-time support, had been good for the both of them.

"I'm glad we could come to this together," Natalie said.

As soon as her mother started scanning the room again, Natalie did some looking around of her own. Where was he? Even though the officers weren't wearing their hats, it still wasn't easy to single out Shane. She couldn't even figure out where they would park his chair.

Was he even there? Could there have been a downturn in his health? Of course not. She was leaping to conclusions faster than a person on that stage could dive into the orchestra pit below. He'd looked just fine each time she'd seen him working with Deborah at the clinic lately, although she couldn't be certain since they hadn't actually spoken. In fact, he'd been so hyperfocused at each of his sessions that she'd never even caught him watching her. She'd done enough looking for both of them.

Elaine was straining her neck searching for Shane.

"Do you think he'll stop by and speak to us before it starts?"

"I'm not sure." Well, she'd hoped so, but as the minutes ticked away, she had her doubts. Could all of her anticipation have been for nothing? She'd thought this would be a perfect time to tell him about all the changes she'd made in her life, that she'd actually *claimed* her life, so she couldn't help feeling disappointed that she might not get the chance.

"Ladies and gentlemen," the announcer called into the microphone, "we'd like to welcome you to this year's Michigan State Police awards ceremony. Each of the individuals we will recognize today exemplifies all of the qualities of our state police value statement.

"In the MSP, we have—" He paused, waiting for dozens of other voices to join him in repeating, "A proud tradition of service through excellence, integrity and courtesy."

Hearty applause followed the opening remarks and continued as the announcer introduced each officer and read the story of his or her heroism. Natalie felt guilty for only half listening to the stories of honor and bravery, but she couldn't focus. Not when she still hadn't seen Shane.

"Now I would like to introduce one of our brothers, who reached out to a domestic-abuse victim at great risk to his personal safety. Let's welcome Shane Warner."

Natalie glanced from one side of the stage to the other, expecting Shane to roll out from one of them. Instead, not one but two men stood up from the front row. Still using a cane to walk but looking stronger than he had even two weeks earlier, Shane crossed to the stage's side stairs. As he passed, fellow officers came to their feet to cheer him on. The other officer, whom Natalie now recognized as Vinnie, helped Shane as he climbed the steps, but the rest he did for himself.

"Thanks so much, everyone," Shane said when he reached the lectern, gripping the sides for balance. "Your support has meant so much to me."

Unlike the other officers being recognized, Shane told his own story, the details giving Natalie gooseflesh just as they had the first time he'd shared it with her.

"And I owe my life to this guy," he said, indicating Vinnie with a wide sweep of his hand. "You'll hear about him next, but first, I wanted to let you know that there's an upside to getting shot."

The crowd laughed and then quieted to hear the rest of his story. Natalie leaned forward in her seat and listened even more closely.

"I never knew this, but getting shot really helps with the ladies," he continued. "It's not what you're thinking. My injury allowed me to meet a special lady. I counted on her to help me walk again, but she has done so much more. She has taught me to forgive myself. Helped me see that I am worthy of forgiveness. And I couldn't be more grateful. So thank you, Natalie Keaton."

Natalie's hand moved to her chest. She couldn't believe it. Maybe he'd forgiven her after all. Like she'd forgiven him.

"Stand up, Natalie," her mother said.

She shook her head, confused. But then she glanced at the stage, where Shane lifted a hand in her direction. The crowd applauded until, embarrassed, she stood. After a few seconds, she sank back into her seat.

Finally, one of the superior officers crossed the stage and presented Shane with his award. Applause broke out for the hero this time, the one who deserved it. Shane slowly returned to his seat, and others were honored, Vinnie and a few more, all who'd performed heroic acts in the service of others.

When the ceremony ended, Natalie knew she should wait, should give Shane the extra time to come to her, but she couldn't sit there any longer. She'd waited this long, had taken the time to focus on getting her own life in order, on doing the things that would make him proud and make her proud of herself. Now she couldn't wait another minute to be near him. And to take a chance.

"I'll be back in a minute," she told her mother.

She hurried down the aisle toward the stage. Shane met her before she'd made it halfway. Others stepped around them, some with open curiosity, but Natalie barely noticed. She was with Shane. Finally.

He smiled at her, and she couldn't help smiling back. Her heart pounded so fast she thought it would beat out of her chest. She couldn't get ahead of herself. She didn't even know what he had to say yet.

With one hand resting heavily on his cane, Shane lifted his other to wave. "Hi."

"Hi." She cleared her throat and shoved her hands in the pockets of the new spring skirt she'd worn just for him. "My mom and I wanted to thank you for the invitation. This was great."

"Glad you could come."

"I've had so many things to tell you," she said, the words rushing from her mouth. "I have my own place now. Mom's doing great on her own. With support. She goes to activities at the senior center on Tuesdays. And I started playing again. On an old upright piano. Everything's good, and I owe it all to you."

When she'd finally run out of words, she looked to him and waited.

"I'm glad you're doing so well."

Polite. Civil. But no more than that. Had she expected too much? Had he just been extending an olive branch and she'd expected an engagement ring? The words he'd said on stage suggested more than that, but maybe she'd just heard what she wanted to hear. So she braced herself for whatever he said next, praying that it wouldn't be goodbye.

"I've missed you."

Her breath caught. Had she heard him right? Did this mean what she thought it meant?

"And I really want to hear all of the things you're telling me, but right now… I just really want to kiss you."

She blinked. He'd surprised her again, but she recovered faster this time.

"Then I guess you'll have to do what you need to do."

He took two steps forward and dipped his head to capture her lips in a kiss filled with passion and promise and, quite possibly, love. As she tilted her head back to fully accept his kiss, she realized with a jolt that it was the first time he'd held her in his arms while both of them were standing. It should have seemed odd, particularly since he was the first man who'd had to bend his head to kiss her, and the badge on his crisp dress uniform pressed into her collarbone as he did it, but this was Shane. He was the man she'd told herself she shouldn't want, and he'd turned out to be the only one she couldn't live without.

"I'm in love with you," he breathed next to her ear before returning his lips to hers.

Her hands had slipped around his neck, her fingers brushing over the newly short-trimmed hair at his nape, when loud applause exploded. They jerked back quickly to find a baker's dozen officers in dress uniforms gathered around them, cheering. Natalie's cheeks burned, but nothing could stop her from grinning.

"And you thought a measly commendation would be the best gift you got today," Vinnie called out, and everyone laughed.

"If one of those comes with a commendation, I'd better get out there and save somebody," someone else piped in.

On one side, the circle of fans split, and Elaine rolled closer.

"Looks like I missed a good show," she said, smiling.

"Well, hello, sweetheart." Shane stepped closer to Elaine and bent to drop a kiss on her cheek.

Natalie crossed to her mother, as well. "Mom, I was just telling Shane about my apartment and the piano."

"And I didn't have the heart to tell her I already knew about all of it," Shane said from beside her.

At Natalie's sidelong glance, Shane explained, "I've been receiving updates."

Her gaze shot back to her mother. "You've been in contact with Shane all this time?"

Elaine gave an apologetic grin. "It would have been a shame to lose contact with my friend."

Natalie turned back to Shane. "You knew all of that, and you still waited until now…?"

"We both needed time to figure our own stuff out."

Natalie nodded. She couldn't disagree with that.

Shane gestured toward the other officers and then the woman Natalie recognized as the wife of his late friend Kent.

"I need to thank some people for coming, okay?"

"We'll be here," Natalie told him and then moved to crouch next to her mother.

If she'd thought her mother had appeared healthy and happy before, now she looked downright giddy.

"You've got one of the good ones," Elaine said as she pressed her cheek to her daughter's. "And so does he."

Natalie kissed Elaine's cheek. Who would have thought that in order to help her mother learn to live again, she'd needed to finally begin living her own life? And open her heart to a man who just happened to adore them both.

She sneaked a peek at him now and caught him staring. As they exchanged a secret smile, her skin warmed under his steady gaze. Her heart was full. They hadn't made any commitments yet, but the promise was there in his eyes.

She wasn't in a rush, either. This most amazing, heroic man loved her, so her life was already nearly perfect. As she watched him, knowing the love shining in his eyes was reflected in hers, she was certain that their lives would only get better.

SHANE STARED AT himself in the mirror of the community church dressing room just four weeks later. Outside, a late-spring thunderstorm threatened, with the temperature dropping ten degrees in the past hour. But inside the tiny church, where he was surrounded by so many friends, it felt endlessly warm.

He brushed off the shoulders of his dress uniform that he'd worn more often in the past few months than he had in all of his years of police work. He'd passed his physical and would return to full duty soon, but he no longer felt the desperation he'd experienced before. He would have a new wife and a honeymoon to enjoy first.

"You okay, buddy?" Vinnie asked as he tightened the tie on his own uniform. "Are you ready for all of this?"

"If I say I can't wait, does that make me a total loser?"

Vinnie nodded into the mirror. "Yeah. Pretty much."

"You know, I'm okay with that."

The dressing room door opened, and Trevor peered inside. "You guys about ready? The chaplain is waiting."

They followed him out and around the piano on

the way to the pulpit where the chaplain had already taken his place. Shane stopped to the right of the chaplain, and Vinnie took his place at his flank.

Because the prelude music was still playing, he had a chance to look out in the small crowd of family and close friends. Well, friends more than family, really. Natalie only had her mother, and he had no one. He scanned the groom's side of the aisle. With so many of the guests in uniform, the few civilians among them stood out even more. Kent's wife, Tammy, and their two kids sat a few rows from the front, and a few of their basketball players were there with their parents, their wheelchairs parked on the outside aisles.

But at the sight of another couple near the back, his breath caught. His brother, Stephen, was there with his wife, Beth. Sure, Natalie had insisted on inviting them, but he'd never expected them to show. That Natalie was right again shouldn't have surprised him. He was going to have to get used to that, though, because she would probably be right more than he would through their next fifty or so years of marriage. He nodded at the thought and smiled. Yeah, fifty years or more sounded perfect.

It was good that the processional music started then, or he might have done something ridiculous and cried over his good fortune. Elaine appeared in the doorway first, her pretty pink dress arranged artfully in her chair. It had been Natalie's idea to have her mother as maid of honor, and once again, she'd made the right choice.

Just as the music changed, Natalie stepped to the auditorium entry. She was so beautiful that he could barely breathe. She wore a simple, silky gown that she'd told him was called a sheath. He definitely approved since it left her shoulders bare. Because she'd given him a vote on her hair, Natalie wore it loose about those beautiful shoulders, under a short veil.

It was all he could do to listen to the chaplain as he said all of those words, but he didn't care what the man said as long as it meant he could take Natalie home forever to be his wife.

NATALIE LIFTED HER head and stared into Shane's mesmerizing eyes. It had been particularly important to him to pass his physical before the ceremony, so she'd helped him gain strength with his exercises. What he might not have fully realized was that it made no difference to her at all. She loved *him*—not the way he moved from one place to the other. But it had been so important for him to return to the job he loved and the place where he could make a difference, and she'd come to want that for him as much as he wanted it for himself.

She stared into his eyes the whole time that the chaplain spoke about the responsibilities of marriage, and then it was finally time for the vows, the ones that Shane had insisted they should write themselves.

"Natalie, I love you," he began. "I had to get shot to meet you, but I would gladly do it all over again if it meant I could get to know such an amazing person. You are beautiful, kind and compassionate. You are my love. Whether I have to walk, ride or even crawl, I'll always come back to you."

Tears already clogging her throat and trailing down her cheeks, Natalie stared into those eyes that had always seen to her very core. She glanced down in her hand at the tiny sheet where she'd copied the vows she'd written and revised dozens of times over the past few weeks. She crumpled up the sheet and tossed it over her shoulder, earning a laugh from their guests.

"And I'll be the luckiest woman in the world to be with a man like you," she said simply.

After the exchange of rings, the chaplain pronounced them husband and wife.

"Kiss her already," someone called out before the chaplain could even say the words.

Laughter filled the sanctuary as Shane drew Natalie into his arms. Everything outside the two of them fell away as he brought his lips to hers. Even as he lifted his mouth away, Natalie stared up at him, mesmerized. She was amazed and so grateful to have him in her life. By opening her heart to forgiveness and stripping away layers of blame, she'd finally made room in her heart for hope and for a future with her own hero in blue.

"Are you ready to go, Mrs. Warner?" Shane pointed to the back of the church. "The guys decorated one of the patrol cars, but you probably want to just take my car."

"Oh, I think we can take the car they decorated," she said. "But on one condition."

"What's that?"

"I want the siren. I married a police officer, and I want everyone to know he's all mine."

* * * * *

Be sure to look for future books in
Dana Nussio's TRUE BLUE series,
as well as her previous title,
STRENGTH UNDER FIRE.

Get 2 Free Books,
Plus 2 Free Gifts—
just for trying the
Reader Service!

YES! Please send me 2 FREE LARGER PRINT Harlequin® Romance novels and my 2 FREE gifts (gifts are worth about $10 retail). After receiving them, if I don't wish to receive any more books, I can return the shipping statement marked "cancel." If I don't cancel, I will receive 4 brand-new novels every month and be billed just $5.34 per book in the U.S. or $5.74 per book in Canada. That's a savings of at least 15% off the cover price! It's quite a bargain! Shipping and handling is just 50¢ per book in the U.S. and 75¢ per book in Canada.* I understand that accepting the 2 free books and gifts places me under no obligation to buy anything. I can always return a shipment and cancel at any time. Even if I never buy another book, the two free books and gifts are mine to keep forever.

119/319 HDN GLPW

Name	(PLEASE PRINT)

Address		Apt. #

City	State/Prov.	Zip/Postal Code

Signature (if under 18, a parent or guardian must sign)

Mail to the Reader Service:
IN U.S.A.: P.O. Box 1867, Buffalo, NY 14240-1867
IN CANADA: P.O. Box 611, Fort Erie, Ontario L2A 9Z9
Want to try two free books from another line?
Call 1-800-873-8635 or visit www.ReaderService.com.

* Terms and prices subject to change without notice. Prices do not include applicable taxes. Sales tax applicable in N.Y. Canadian residents will be charged applicable taxes. Offer not valid in Quebec. This offer is limited to one order per household. Books received may not be as shown. Not valid for current subscribers to Harlequin Romance Larger Print books. All orders subject to credit approval. Credit or debit balances in a customer's account(s) may be offset by any other outstanding balance owed by or to the customer. Please allow 4 to 6 weeks for delivery. Offer available while quantities last.

Your Privacy—The Reader Service is committed to protecting your privacy. Our Privacy Policy is available online at www.ReaderService.com or upon request from the Reader Service.

We make a portion of our mailing list available to reputable third parties that offer products we believe may interest you. If you prefer that we not exchange your name with third parties, or if you wish to clarify or modify your communication preferences, please visit us at www.ReaderService.com/consumerschoice or write to us at Reader Service Preference Service, P.O. Box 9062, Buffalo, NY 14240-9062. Include your complete name and address.

HRLP17R

Get 2 Free Books,
Plus 2 Free Gifts—
just for trying the Reader Service!

YES! Please send me 2 FREE Harlequin Presents® novels and my 2 FREE gifts (gifts are worth about $10 retail). After receiving them, if I don't wish to receive any more books, I can return the shipping statement marked "cancel." If I don't cancel, I will receive 6 brand-new novels every month and be billed just $4.55 each for the regular-print edition or $5.55 each for the larger-print edition in the U.S., or $5.49 each for the regular-print edition or $5.99 each for the larger-print edition in Canada. That's a saving of at least 11% off the cover price! It's quite a bargain! Shipping and handling is just 50¢ per book in the U.S. and 75¢ per book in Canada.* I understand that accepting the 2 free books and gifts places me under no obligation to buy anything. I can always return a shipment and cancel at any time. Even if I never buy another book, the 2 free books and gifts are mine to keep forever.

Please check one: ☐ Harlequin Presents® Regular-Print ☐ Harlequin Presents® Larger-Print
                              (106/306 HDN GLP6)   (176/376 HDN GLP7)

Name _____ (PLEASE PRINT) _____

Address _____ Apt. # _____

City _____ State/Prov. _____ Zip/Postal Code _____

Signature (if under 18, a parent or guardian must sign) _____

Mail to the **Reader Service:**
IN U.S.A.: P.O. Box 1867, Buffalo, NY 14240-1867
IN CANADA: P.O. Box 611, Fort Erie, Ontario L2A 9Z9

Want to try two free books from another series? Call 1-800-873-8635 or visit www.ReaderService.com.

* Terms and prices subject to change without notice. Prices do not include applicable taxes. Sales tax applicable in N.Y. Canadian residents will be charged applicable taxes. Offer not valid in Quebec. This offer is limited to one order per household. Books received may not be as shown. Not valid for current subscribers to Harlequin Presents books. All orders subject to credit approval. Credit or debit balances in a customer's account(s) may be offset by any other outstanding balance owed by or to the customer. Please allow 4 to 6 weeks for delivery. Offer available while quantities last.

Your Privacy—The Reader Service is committed to protecting your privacy. Our Privacy Policy is available online at www.ReaderService.com or upon request from the Reader Service.

We make a portion of our mailing list available to reputable third parties that offer products we believe may interest you. If you prefer that we not exchange your name with third parties, or if you wish to clarify or modify your communication preferences, please visit us at www.ReaderService.com/consumerschoice or write to us at Reader Service Preference Service, P.O. Box 9062, Buffalo, NY 14240-9062. Include your complete name and address.

HP17R

Get 2 Free Books,
Plus 2 Free Gifts—
just for trying the Reader Service!

HARLEQUIN

HEARTWARMING™

YES! Please send me 2 FREE Harlequin® Heartwarming™ Larger-Print novels and my 2 FREE mystery gifts (gifts worth about $10 retail). After receiving them, if I don't wish to receive any more books, I can return the shipping statement marked "cancel." If I don't cancel, I will receive 4 brand-new larger-print novels every month and be billed just $5.49 per book in the U.S. or $6.24 per book in Canada. That's a savings of at least 19% off the cover price. It's quite a bargain! Shipping and handling is just 50¢ per book in the U.S. and 75¢ per book in Canada.* I understand that accepting the 2 free books and gifts places me under no obligation to buy anything. I can always return a shipment and cancel at any time. Even if I never buy another book, the 2 free books and gifts are mine to keep forever.

161/361 IDN GLQL

Name	(PLEASE PRINT)

Address		Apt. #

City	State/Prov.	Zip/Postal Code

Signature (if under 18, a parent or guardian must sign)

Mail to the Reader Service:
IN U.S.A.: P.O. Box 1867, Buffalo, NY 14240-1867
IN CANADA: P.O. Box 611, Fort Erie, Ontario L2A 9Z9

Want to try two free books from another line?
Call 1-800-873-8635 today or visit www.ReaderService.com.

* Terms and prices subject to change without notice. Prices do not include applicable taxes. Sales tax applicable in N.Y. Canadian residents will be charged applicable taxes. Offer not valid in Quebec. This offer is limited to one order per household. Books received may not be as shown. Not valid for current subscribers to Harlequin Heartwarming Larger-Print books. All orders subject to credit approval. Credit or debit balances in a customer's account(s) may be offset by any other outstanding balance owed by or to the customer. Please allow 4 to 6 weeks for delivery. Offer available while quantities last.

Your Privacy—The Reader Service is committed to protecting your privacy. Our Privacy Policy is available online at www.ReaderService.com or upon request from the Reader Service.

We make a portion of our mailing list available to reputable third parties that offer products we believe may interest you. If you prefer that we not exchange your name with third parties, or if you wish to clarify or modify your communication preferences, please visit us at www.ReaderService.com/consumerschoice or write to us at Reader Service Preference Service, P.O. Box 9062, Buffalo, NY 14240-9062. Include your complete name and address.

HWI7

Get 2 Free Books,
Plus 2 Free Gifts—
just for trying the Reader Service!

HARLEQUIN

I N T R I G U E

YES! Please send me 2 FREE Harlequin® Intrigue novels and my 2 FREE gifts (gifts are worth about $10 retail). After receiving them, if I don't wish to receive any more books, I can return the shipping statement marked "cancel." If I don't cancel, I will receive 6 brand-new novels every month and be billed just $4.99 each for the regular-print edition or $5.74 each for the larger-print edition in the U.S., or $5.74 each for the regular-print edition or $6.49 each for the larger-print edition in Canada. That's a savings of at least 12% off the cover price! It's quite a bargain! Shipping and handling is just 50¢ per book in the U.S. and 75¢ per book in Canada.* I understand that accepting the 2 free books and gifts places me under no obligation to buy anything. I can always return a shipment and cancel at any time. Even if I never buy another book, the two free books and gifts are mine to keep forever.

Please check one: ☐ Harlequin® Intrigue Regular-Print   ☐ Harlequin® Intrigue Larger-Print
                                    (182/382 HDN GLP2)   (199/399 HDN GLP3)

Name _____ (PLEASE PRINT) _____

Address _____ Apt. # _____

City _____ State/Prov. _____ Zip/Postal Code _____

Signature (if under 18, a parent or guardian must sign) _____

Mail to the **Reader Service:**
IN U.S.A.: P.O. Box 1867, Buffalo, NY 14240-1867
IN CANADA: P.O. Box 611, Fort Erie, Ontario L2A 9Z9

*Terms and prices subject to change without notice. Prices do not include applicable taxes. Sales tax applicable in N.Y. Canadian residents will be charged applicable taxes. Offer not valid in Quebec. This offer is limited to one order per household. Books received may not be as shown. Not valid for current subscribers to Harlequin Intrigue books. All orders subject to credit approval. Credit or debit balances in a customer's account(s) may be offset by any other outstanding balance owed by or to the customer. Please allow 4 to 6 weeks for delivery. Offer available while quantities last.

Your Privacy—The Reader Service is committed to protecting your privacy. Our Privacy Policy is available online at www.ReaderService.com or upon request from the Reader Service.

We make a portion of our mailing list available to reputable third parties that offer products we believe may interest you. If you prefer that we not exchange your name with third parties, or if you wish to clarify or modify your communication preferences, please visit us at www.ReaderService.com/consumerschoice or write to us at Reader Service Preference Service, P.O. Box 9062, Buffalo, NY 14240-9062. Include your complete name and address.